The Way You Look Tonight

He lightly touched her jaw. "Your skin is beautiful," he said softly.

She wrapped her fingers around his wrist as a warning bell sounded in her brain that she was too close to the edge of that slope again. *Don't slip*, she cautioned herself. *Whatever you do, don't slip.* "Freckles," she protested lightly, trying to divert him.

"I like them." The pulse in his wrist pounded beneath her fingertips. "Are you that type of woman, Jordan?" he asked.

"I don't think—"

"I do." He pressed the pad of his thumb to the corner of her mouth. "I sensed it the day I met you. Excessive passion."

MacKENZIE TAYLOR

The WAY YOU LOOK TONIGHT

AVON BOOKS
An Imprint of HarperCollinsPublishers

This is a work of fiction. Names, characters, places, and incidents are products of the author's imagination or are used fictitiously and are not to be construed as real. Any resemblance to actual events, locales, organizations, or persons, living or dead, is entirely coincidental.

AVON BOOKS
An Imprint of HarperCollins*Publishers*
10 East 53rd Street
New York, New York 10022-5299

Copyright © 2003 by P.R.S., Inc.
ISBN: 0-380-81938-4
www.avonromance.com

First Avon Books paperback printing: March 2003

Avon Trademark Reg. U.S. Pat. Off. and in Other Countries, Marca Registrada, Hecho en U.S.A.
HarperCollins® is a registered trademark of HarperCollins Publishers Inc.

Printed in the U.S.A.

10 9 8 7 6 5 4 3 2 1

Chapter One

𝄞

His FIRST IMPRESSION HAD BEEN RIGHT, SIMON thought grimly. Jordan Morrison was a woman of excessive passion.

And excessive passion was the one thing that scared the hell out of him. In his experience, it was messy. It made intelligent men act like idiots, and it made intelligent women make bad choices. It started wars and burned bridges. It ended careers and ruined lives. Excessive passion carried more baggage than the cargo hold of a 747. His usual rule of thumb was to avoid it at all costs.

But that didn't mean it wasn't damned attractive. Which obviously explained, he thought cynically, why he had been unable to shake her image from his mind for the past two weeks. He watched her now, having finally caught up with her at this dingy theater in Boston's South End, and felt the same tug of attraction he'd felt the day he met her.

She and a young African-American boy were seated at a piano that appeared to predate Paul Revere, playing impossibly complex music on the ancient instrument. Simon set the child's age at about eight, judging from the fact that his feet didn't even reach the floor, yet he and Jordan were weaving the most complex duet of—Simon caught the melody thread and shook his head in appreciation.

Chopsticks.

He had to hand it to her. If Jordan could take something as simple as the childlike song and turn it into something enticing, it was no wonder her cousin thought so highly of her. He braced one shoulder against the doorframe and studied the woman he was beginning to see as his last hope.

Nothing about her demeanor, the machine-gun pace of the music, or the slightly flushed tint of her skin could be categorized as "playing." Jordan didn't play the piano—she seduced it. Like a practiced lover coaxed delight from his partner, her fingers caressed and stroked the keys until they seemed to quiver for her. For the first time he understood why the Victorians found the piano so scandalous. Of course, he thought wryly, no Victorian woman in layers of petticoats and voluminous skirts would have looked this alluring.

Simply dressed in faded jeans and a sweatshirt, Jordan had an earthy, natural appeal that had intrigued Simon from the moment he met her. That day she'd worn a long fringed sweater and an impossibly wrinkled skirt. Simon was fascinated that she managed to make it look right and not like it had spent the last nine months in a suitcase.

But then, as now, he'd noticed that it wasn't what she wore, it was the way her clothes modestly emphasized generous womanly curves that had the most impact. Granted, she was curvier than the current fashion found acceptable, but then Simon had never found rail-thin women attractive. To him, they lacked the softness that gave a woman her sex appeal.

Jordan's sweatshirt had obviously seen better days, and the butter-soft fabric clung to her—not too tight, but not baggy, either. Her hips swelled enticingly in a pair of faded jeans. The denim tapered quickly to slim ankles and bare feet. A pair of battered leather clogs sat under the piano bench. He traced her shape from toe to head with the satisfaction that at least his memory had served him well: there wasn't a hard angle on the woman.

The exertion of the piece had left a fine sheen of perspiration on the nape of her neck. The sun pouring through the dingy windows at the back of the warehouse-type room highlighted her dark hair and the few damp tendrils that curled against her face. The hair, a short cut with too much curl and too much disorder, should have looked untidy and unflattering. Another paradox, Simon mused. She somehow managed to look mussed. Just-out-of-bed mussed. Just-made-love mussed.

He'd wanted to feel those curls twined around his fingers from the moment he met her.

Jordan and her young friend completed the duet. Laughing, they hugged enthusiastically.

"Spectacular, Darius," Jordan told him. "I can tell how much you've practiced."

"I keep missing that middle part," the child told her. "I can't get the fingering."

Jordan played a few notes slowly. "It's hard for you. Your fingers are smaller."

He picked up the sequence an octave higher and mimicked her. "I'll keep practicing."

"I don't doubt it," Jordan assured him.

Realizing the practice session was over, Simon abandoned his position by the door and made his way toward the piano. "Hello."

Jordan jumped and turned to face him. She didn't seem to recognize him for a brief second. He found that irrationally annoying. Her eyes widened as recognition dawned. "Ezekiel's wheels, Simon," she muttered. "You scared me to death."

"Sorry." He glanced at the piano. "I was enjoying the concert."

Darius had turned on the piano bench to study him. "Who's that man, Jorie?"

"He's a friend of the man Lily wants to marry," Jordan explained.

Simon extended his hand to Darius. "Simon Grant."

The child studied him a moment, then gravely shook his hand. "Darius Jackson."

"Nice to meet you." Simon tipped his head toward the piano. "You're very talented."

"Jorie's been teaching me."

A smile played at the corner of Simon's mouth. "She's obviously doing a good job."

Darius grinned at him. "I keep hoping she'll teach me blues and stuff, but she won't. Not yet."

"Yeah?"

"Uh huh," Darius assured him. "She's good at it. You ever heard her?"

Simon shot Jordan a quick glance. "No. I haven't."

Darius shook his head. "You should, man. She's fly. My friend Remo says Jorie is one hot chick when she tolls on the blues."

"Darius." Jorie thumped him on the shoulder. "Cut it out."

"He does," Darius insisted. He swiveled on the piano bench and played a driving bass line. "It's way phat," he informed Simon as he stopped abruptly. "But that's all I know."

"She won't teach you?"

"Just classic stuff." He indicated the piano with a tip of his head. "The chopsticks thing is just for fun. We're playing a fund-raiser."

He said that with the finesse of Van Cliburn announcing that he was playing with the Boston Symphony. "No kidding?" Simon asked.

"Nope," Darius said. "Three weeks. We're headlining."

"Darius," Jordan said firmly, "why don't you get your backpack so we can go?"

Darius slipped off the bench. "Okay. Can we stop at Mr. Lee's for ice cream?"

Jordan flashed him a brief smile. "And who's going to explain to your mother when you don't eat dinner?" She reached for an enormous purse and began stuffing music books into it.

"I'll eat," Darius assured her. "I promise."

"Um hmm," she said skeptically. "We'll see. Go grab your books."

The child nodded and hurried toward the back of the theater. "Tim," he called. "I need my backpack."

Darius disappeared into the dim wings.

"So," Jorie asked him as she pulled her clogs from under the bench. "What brings you way out here to the South End?"

"I want to talk to you about Lily and James."

Jordan shot him a dry look. "Still opposed to the wedding, Simon?"

"Still opposed to them getting married three months after they met," he said tightly.

Jordan sighed and leaned back on the piano bench. "They're old enough to make their own decisions," she insisted.

He jammed his hands into his pockets. "And this is a hasty one."

She hesitated a moment, then nodded. "I agree."

Relief and satisfaction filled him. His instincts had been correct. What he'd seen in Jordan's eyes the day James introduced them had been a wary look that told him she wasn't any more comfortable with the pace of her young cousin's relationship with his former ward than Simon was. "I'm glad to hear that."

"However," she said shortly, "I don't see any reason to be Draconian about it."

"I beg your pardon?"

"You know what I mean." She waved a hand in his direction. He noted the elegance in her long, musician's fingers. "Lily says you could cut off James's access to his father's money if you wanted to."

"I could," he agreed.

Her gaze narrowed. "Would you?"

"Depends."

"It's his life."

"It's also his father's legacy." Simon jammed his hands into his pockets. "James's father trusted me to ensure that Wells Enterprises survived and prospered. I'm doing my job."

"Sounds to me like you're enjoying it, too."

The characterization grated on his nerves. "I'm not trying to stand in the way of James's happiness."

"Just his marriage to my cousin?"

"You said you had concerns of your own," he pointed out. "You agree they're being hasty."

"Sure." She nodded. "But who am I? I don't control Lily's life."

"Believe it or not, I don't control James's, either."

"Just his money."

Simon squared his jaw. "Just his father's corporate interests. What James does with the rest of his inheritance is his business."

She appeared to think that over. "You have to see, though, that Lily and James think you're being positively medieval about this."

"I don't consider requiring a prenuptial agreement unreasonable. If Lily loves James, she shouldn't balk at the idea of protecting him."

She visibly bristled. Simon immediately knew he'd made a serious tactical error. "Of course she loves him," she said hotly. "If you think Lily would marry James for his money—"

Excessive passion, Simon reminded himself. Messy and complicated. He moved quickly to head off her tirade. "I didn't mean to imply that your cousin's interest in James was mercenary."

Her face had flushed slightly, giving her a peachlike hue that sparked an illicit vision in his mind. "I hate to break this to you, Simon, but that's exactly the way it sounds."

"Then my apologies," he said smoothly. "Maybe I've been his lawyer for too many years. I have a gut instinct for protecting James from anything that might hurt him."

She was probing him, searching his eyes for something, and he found himself worried that she might not find it. Finally she nodded briefly, apparently satisfied. "I can understand that. Sometimes I feel more like Lily's mother than her cousin." Her lips twitched at the corner. "And if you use that against me, I'll kill you."

"I'm sure you would."

"Even if I agree with you that they're rushing this, I'm not going to alienate Lily just because I think she's being a little rash."

"I wasn't asking you to." What she didn't know was that he was too good at strategy to even consider the possibility. Jordan, he knew, though twelve years older than her cousin, was very close to the girl. Lily Benton had been a newborn when Jordan came to live with her aunt and uncle in Boston. Though James had known only sketchy details of the story, he had told Simon that Jordan's parents were missionaries. When Jordan turned twelve, they'd decided she needed the security and quality of an American education, and had sent her to live with the Bentons. Alone and probably feeling abandoned, Jordan had bonded with her infant cousin.

"What both of us are going to have to accept, Simon," Jordan was telling him now, "is that they're old enough to make their own decisions."

"I'm aware of that," he said tightly. "That doesn't mean I wouldn't like to keep him from making a mistake like rushing into marriage with a woman he barely knows." If his suspicions about Lily's sudden emergence in James's life proved to be correct, he'd go to extraordinary lengths to ensure that James came away from the relationship relatively unscathed. Broken hearts healed. Bad decisions, Simon knew, could last a lifetime.

Jordan studied him a moment, then exhaled a long breath. "This really isn't personal, is it?"

"Personal about Lily, you mean?"

She nodded. "Yes."

"Of course not. I like her."

Her lips twitched again. "She certainly doesn't think so."

"Then she's mistaken. James could have done far worse."

"I'm glad you see that. Lily is convinced you think she'll ruin James' life."

"She's wrong."

"That's what I told her." She dug through the purse a moment, then produced a tube of lip balm. She applied it with an efficient flick of her wrist. Simon had a brief memory of watching his last date go through the apparently painstaking process of applying lipstick. The contrast between the brittle artificiality of the women he knew and Jordan's artless grace, he realized, was precisely what James was talking about when he waxed on about how different Lily was from the other girls he'd known. Jordan evidently had had a positive influence on her cousin's life. She dropped the lip balm back in her cavernous purse. "And for what it's worth," she told Simon, "I like James. He's a great kid."

"What's not to like?"

That made her smile. "Spoken like a true friend. He suits Lily. He's . . . gentle."

"Naïve, you mean?"

"No," she mused, "I wouldn't say naïve. Just not polished like most of the guys Lily knows. He seems real. Genuine. I like that."

"James is a pretty basic kind of kid. In some ways he's incredibly mature—"

"Losing both your parents so young will do that to a person," she said softly.

Simon nodded. "But socially"—he shrugged—"let's just say that wasn't a big priority in James's life."

"Which is why you're concerned," she mused.

"He's vulnerable. Someone could take advantage of him by playing his heart."

"Lily wouldn't do that."

"But I have no way of knowing that, do I?" he countered, not ready to tell her it was Lily's father he didn't trust.

"No. I suppose you don't."

"As James's attorney, it's my job to worry about his legal protection. That's why I want a prenuptial agreement."

"You can understand why James and Lily both think it's unromantic."

They wouldn't be worried about that, he thought silently, if their marriage blew up in a few years. "I'm also James's friend," he told her honestly. "And I'm more concerned about his heart than his finances."

Jordan's eyes widened. "Why, Simon. That's almost sensitive."

He had an odd feeling that he'd just passed a test of some type, and it grated on him. Before he could respond, Darius returned, backpack in hand. "Ready," the child announced.

"Did you thank Tim for the use of the piano?" Jordan asked him.

"Yeah. He said the chopsticks thing kicks, but the blues would sound better."

She laughed. "I told you. Not until after you prove to me that you can do Chopin." She stood, scooping up her bag. She slung it over her shoulder, and Simon wondered why it didn't knock her off balance. "Okay," Jordan said, "let's hit it." She looked at Simon. "Look, I hate to cut you off, but I've got to take Darius home. Was there something specific you wanted? Or were you just interested in my opinion about the lovebirds?"

"Is your car here?" he asked.

She gave him a wry look. "That would mean I have a car, and that I actually found a parking space here. Since I'm not talented enough to park it, I don't bother owning one. We took the T," she said, referring to Boston's infamous subway system.

"My car is out front," Simon informed her. "I'll take you, and we can continue our talk."

Her eyebrows lifted. "If you parked it out front, what makes you think it's still there?"

"Confidence." Simon indicated the door with his hand. "Please, Jordan," he prompted. "There are some things I want to discuss with you before their engagement party tomorrow night."

Jordan hesitated a moment longer, then nodded. "Okay, but we have to stop at Mr. Lee's Market for ice cream."

"Yes," Darius said, pumping the air with his fist.

"No problem," Simon assured her.

Darius grinned at her. "Thanks, Jorie."

"Just don't forget your promise about dinner. Your mama will have my head."

"I won't. I swear."

"You're going to regret that if she serves carrots," Jordan quipped as she started toward the door. She glanced over her shoulder at the battered piano. "Thanks, Tim," she called into the shadows.

"Any time, Jorie," came a voice from the darkness.

Darius slipped his hand into Jordan's as they made their way in front of the stage to the side door of the theater. "Jorie?"

"Hmm?"

"When we get to Mr. Lee's, can I have the colossal?"

"Don't push your luck, kid."

Simon swung the door open. Joe Baxter, his driver and personal assistant, was leaning against the side of the town car Simon used for most of his business in the city. Joe acknowledged him with a slight nod of his head.

Darius pressed his point about the ice cream. "I was just thinking—" He stopped abruptly when he saw the sleek black sedan. "Whoa. Is that a limo?"

"No," Jorie told him. "It's smaller."

Joe rounded the car to open the doors. "I see you found her, Simon."

"Finally," Simon told him. He indicated the front seat with a wave of his hand. "Darius, why don't you sit in the front so you can tell Joe how to find Mr. Lee's?"

Darius's eyes widened as he looked at the luxurious interior. "Man, this is phat. Are you really loaded?"

"No," Simon assured him. "I'm really busy."

Joe closed the door when Darius was seated. Jordan slipped into the backseat and slid across to make room for him. "You know how hard it is to park down here, Darius?" Simon asked the child.

"Sure. Mama says she's glad we don't got a car. You can't park it anyway."

Simon nodded. "That's why Joe helps me," he told Darius as Joe slid into the driver's seat. "I can get work done while Joe looks for a place to park."

"What if there ain't nowhere to park?"

Joe flashed Darius a grin. "Then I drive around the block until he's ready to leave."

"Dude." Darius settled back in his seat and snapped his seat belt into place. "Sucks to be you."

Joe laughed.

"Darius," Jordan prompted gently.

"It's all right," Simon assured her. "Joe probably feels the same way."

Joe met his gaze in the rearview mirror. "I told you I should get a raise, Simon."

"Don't let it go to your head."

Joe indicated Darius with a nod as he pulled

away from the curb. "I'm going to get the kid to lobby for me." He looked at Darius. "Where to, sir?"

Darius glanced at Jordan. She nodded. "It's okay. Do you know the way?"

"Sure. Between here and the T." He looked at Joe. "Straight down this street to the end, then turn that way. Mr. Lee's is on the right."

Joe guided the car into the traffic and expertly engaged Darius in a conversation about the Boston Celtics. Simon leaned back in his seat and looked at Jordan. "For what it's worth," he said, "James can't give me a single explanation about why he feels like they've got to rush down the aisle."

Jordan rolled her eyes. "Of course he can't. They're young and they're in love," she said with a dismissive wave of her hand. "Don't you remember it? Everything seems so dire and urgent."

"No," he said flatly. "I can honestly say I do not remember ever putting reason aside for passion."

Her laugh was a bubble of mirth. "I'll bet."

He gritted his teeth as the barb chafed him. James had to be his first priority. If the passionate Jordan Morrison found him ridiculous, that was her problem. "And Lily and James won't, either, if they're wise."

"I hate to break this to you, Simon, but I don't think wisdom is uppermost in their minds right now."

He would have responded, but Joe glided to a stop in front of Mr. Lee's Market. Darius was already on the sidewalk as Jordan pushed her door open. "I think Lily's right," she said over her shoulder. "You *are* a lost cause." She tapped Joe on the shoulder. "Ice cream?"

"Chocolate," he assured her.

Jordan glanced at Simon. "I'll pass," he told her, unreasonably irritated by her teasing.

"Suit yourself."

He watched her as she slid from the car with effortless grace. He wasn't sure why he let her get under his skin. He'd never known a woman who bothered him the way Jordan did. It wasn't a bad kind of bothered, he admitted, just a nagging sort of awareness that her opinion mattered more than it should.

He watched her follow Darius into the convenience store. He liked the way she moved. He had noticed it the day he'd met her. James had brought Lily downtown for lunch that day to meet Simon. James had selected a small bistro several blocks from their corporate headquarters at Wells Enterprises—the vast technology firm he'd inherited from his father. To Simon's surprise, and if the slightly suspicious look in her eyes was any indication, to Jordan's surprise as well, she had joined them a few minutes after they were seated.

Simon saw her when she'd entered the restaurant. The first thing that struck him was the paradox of the woman in the wrinkled skirt and baggy sweater, with the impossibly large purse and unruly hair, who moved with the grace of a ballerina and drew every eye in the place. He'd caught the slightly nervous look Lily had given James before she'd risen to meet her cousin. Jordan had glanced at Simon, then given Lily a slightly chastising look.

But she'd been charming and energetic at lunch, talking with James about the computer program he was designing, asking Lily about her plans for the engagement party. Simon had noted, however, that she'd seemed to avoid meeting his gaze. At first he'd wondered if she found him intimidating. That thought had died when he'd capitalized on James's comment that, having just met Lily several weeks before, he was not yet sure what her preferences might be for the wedding. Simon had seized the opportunity to indicate the wisdom of a prenuptial agreement given the pace of their march down the aisle. That comment had earned him a withering look from Jordan that might have melted a lesser man.

Instead, Simon found it intriguing. He had an exceptional and well-honed talent for reading people, and he'd bet real money that she was no happier with the young couple's mad dash toward matrimony than he, yet she'd risen quickly to her cousin's defense when James had insisted that he trusted Lily implicitly and that no agreement was necessary.

Jordan's look of distaste had told Simon precisely what he wanted to know. He knew from James that she had enormous influence in Lily's life. The two were closer than most sisters. If he wanted to count on that bond to achieve his objectives in the next few weeks, he'd have to use a strategy other than logic to win her cooperation.

Simon had factored that piece of information into his developing strategy as he'd contemplated how best to proceed. At any cost, he was determined to find out what Lily and her father stood to gain from her marriage to James. Jordan could be a valuable ally, he knew.

"So what do you think, boss?" Joe asked from the front seat as they watched Jordan walk into the crowded market with Darius.

Simon met his driver's gaze in the rearview mirror. "I think she's trouble."

That made Joe laugh. "Yeah, me too."

Simon looked at Jordan again. He could see her through the plate-glass windows as she placed the ice cream order. She had drawn the attention of most of the customers as she laughed with the clerk.

"You still want her?" Joe asked.

He had no idea, Simon thought. "If she'll take the job."

Jordan and Darius returned to the car with three large cones. She passed Joe a double chocolate scoop through his window before sliding in next to Simon again. "Hold this a second," she told him, pressing the cone of pink and green sherbet into his hand. "And don't lick it." While she fumbled with her seat belt, she instructed Darius. "Let Joe hold your cone, D, and put your seat belt on."

The child complied. Jordan took her cone from Simon and swirled her tongue around the top with a sigh of delight. "Passion fruit," she told him. The tip of her tongue darted out to lick the corner of her mouth. "You have no idea what you're missing."

Simon had long suspected that all women secretly knew that men found the sight of them licking ice cream nerve-wrackingly erotic, despite—or maybe because of—the complete innocent enjoyment in their eyes when they did it. But Jordan raised the standard. Each peek of her pink tongue tightened his gut. "I'll take your word for it," he drawled.

Joe asked Darius for his address, then eased the car into the heavy afternoon traffic. Jordan licked a drip off the back of her hand. Simon suppressed a groan. "So, James and Lily," she said. "What made you come all the way down here to tell me that you think they're rushing things? I already knew that."

Simon carefully planned his next words. The strategy of the next few moments, he knew, was crucial to his success. And he excelled at strategy. "I had the impression that day at lunch that you agreed with me." He looked at her closely. "I'm relieved to know I was right."

Jordan shrugged. "Whether I agree or not doesn't really seem to matter. Lily's a very independent girl. She's going to do what she wants."

"So is James."

"Then you should know that if you put pressure on them, it's only going to make them more determined. If you make it too hard, they might just ditch the wedding altogether and elope."

"I've considered that."

"Glad to hear it." She took a large bite of the pink sherbet, then licked her lips.

Simon shifted slightly in his seat. "I've said what I need to say to James. He knows I think he's being unwise."

"Then let it go. That's my advice."

"Have you?" he prompted.

"Have I what?"

"Let it go?"

Jordan nodded. "Lily hasn't asked for my opinion yet. When she does, I'll tell her. In the meantime I'm not going to make her miserable when this should be one of the happiest times of her life." She shook her head slightly. "She really loves him, Simon."

He looked at her closely, relieved at her ingenuous tone and the lack of duplicity he saw in her eyes. His instincts about her were correct. "Love can be messy, Jordan," he said quietly.

"And wild and uninhibited and glorious."

Excessive passion, he recalled grimly. His throat felt suddenly tight.

"We're here," Joe announced as he glided to a stop in front of a run-down apartment building.

Jordan held Simon's gaze a moment longer, then looked at Darius. Her slight laugh broke the bubble of tension. He had a ring of chocolate ice cream around his mouth. "Hang on, Darius. You've got incriminating evidence all over your face." After a brief foray into the purse, she produced a premoistened wipe. "Use this." She handed the foil packet to Darius.

How in the hell, Simon wondered, did she find stuff in that bag? She looked at Simon as Darius cleaned his face. "I guess I wasn't much help to you."

"I wouldn't say that," he assured her.

Darius balled up the wipe and handed it to Jordan. "Okay?" he asked.

She nodded. "Better."

"You still coming to dinner?"

"Yes." She reached for the door handle as she glanced at Simon again. "Was there something else you wanted?"

Definitely. "I have a proposition to make," he

told her. "I had hoped we'd have time to discuss it before the engagement party tomorrow night."

She winced. "My day is horrific tomorrow. My boss has a press conference Monday, which means he'll put his foot in his mouth like always. Which means that I'll be on the phone for the rest of the week doing damage control. Anything I hope to get done, I'd better finish this weekend." She worked, James had told him, as the media and policy director for a small nonprofit children's advocacy firm. "I might have some time in the afternoon."

Darius had climbed out onto the sidewalk where several young boys were admiring Simon's car. Darius was preening for his audience. Simon decided to press his advantage. He pushed the button to electronically roll down his window and spoke to Darius. "You want to show them the inside?"

Darius's eyes widened slightly. "Can I?"

Simon shrugged. "Sure."

Jordan frowned at him. "Simon—"

He cracked open his door and stepped onto the curb. Darius instructed his friends to line up. "Don't touch anything," he warned. "It's buff, and I don't want you getting it dirty in there."

Jordan got out of the car on her side and glared at Simon over the roof. "What are you doing?"

Darius held one boy back as the first climbed through the car, admiring the leather interior and chrome trim. "One at a time, man. This is my boy Simon's car. Show some respect."

"Thanks," Simon told Darius.

"Sure. You know how they are. They'd trash it if you don't watch 'em." Darius let the next boy in, then leaned down to smack his hand when he would have palmed a leather business card case he found wedged into the seat. "Don't touch."

The boy glared at Darius, but moved through the vehicle without further comment.

Darius rolled his eyes. "They don't mean nothing by it," he explained to Simon. "Just nobody ever learned 'em better."

Simon slipped his hands into his pockets. "Who taught you?"

"Mama." Darius grinned at him as he let the next boy into the car. "Mama would have skinned the black right off of me if she caught me stealing something."

"Sounds like a smart woman, your mother."

Darius's nod was solemn. "The best."

"I'd like to meet her."

Darius seemed to consider that. "You want to stay for dinner?" he asked.

Jordan groaned. Simon slid her a knowing look. "Actually," he told Darius, "if it's all right with your mother, I'd love to."

Lavonia Jackson, it turned out, seemed thrilled to have Simon added to her dinner table. He'd told Joe to head home after Darius's impromptu tour. He'd take a cab when the time came. Lavonia had looked from Simon to Jordan and back again with a broad smile and a knowing twinkle in her eye. Simon had the distinct impression that if Jordan had been wearing high heels and not the leather clogs, she'd have buried her heel in the arch of his foot.

Dinner was pleasant and comfortable, and Simon found himself almost unaccustomedly relaxed. There was a homey feel to listening as Lavonia questioned Darius about his day, cautioned him about a group of friends he'd begun to hang with at school, and generally probed him for the details of his world. She and Jordan talked about their respective work. The two women had met, Simon gleaned, when Darius's case had landed on the desk of one of Jordan's coworkers. Her firm specialized in advocacy for kids like Darius who were gifted in the arts but at risk of falling through the cracks of the system. Lavonia was working toward her GED and worked a retail job. She had a child care arrangement of sorts with her local church where Darius went after school while his mother was working. There he'd learned to play the piano. When the pastor had recognized that Darius had an extraordinary talent, he'd referred the case to Jordan's firm.

The two women had struck up an immediate friendship. James had told Simon that Jordan had a college degree from Boston's prestigious Berklee College of Music. She'd taken an interest in Darius at the request of one of the conuselors and begun giving him lessons. Lavonia didn't have a piano, and there had been a funeral that afternoon at the church where they usually had lessons—which explained why Simon had found Jordan at the theater on the South End.

Lavonia looked at him now and asked, "So you've heard the duet?"

Simon nodded. "It's good," he assured her. "A showstopper, definitely."

"See, Mama," Darius said. "I been telling you."

"So you have." Lavonia leaned back in her chair. "Jordan's been wonderful for him."

"He's got a lot of talent, Lavonia," Jordan said. "And we need to find him a teacher who actually knows how to teach." At Simon's raised eyebrow, she shook her head. "I know how to play. It's not the same thing."

"You teach good, Jorie," Darius insisted.

"Thanks," she told him, "but you're going to outgrow me soon." She looked at Simon. "Darius is talented enough to earn a college scholarship if he sticks with his playing and gets some formal training. We have some teachers we refer kids to, but no one at his level."

Lavonia sighed. "I know the Lord will work it out somehow, but right now I can't afford the extra cost of lessons. Not even with the supplement

Art-Is-In will provide. I wish he had a piano to practice on here. I can't always get him down to the church."

Jordan covered her hand with a reassuring squeeze. "We'll find the right teacher. Then we'll work out the rest of the money."

Lavonia hesitated a moment, then shook off her grim mood with a determined nod. "I'm sure you're right." She looked at Simon. "So tell me, Mr. Grant—"

He held up his hand. "Simon, please."

"Simon," she acknowledged. "What is it that has you tracking Jordan all the way down to a theater in the South End and driving my boy home in a limousine?"

"It's a town car, Mama," Darius said, pained.

"Somebody other than you drove it, didn't they?" she asked.

Darius nodded. "Joe drives it."

"Then it's a limousine." She looked at Simon again. "Does this have to do with Lily and your young friend?"

"Yes." He looked at Jordan. "The engagement party is tomorrow night."

Lavonia whistled softly. "She's really going to marry that boy?"

Jordan nodded. "Looks like it."

Strategy, Simon reminded himself. What he needed here was strategy. "Unlike Lily, James doesn't have a large extended family."

Lavonia laughed. "That might not be such a bad thing. I'm sure poor Lily would like to get rid of some of hers."

Jordan rolled her eyes. "I can't say I blame her. They're my family, but there're a handful of them that are just plain nuts."

Lavonia looked at Simon. "Is James sure he wants to marry into that?"

"He seems to be," Simon said carefully.

"After he meets them all at that party tomorrow night," Lavonia asserted, "he might change his mind."

Jordan was watching Simon carefully. He spread his hands palm down on the table and studied his fingers. "I don't think so."

"He hopes so," Jordan said to Lavonia. "He thinks they're moving too fast."

"They are," Lavonia agreed. "It's not going to kill either one of them to wait a year or so. Does that girl have any idea how serious marriage is?"

"Lily's very levelheaded." Jordan leaned back in her chair. "I think she's thought all this through and decided that if James is right for her, there's no point in waiting."

Lavonia clucked her tongue. "Sounds like Lily." She looked at Simon. "Are you trying to talk James out of it?"

"I've asked him to be cautious," Simon said.

"He could cut off James's inheritance," Jordan said.

Lavonia gave him a shrewd look. "I see."

Darius interjected, "You don't want Lily and James to get married? How come?"

"It's my job to protect Wells Enterprises," Simon clarified. "If I think James is jeopardizing the future of the company, I can restrict him." He gave Jordan a close look. "I'm not going to make him destitute."

"Just unemployed."

He held on to his patience. "I'm confident it won't come to that."

Lavonia clucked her tongue. "You push too hard, you'll make him mad."

Simon glanced at Jordan. "That's what I hear."

"So that still doesn't answer my question," Lavonia persisted. "What do you want with Jorie?"

A smile played at the corner of his mouth. She had no idea how complicated that question was. "I want her to make me look charming," he said simply.

Chapter Two

𝄢

JORIE CHOKED ON HER SWALLOW OF ICED TEA. The day she'd met him, she'd understood why Lily found him intimidating. Simon Grant was the kind of man who knew exactly what he wanted and exactly how to get it. He was bold, determined, and absolutely self-confident, which made him indomitable.

And sexy.

He exuded a something Jordan called self-power awareness, meaning he knew exactly what kind of impact he had on a room, and never hesitated to use it. Jordan found him incredibly attractive, in a forbidden-fruit sort of way. She wouldn't describe him as handsome; the word seemed too soft for his angular features, and for him in general. By far his most striking feature was his eyes.

The color of wet leaves, his deep green eyes seemed fathomless. Even the wire-frame glasses he wore did nothing to mask the unusual and beautiful color, or the type of luxuriant lashes that were entirely wasted on men. Framed with thick hair, too dark to be called brown and too subtle to be called black, his face was a fascinating plane of angles and lines. The absolute and irrefutable masculinity of his face, she'd decided, simply set off the beauty of his eyes.

But beneath the surface, Simon had an edge to him, something that said he'd achieved his success through hard work and determination, not through the advantages of a well-to-do family and political connections. Though his external packaging suggested wealth, Jorie recognized the sharpness in his gaze. She saw it almost every day in the eyes of the people she worked with. It said that wherever he'd come from, he wasn't going back.

She looked at him now, searching for something, anything, that might tell her what he was up to. "You can't be serious," she said carefully.

His grave nod told her he was completely serious. "With the exception of his Uncle Howard, I'm the only family James has. I've been to enough weddings to know that the groom's family has some responsibilities for all this. I don't want James to feel uncomfortable."

Jordan studied him. In the cheery light of Lavonia's kitchen, his forest green shirt made his broad shoulders look broader and, somehow, his eyes look even greener. This, she thought dryly, from the man who'd charmed his way into a dinner invitation from Darius. Lavonia had been happy to feed him, more than a little intrigued by the man Jordan had told her was both arrogant and narrow-minded.

Simon elaborated. "Because of your relationship with Lily, you seem like the most natural choice."

Jorie frowned. "Choice for what?"

He made a slight gesture with his hands. "You're a public relations director. I want you to help me publicly relate."

Lavonia laughed. "Lord, Jorie. How are you going to say no to an offer like that?"

"You have got to be kidding," she said to Simon.

"I don't kid."

She could believe that. "You don't expect me to believe that you need etiquette lessons."

"What's etiquette?" Darius probed.

His mother shot him a dry look. "It's manners for rich people."

That made Darius frown. "How come they can't have regular manners like the rest of us?"

Lavonia pointed to his plate. "Eat, Darius. You've still got homework."

Simon held Jorie's gaze. "There's a lot of entertaining involved in this."

"What you need is a professional party planner. Not me."

"I'll have to interact with your family."

Lavonia snorted. "He's got a point there, Jorie. Nobody handles that crowd like you do."

Jorie shook her head. "I don't think James is expecting—"

"I don't think James should be deprived of the normal trappings simply because he was orphaned at fourteen," Simon said smoothly.

The fiend, Jorie thought. He'd played that card with an absolutely emotionless face, as if he hadn't known he was pulling out the heavy artillery. He knew he'd strike a soft spot and he'd never even hesitated. An inner voice warned her that Simon would never be the kind of man who hesitated. He saw what he wanted, and he seized it. In her cautious, simple world, he'd cause havoc. "That's a little melodramatic, don't you think?" she said softly.

Simon shrugged. "I'd rather have someone who knows Lily well, who knows what her preferences might be, than a complete stranger."

The day she'd met him, she'd known he was trouble. Something in his expression as he'd listened to James explain his plans to marry Lily by the end of the summer had haunted her. She hadn't been able to put her finger on it then, but she was beginning to realize it was the slight vulnerability behind the stoic mask that had struck her as so incongruous. And utterly irresistible. She banished the thought as quickly as it occurred to her. Simon Grant was trouble—big trouble. No matter how vulnerable or wounded he might look, she could not, *would* not succumb to the urge to rescue him. He didn't want rescuing. She'd do well to remember that. "Really, Simon, all you have to do is host the rehearsal dinner. Any competent planner could—"

"But there are Lily's parties. Family events." Simon leaned forward and braced his elbows on the table. "Like the engagement party tomorrow night. You said yourself that if I give James the impression that I'm completely opposed to the wedding, he'll resent me for it. He'll probably rebel. So the best way to prove to him that I'm supportive is to build bridges with Lily's family."

Jorie probed his expression warily. Though he looked ingenuous, something told her there was a deeper reason for his apparently simple request. "What, exactly, do you want me to do?"

"Go with me to a couple of events. Introduce me around. Help me provide Lily and James with whatever's expected of James's family." He shook his head, and a wave of dark hair tumbled over his forehead. That, Jorie figured, probably drove him crazy. She had a strong feeling that Simon didn't like things to be out of control. "Lily trusts you. Consequently, so does James."

"And?"

"And I think right now they see me as the enemy."

"I wouldn't say that—exactly."

"No? You said yourself that Lily thinks I don't like her."

"James thinks you don't see him as an adult."

"He's wrong."

"I think Lily's a little intimidated by you, but I wouldn't call you the enemy."

"You see? What I have is a bad image. Images are fixed by public relations experts."

Lavonia's expression turned gloating. "He's got you there, girlfriend."

"I hate to break this to you," Jorie told him, "but I don't think there's enough spin in the western hemisphere to dig you out of the pit you created when you started demanding prenuptial agreements."

"Oh Lord," Lavonia said. "Don't tell me."

"What's that?" Darius probed.

"It's like a contract," Jorie told him. "People sign it before they get married so that if they get divorced, neither one gets to keep the other one's stuff."

Darius's expression turned puzzled. "If you gotta have a contract for that, I don't think you should get married at all."

"Thank you," Jorie told him.

"Eat, Darius," his mother instructed.

Jorie looked at Simon. "You see? It's a bad idea."

"I didn't insist on it," he said tightly.

"You just intimated," Jorie pointed out, "that without it, you'd consider restricting James's role at Wells Enterprises."

"Temporarily. I said I'd consider restricting it temporarily."

"If you were twenty-two, how would you react to that?" Jorie asked him.

He never would have gotten himself in James's position in the first place, Simon thought. He didn't let other people have control over his life or his choices. But James was tender, different, and if he had to vilify himself to do it, Simon was determined to protect him.

He realized Jorie was waiting for an answer. "Probably no better than James," he admitted. "Which is why I didn't simply tell him he couldn't marry her."

"Good thing," Lavonia said.

"I could have, you know," Simon pointed out.

Jorie rolled her eyes. "That's not the point. The point is that when you told James he needed to make Lily sign an agreement, he immediately took that as your opposition to *Lily*, not as opposition to the idea of his marrying her too quickly. And so did Lily."

"And neither of them," he concurred, "is going to listen to anything else I have to say."

"That's right. All they hear right now is that you don't like Lily and you think she's wrong for James."

"Which is why I need you." He gave her a satisfied look. "Until they believe that this has nothing to do with them individually, I have no chance of influencing their decision."

He was right, and she knew it. Though Simon's concerns about the relationship were different from hers, she had worries of her own. If he exercised anywhere near the amount of influence on James that she suspected, he could prove to be an invaluable if unlikely ally. Simon seemed to sense her indecision and capitalized on it. "We'll be stronger as a team," he insisted.

She frowned. "Besides weeks of frustration and anxiety, what's in this for me?"

"In addition to access to my dynamic personality?"

At the taunt, she felt a slight smile play at the corner of her mouth. Damn the man. He reminded her of an elephant—tactless, methodical, unwieldy, overpowering, and utterly adorable. "That, too."

"Well, how about a four-hundred-thousand-dollars donation from Wells Enterprises to your foundation?"

Her mouth dropped open. "Four hundred *thousand* dollars?" Jorie quickly calculated the amount in her mind. It would cover the agency's overhead for a year, allowing them to divert grant money to several underfunded projects.

"Yes." He nodded slightly.

"Five zeros?"

"I'll make out a contract if you'd like."

"Simon, I can't—"

"And"—he tipped his head toward Darius— "a piano. For Darius."

The following evening, Jorie scanned the crowd at Lily's engagement party with unease. Not, she admitted to herself, an entirely bad feeling. More like nervous anticipation. After Simon's bombshell the night before, she had spent a mostly sleepless night weighing the pros and cons of his offer. Common sense told her it was nothing more than a simple bargain. Simon was trying to do his best by James. He realized he'd lost ground when he'd raised the issue of the prenuptial agreement, and the only chance he stood of getting James to heed his advice was to prove that he had nothing against Lily.

Jorie could help him with that, since the young couple trusted and liked her, and since Lily had always relied heavily on her advice. In exchange for her help, he was willing to authorize a hefty, tax-deductible donation to Art-Is-In, the nonprofit advocacy group where Jorie worked. It should be simple.

It didn't feel simple. She couldn't shake the

idea that, though he seemed plainspoken enough, he had not yet revealed his hand.

She had pounded her pillow and chastised herself for blowing the entire episode out of proportion. Sometime around four in the morning, she'd fallen into a fitful sleep, hoping that the next day would bring a sign that might make the decision easier. It had come by way of a bankruptcy declaration from one of the agency's major funders. If Simon's offer was tempting before, now it appeared to be heaven-sent.

Jorie had called him that afternoon and told him she'd meet him at the party tonight if she could pick up the check within the next two weeks. Looking now at the large crowd, she felt a flutter of anticipation. For the first time in years, she was actually looking forward to one of her Aunt Nora's soirees. No doubt she'd cause enormous speculation once people began to realize she was there with Simon. And she was sure her aunt would have something to say about that. Nora seemed to viscerally despise poor Simon. Lily had reported her mother's increasingly derisive opinions about the man who was standing in the way of Lily's nuptial bliss. Nora would have plenty to say, Jorie knew, about her apparent alliance with him.

The thought gave her a sense of smug satisfaction for which she sent up a quick prayer of repentance. She and her aunt had clashed many times, but Nora had always taken care of her basic needs. Vengeance, her father would tell her, belonged to the Lord. That didn't mean, however, that Jorie didn't enjoy the opportunity to play a small part in it. There was nothing, she thought devilishly, like creating a disturbance to liven up a party.

Jorie spotted Nora across the room. Her mother's only sister, Nora was the one member of the vast Ludwell clan that had chosen a traditional path to success. She'd married money. Lots of money. And she'd made no secret of her disapproval of her sister's choice of husband and profession. Long ago, Jorie had learned that the easiest way to keep Nora from getting under her skin was to stay out of her way. As long as her aunt didn't manipulate her into an impromptu piano concert, Jorie might escape the evening in a relatively decent mood.

Finally she located Nora standing near the entrance to the dining room surrounded by a cluster of her husband's business associates. In her element, her aunt was holding court. Jorie had a brief vision of the comfort and simplicity of Lavonia Jackson's home. Compared to the opulence in Nora Benton's Avon Hill residence, Lavonia's life seemed humble, simple, and far more welcoming. And happier, Jorie added when Nora spotted her and acknowledged her with a brief nod.

Safe, Jorie thought. For the moment. Lily truly

had no idea how much Jorie loved her to endure one of these events at her aunt and uncle's house. Crowds bothered her enough as it was, but Nora's parties made her downright nuts. Too many times, Nora had held her up as a specimen to be examined and talked about. Though she knew Nora hadn't intended to make her feel so freakish, at twelve she hadn't understood her aunt as well as she did now. Still, she'd learned to loathe these events, and if that wasn't enough to have her edgier than usual, tonight she had Simon Grant to deal with.

"You look better."

At the sound of the deep voice in her ear, Jorie started. She turned to find Simon standing behind her. "Better than what?" she prompted.

"Than before."

She wondered if the man had even the slightest clue how absolutely maddening he was. "Maybe you need more help with etiquette than I thought," she quipped.

"I didn't mean it like that," he insisted and pressed a glass of iced tea into her hand. "I saw you come in earlier." When she didn't respond, Simon prompted, "The rain."

With a laugh, Jorie's hand flew to her hair. "Oh Lord, you mean Noah's flood?" She'd arrived at the Bentons thirty minutes ago, running late and drenched to the skin. A cold front had come through that day, bringing torrential downpours in its wake. Trapped at the office with no umbrella, she'd dashed for the T with a piece of newspaper to keep her hair dry. The paper had failed before she made it down the first block, leaving her hair a tangle of wet curls. The walk from the station to the Bentons undid whatever repairs she'd been able to make during the short subway ride.

"Can I say you did a remarkable job in"—he checked his watch—"twenty-eight minutes?"

"Practice," she assured him. "Thank goodness I had the foresight to bring my dress with me rather than changing at the office." The vintage 1940s dress she'd picked up at a thrift store was one of her favorites. The rich gold fabric complemented her coloring, and the sleek cut flattered her.

He gave her an appraising look. "Nice dress. Old?"

Jorie stifled a groan. What in the world had she gotten herself into? "Do you get many dates with lines like that?"

He gave her a blank look. "It wasn't a pickup line."

"Thank God," she muttered.

"I just wondered if it was a vintage piece." He touched the hem of the sleeve where a fringe of beads lay against her arm. His fingers were impossibly warm, and Jorie felt a path of goose bumps trail down her arm. "It looks old."

With a brief shake of her head, Jorie handed

him the tea and went back up two steps. "Let's start over," she told him. "I come down," she said, her hand on the railing. "You approach and say, 'Miss Morrison, you look fabulous.' "

A devilish smile played at the corner of his mouth making him look incredibly sexy. "You do, you know?"

Easy, Jorie, she warned herself when her heart flipped. She couldn't afford to let him any closer than arm's length. Her resolve was strong enough when he was annoying her, but one flash of that enticing grin, and she felt herself nearing the slippery slope of disaster. She mentally pulled herself together. "Now you offer me the tea."

He extended it to her. "Tea?"

"Why thank you, Mr. Grant. You look very nice yourself."

"Good," he said simply, and turned to scan the room.

Jorie rolled her eyes. "Almost," she mumbled.

He glanced at her. "What?"

"Nothing."

Simon shrugged and surveyed the large crowd again. "I haven't seen James and Lily yet," he told her.

Which was probably a good thing, Jorie thought. In tailored black trousers, a snow white shirt, and a green tie, he looked sophisticated, poised, and unapproachable. He'd probably give

Lily the hives. Jorie took a fortifying sip of her tea, then met Simon's gaze again. "We'll find them sooner or later," she assured him. "Lily may not have come down yet."

"How much longer?" He sounded irritated.

"Have you always been this antisocial?"

"I hate parties."

"Me too," she assured him, "but I know better than to act like it in public."

His sour expression didn't change. "I've never seen the point in pretending to be something I'm not."

Lord, the man was exasperating. "I'm not suggesting that you do," she told him. "I'm saying that for the sake of those around you, you might want to consider losing that expression."

"What expression?"

"The one that says, *Talk to me and die.*"

He looked momentarily stunned. "It does not."

"Looked in a mirror lately?"

He frowned at her teasing rebuke. "Simon," she said chidingly, "parties are for having a good time. You're supposed to enjoy yourself."

"I've read that somewhere."

Did he have any idea, she wondered, how unbearably cute he was with that slightly pained expression on his face? She laughed and held up her hands in surrender. "Okay. Okay, you win."

His grim expression eased a bit. He gave her a

rueful look. "Sorry. You can imagine how much of this goes on in James's life. I've been enduring it for years."

"Then the next few months are going to be very hard on you. You'll have to do a lot of this."

His shoulders lifted in a motion far too graceful to be called a shrug. "I'll get over it. I'm used to it."

The hollow sound of his voice arrested her teasing. Jorie had spent too much time at Nora's parties feeling miserable and uncomfortable not to sympathize with him. She was always nervous in large crowds, and the crush often became stifling to her as the evening wore on. "I understand." When he looked at her sharply, she nodded. "I do. I'm kind of crowd phobic, actually."

He raised an eyebrow. "You?"

"You look surprised."

"You like people."

"That doesn't mean I want to be surrounded by them all the time." She tipped her head to one side. "Don't you like people, Simon?"

"Not many," he admitted.

That made her laugh. "I'm sorry," she said at his sudden fierce frown. "I'm not laughing at you, I swear." She suppressed her mirth and laid a hand on his sleeve. "You're just very . . . honest. Sometimes it catches me off guard."

"Do you know a lot of dishonest people?" he probed.

"Sure. Most people are honest about nearly

everything except their feelings. They don't think it's socially acceptable to say how they feel."

"I've never understood the point of artifice."

The angles of his face seemed to have sharpened. Jorie found herself struggling to resist the urge to smooth the sharp crease from his forehead with her fingertip. She glanced around the room and, not seeing James and Lily, decided she and Simon could safely slip away for a brief respite without being noticed. "Come with me," she said softly, and led the way to one of the many places she'd used as a refuge in the past.

Simon threw a quick glance over his shoulder, then followed her. Jorie stopped several times to introduce him to a relative or make small talk with one of her uncle's business associates. She answered questions about her work, deftly avoided questions about her private life, and made steady progress toward the small hallway near the back of the entry foyer.

"Jorie?" An older woman grabbed her forearm.

Five more steps, Jorie calculated, and they'd be free. She smiled at her cousin. "Hello, Edna."

"Dear, where in the world have you been? I haven't seen you for months."

"Staying busy as usual." Jorie patted Edna's hand. "I was just on my way to look for Lily," she said smoothly. "Did you need something?"

Edna gave Simon a curious look. "Do you finally have a man in your life?" she said bluntly.

Jorie laughed. "Edna, just because you haven't met them doesn't mean there aren't men in my life."

Her elderly cousin shook her gray head as she looked at Simon. "She needs to settle down," she told him. "She's way too old to be running around on her own."

Simon gave Jorie a dry look. "Is that so?"

"Now, Edna," Jorie said indulgently, "that's not true and you know it. You never got married."

"And look how I turned out," Edna said. "Cantankerous and inflexible."

Jorie smiled at her. "You are not. You're eccentric. That's not a bad thing."

"Hmm. Ask your aunt about that."

"I'd rather not," Jorie admitted.

Edna waved her cane in Simon's direction. "This one looks fine enough. Anything wrong with you?" she asked him.

"Not that I know of," Simon assured her.

Edna nodded. "Then I'd grab him if I were you." She patted Jorie's arm. "Or I might just go after him myself."

Jorie laughed. "I'll remember that." She gently disengaged herself from the woman's grip on her arm and eased the final few feet to safety. Tucked beneath the curve of the stairs, mostly hidden by a large potted fern, was a secluded marble bench. Jorie held back the fern and motioned for Simon to precede her into the small alcove. She let the fern drop behind her as she joined him in the intimate space. "We can rest in here for a few minutes. I don't think anyone will miss us."

Simon sat on the bench. "You've been here before," he said quietly.

Jorie smiled as she sat behind him. "Many times. After two or three hours of standing in three-inch pumps, it's a great place to take a break."

"Next time I wear high heels," he said, his expression utterly serious, "I'll remember that."

"Good God, Simon, are you teasing me?"

"No matter what Lily might have told you," he said dryly, "I do have a sense of humor."

She was sure she heard a slight rebuke in his voice. "I wasn't—"

Simon shook his head. "Sorry. I didn't mean to sound irritated. Parties make me edgy."

"I understand."

"And, frankly, I'm a little weary of the overbearing guardian stereotype. It doesn't fit me."

She winced, aware that she'd fallen just as neatly into the trap of making suppositions about him as Lily. "I'm sorry," she said quietly. "I don't want you to think—"

He held up a hand. "No apology necessary. I created this mess when I reacted to James's announcement the way I did. I should have played it differently."

"It shocked all of us," she commiserated.

He tipped his head back against the wall and

momentarily shut his eyes. "I used to think that when James became an adult, I'd quit worrying about him. Instead it's worse. I feel like an old woman."

"Hmm," she said with a knowing smile. "Welcome to parenthood."

"When James was a child, I used to listen to his father, Peter, tell me how much he worried about him. I thought he was crazy. I had no idea."

"How old were you when you became James's guardian?"

"Twenty-nine. It scared me to death."

"I'll bet. That's a lot of responsibility."

"It was easy with James. He's a good kid. His father raised him well."

She shot him a knowing look. "I think he'd agree that you had something to do with it, too."

Simon's expression turned contemplative. "When Peter died, I knew a lot about the law and a lot about Wells Enterprises, and absolutely nothing about teenage boys. I just had to figure it out as we went along."

"Like the parents of most teenagers."

"Maybe." He took a swallow of his drink. "I made my share of mistakes."

"Like the parents of most teenagers," she repeated.

That won a slight smile. "I guess." He glanced at her. "It definitely could have been a lot harder.

James was more interested in playing with his computer than getting into trouble."

"Even when he discovered girls?"

Simon's eyes twinkled. "I'm pretty sure James didn't discover girls until he went to college. He was more serious than most of peers, which is understandable given what he went through. Normal high school girls didn't hold a lot of appeal for him. He didn't have a lot of patience with immaturity."

She shot him a brief smile. "Correct me if I'm wrong, but I'm guessing that when you were in high school, girls held plenty of appeal for you."

"My mother was a single parent. I grew up around a lot of women." He paused and gave her a dry look. "I always notice women."

Jorie swallowed. His eyes had that same smoldering look she'd noticed the night before. Like banked fire. Hot and smoky and ready to ignite. She leaned back against the curve of the stairs and resisted the urge to fan her suddenly warm face. "So, er, how did you meet Peter Wells?"

"My mother worked on his father's estate. She was a maid. Her compensation package included live-in quarters."

The play of emotions across his face fascinated her. A wealth of secrets lay behind that simple explanation. "Did you live there all your life?"

"I was eight when my mother got that job."

"Is she still living?"

"Died five years ago." His voice was utterly flat, as if he'd just delivered a stock report.

"Oh Simon. I'm sorry."

"It's all right," he assured her. "My mother lived a very fast life. People who live at that speed usually don't live long. I never expected her to."

Jorie's heart squeezed tight, but she heeded an inner warning to let the comment pass. Simon wasn't ready to trust her with the wounds beneath the carefully worded explanation. "So you met Peter at the estate?"

He blinked as her question brought him back to the present. "Oh. Yes. His father took an interest in me the day he caught me trying to steal a candlestick from his silver cabinet."

"I'll bet. What did he do to you?"

"He put the fear of God into me. He told me if he caught me doing anything like that again, he'd fire my mother and kick us off the estate." He scrubbed a hand over his face. "We'd never lived in a place that nice, and besides the fact that I didn't want to go back to rent-control apartment housing, I knew my mother would kill me."

"And you abandoned your life of crime?"

His eyes had regained their twinkle. "Not hardly. I just made sure old man Wells didn't catch me. It's amazing what you can get away with when you seduce the staff."

Jorie laughed. "No wonder you became a

lawyer. You'd have spent a fortune on legal fees bailing yourself out of trouble."

His expression turned serious again. "Actually, that was because of Peter. He was good to me, kind of like an older brother. He was home from school one summer, and he asked me to go with him and a bunch of his friends sailing. I'd never even seen the ocean until that day."

The image of a dark-haired little boy with deep green eyes, desperately trying to fit in with Peter Wells's friends, made her smile. "How old were you?"

"Ten."

"That was very generous of Peter."

"Yes." Simon fiddled with the end of his tie a moment. "I was nervous. I was afraid I'd look like a fool around all those older kids, but I wanted to be with Peter badly enough that I agreed to go."

Jorie watched the shadows moving across his expression. The noise of the party had escalated, and she had to lean closer to hear him. She caught the slightest whiff of his scent, clean and soapy and utterly masculine. In the intimacy of their hiding place, it made her head swim. She found herself wanting to unbutton his snow white shirt and find the source of it. "How did it turn out?" she questioned him. Her voice, she noted, had turned slightly raspy.

"I didn't fall in the water at least," he said with a slight laugh. "Peter taught me how to manipulate the sails. It was probably one of the best days of my life."

Jorie shifted on the small bench so she could see his face more clearly. "You idolized him," she said softly.

He raised his warm hand to rest on her shoulder. His fingers skimmed the edge of her dress where it lay against her collarbone, leaving a trail of goose bumps in their wake. For a long second he idly traced the line with his fingertip. "No one had ever taken an interest in me like that."

Jorie's heart twisted. "A lot of the kids my agency works with go through that. Darius has his mom, but some of them have never been encouraged or nurtured. It's very sad."

"But they survive."

"Everyone deserves to be loved, Simon."

He dropped his hand as his enigmatic mask slid back into place. "It wasn't easy for my mother," he told her. "Making ends meet was a priority. I had warm meals, a usually dry roof, and clothes on my back. That's more than a lot of kids."

Jorie laid her hand on his arm. "Of course. I wasn't suggesting—"

Simon shook his head. "I know. I just don't want you to think I have nothing but bad memories of it. It wasn't like that."

"Because you had Peter."

"I had Peter." Simon's expression turned rueful. "Although I'm pretty sure if I'd known what his ulterior motive was in taking me sailing that day, I might not have gone."

"One of life's harder lessons?" she guessed.

"The good ones usually are. After everyone left, Peter made me stay to help him clean the boat. It was the end of the summer, and he was getting it ready for winter dock. It's backbreaking work. I scrubbed deck boards until my fingers turned raw."

She nodded sympathetically. "I've done that before. It takes some of the allure out of sailing when the salt water feels like it's going to burn your fingertips off."

"Exactly. And Peter took the opportunity to point out to me that if I didn't straighten up, get an education, and make something of my life, then I could probably count on doing that kind of work until I died."

Jorie's eyebrows lifted. "I'm sure that had an impact."

"My mother cleaned houses and office buildings for a living. It's an honorable profession, but I knew I didn't want to do it. Peter told me that if I were smart enough to figure out how to pilfer stuff out of his house without getting caught by his dad, then I was probably smart enough to make decent grades in school. He promised me that day that if I graduated from high school without getting expelled, and with a decent enough GPA to get into school, he'd help me find the money."

"How old was Peter at the time?"

"Twenty-one. James is a lot like his father," Simon said. "Very wise and very mature in many ways, and not so much in other ways. James has his father's heart—huge and full of compassion." Simon paused. "And easily broken."

Jorie nodded. "Lily says that about him. He's a very sweet young man."

"Yes," Simon said carefully. "And Peter was the same way. He convinced his father to help me get a scholarship to college. Peter had already taken control of Wells Enterprises by then, and when I enrolled at Boston, he extended his promise. If I graduated in four years with a 3.0 average, he'd put me through law school."

"Some deal."

Simon laughed. "With a lot to his benefit," he told her. "James may have Peter's heart, but Peter had his father's head for business. In exchange for the free ride through law school, I had to agree to work for the company for at least five years as a contract attorney."

She studied him closely. "But he obviously loved you, or he wouldn't have named you as James's guardian."

"Peter trusted me," he said. "And I trusted him. That can be a tighter bond than love."

His expression had turned mercurial. The memories had obviously been bittersweet for him, and Jorie longed to reach up and smooth the wrinkle from his forehead. Every nurturing instinct she had roused to the image of a little boy, lonely and afraid, who desperately needed someone to love him.

He leaned closer to her, his gaze intent. "Or aren't you the kind of woman who knows the difference?"

Her lips parted slightly. "What kind of woman doesn't know the difference?"

He lifted a hand to toy with one of her dangling earrings. The feel of his warm fingers so close to her face made her skin tingle. "The kind that thinks with her heart," he said, "and not with her head." He lightly touched her jaw. "Your skin is beautiful," he said softly.

She wrapped her fingers around his wrist as a warning bell sounded in her brain that she was too close to the edge of that slope again. *Don't slip*, she cautioned herself. *Whatever you do, don't slip.* "Freckles," she protested lightly, trying to divert him.

"I like them." The pulse in his wrist pounded beneath her fingertips. "Are you that type of woman, Jordan?" he asked.

"I don't think—"

"I do." He pressed the pad of his thumb to the corner of her mouth. "I sensed it the day I met you. Excessive passion."

Her eyes drifted shut as he tipped his head toward her. "Simon—"

She felt his breath whisper across her lips an instant before she was startled by the sound of her name.

"Jorie?"

Jorie jumped when she recognized Lily's voice. "It's Lily," she told Simon. He hesitated, then moved slightly away.

The fern shifted. "Jorie, are you back there?"

Jorie stood quickly and moved toward the opening. "I'm here."

"I thought you might be." Lily's gaze turned curious as she spotted Simon. "Am I interrupting?" She glanced at Jorie. "You seem . . . engrossed."

Jorie shook her head as she emerged from the alcove. "No, not at all. Simon was just telling me about how he met James's father."

"I see," Lily said, her wary gaze darting to Simon again. He let the fern fall back in place as he joined Jorie in the hallway. "Hello, Simon."

"Lily," he said.

Her cousin looked, Jorie noted, as lovely as usual. Her blond hair was pulled back in a flattering style, and her blue dress emphasized her slender figure and her delicate coloring. With wide blue eyes and porcelain skin, Lily was as lovely as she'd ever been. Jorie felt a familiar twinge of melancholy. It was hard to believe twenty years had passed since she'd come to the Bentons' home as a lonely twelve-year-old girl who'd found solace in caring for and loving the newborn Lily.

Lily laid her hand on Jorie's arm. "I've been looking for you."

"Just taking a break," Jorie told her. "You know how I am with large crowds."

Lily glanced over her shoulder. "I was half tempted to join you. I think my mother got a little carried away with the invitations."

"She wanted to show you off. And I can't say I blame her. You look fabulous."

"Thanks. So do you."

Jorie felt a smile tug at the corner of her mouth. "How appalled do you think your mother is going to be about this dress?"

Lily laughed. "At least it's in style."

"Pure luck, I swear."

"And you look absolutely glamorous in it."

"You know how much of a priority that is for me," Jorie quipped airily.

Lily shook her head. "Sometimes I think you just enjoy rankling Mother. But if you're worried about it, I think she's too uptight about Dunstan to care what you're wearing tonight."

"Oh Lord." Jorie glanced past Lily's shoulder to the ever-growing crowd. "Is he here?" Of the entire extended family, her cousin Dunstan held the record for most tedious and most bizarre. The last time she'd seen him, he'd been trying to sell stock in a time-travel machine he claimed to have invented.

"Right now, Dad has him trapped in the study trying to fix the computer."

"What's wrong with it?"

Lily's eyes twinkled. "Nothing. James created a few problems for Dunstan to work on. He'll fix it later."

"At least he's found the way to Nora's heart."

"You have no idea." Lily looked at Simon again. "I'm glad you could make it," she told him. "James said you might not."

"I told him I'd be here. You look nice."

At the simple compliment, Jorie stifled a sigh of relief. So far, so good. He'd made it through two entire minutes of dialogue without saying anything offensive.

"Thanks," Lily said. "James said you'd like this dress because it doesn't make me look old enough to be married."

Simon's expression didn't alter. "I see."

"That's a joke," Lily insisted. "Honest."

Jorie exhaled a frustrated sigh. "Don't tease him, Lily. He's trying."

Lily looked momentarily baffled, then curious as she glanced between the two of them. "Jorie—"

Jorie sensed the direction of her cousin's thoughts and moved to intercept her. She looped her arm through Lily's elbow and turned to face the room. "Just promise me," she said quietly, "that your mother isn't going to make me play tonight."

Lily looked warily at Simon for a second longer, then smiled at Jorie. "I made her swear. I told you I would. But you know how she is."

Jorie nodded thoughtfully. "I'll try to slip out before things really get wound up."

"You can't leave before the announcement."

"I doubt your mother will ask me to play before the announcement."

"Good point." Lily smoothed her hands over her dress. "I really do appreciate your coming, Jorie. I know you'd rather be almost anywhere else right now."

"It's your party, Lily," Jorie insisted. "I wouldn't have missed it."

"Which means a lot to me." Lily gave her a quick hug and whispered in her ear, "Thanks for taking charge of Simon. I'm not looking forward to his meeting Mother."

"Lily—"

"I've got to go check on Aunt Martha," her cousin continued. "Mother swore she'd kill me if I let her corner any of Dad's business associates."

"You'd better hurry, then. I saw her toddling toward the den earlier."

"Oh, Lord help us, I'd better go get her." Lily started away, then shot Simon a look over her shoulder. "Thank you again for coming, Simon. It means a lot to James."

"I think she likes me," Simon said under his breath as Lily eased back into the crowd.

"The way I see it, no one drew blood, no one cried, and nothing got broken. Given the circumstances, I don't think we could have asked for more."

That made him laugh. He looked younger when he laughed, she noted. It warmed his eyes. "I'm glad to know your standards are so high."

"At least this won't be boring."

"Actually, I have it on excellent authority that I'm boring as hell."

"Who says?"

"The last woman I considered marrying."

Jorie's response was forestalled by the arrival of Linwood Hayes, one of her uncle's business associates. He greeted her briefly, then turned to Simon. "Grant—I had no idea you were in town."

Simon slipped his fingers beneath Jorie's elbow as he turned to address the comment as if he feared she'd use the excuse to slip away from him.

Utterly fascinating, Jorie thought with a sinking feeling. Since the day she'd met him, he'd had her off balance with that pure, adrenaline-pumping, stomach-fluttering excitement she felt just before falling hard for a man who would eventually break her heart. That day after lunch, she'd given herself a stiff talking-to. She'd actually managed to convince herself that the light-headed feeling she had came from waiting too long before she'd eaten lunch. But a nagging suspicion told her it had more to do with that lonely, stoic look on Simon's face.

Fool, fool, fool, a voice inside her warned. Under no circumstances could she afford to fall for him. In the past she'd taken on hopeless cases and strays with the same optimism that made her good at her job. She liked to salvage people. She'd met and casually dated several men who'd simply needed a little fixing. Most of them, she'd successfully paired off with women who had simply needed a little push to recognize the value in a fixer-upper kind of relationship.

But Simon was different. He was no weekend project she could take to heart and then release without a qualm. No, he was the lifelong kind of project, the kind that used his emotional detachment as armor and resisted every effort to peek behind the façade. He wouldn't go gracefully. Chances were, he wouldn't go at all. And the woman who tried would probably get seriously wounded in the process.

Her resolve had taken a serious blow when he'd asked her to help him. It hadn't been the request that had done it, however; it had been the slightly haunted look in his eyes. That, she admitted to herself now, was what had kept her up until the small hours of the morning. That look that said he had his own vulnerabilities, no matter how well masked. That look that said he had painful secrets he rarely revealed. That look that said he'd felt bitterly lonely and afraid and uncertain at one time in his life. It tempted her like Pandora's Box. She knew it was dangerous, but she desperately wanted to open the lid.

Jorie had never been able to resist that look. She could have spared herself several sleepless nights if she had. Jorie had decided long ago that saving herself from anxiety wasn't worth giving up the great joy of investing herself in people. A few days of tears, a long hot bath, a couple of pints of chocolate ice cream, and some concentrated time with her friends usually renewed her enough to make her feel like she'd survive 'till the next time. Before long another tortured soul would appear, and she'd find herself falling right down the same rabbit hole.

But some self-preservative instinct warned that Simon Grant was different. She remembered a friend in college who'd been unable to resist taking in strays. One after another, Candace would come home with lost cats, birds with broken wings, homeless dogs, and whatever other wounded creatures came her way. She'd work tirelessly until she placed each one with a new owner, only to come home a day or so later with another "project." Vividly, Jorie remembered the day a shaken Candace had burst through the front door during a heavy thunderstorm and headed for the telephone. She'd called animal control to alert them about an injured dog she'd seen limping along the road. When Jorie pressed her on why she'd failed to bring the dog in from the rain, Candace had explained that the secret to helping strays was knowing which ones needed nurturing and which ones were dangerous.

Simon Grant, she had a feeling, was of the latter variety. Under no circumstances could she afford to fall for him. No matter how irresistible he looked.

"Jordan?"

His voice startled her. She hadn't realized he'd finished his conversation. "Sorry," she told him. "I drifted."

Simon looked at her curiously. The banked fire was back in his gaze again, warming her skin and making her spine tingle. He indicated the landing at the top of the stairs with a wave of his hand. Lily and James, flanked by Nora and William Benton, stood looking down on the large crowd. "I think we're about to have an announcement," he told her.

Definitely the dangerous type, she thought, studying the brooding look in his eyes. He looked at her curiously as William Benton struggled to get the crowd's attention by tapping on a wineglass. "What are you thinking?" he asked.

"This is a good time to smile, Simon."

Later that night, Jorie sank onto the overstuffed sofa in her small apartment with a weary sigh. Under the best of circumstances, Nora's parties never failed to wear her out. Tonight she'd had the added complication of her mounting attraction to Simon Grant and her increasing determination to fight it.

War, she'd decided, was exhausting.

She slipped off her shoes and rubbed the balls of her feet as she idly sorted her mail. Though her quiet home on the west end of town usually felt like a haven, she felt distinctly on edge.

The feeling had lingered since Lily had interrupted them in the alcove. At least, Jorie thought, she'd managed to avoid a confrontation with her aunt. The party had gone well, better, actually, than she'd expected. Usually when Nora tried to mix her family and her friends, something went awry. William Benton's business associates had difficulty accepting the eccentricities of his wife's large, unusual family, while Nora's relatives found her husband's colleagues unbearably conservative and close-minded.

But Lily was loved by all.

So for her sake, both sides had managed to play nicely, and Lily had looked happy, content, and utterly in love with James Wells.

Jorie continued to sort the mail, finding the simplicity of the task calming. She tossed two coupon circulars onto the to-be-read pile. Why she bothered, she had no idea. She had an eight-inch stack of clipped coupons in her pantry she never remembered to take to the store. Still, guilt made her keep clipping them because her father had always said . . . She reached a pale blue airmail envelope with her parents' address and stopped. Her mother hadn't written in a while. It might be nothing more than an update on how their latest project—a children's clinic in China—was progressing.

Or, she thought, tapping the letter absently on the back of her hand, it could be another lecture from her mother about the importance of duty and family responsibility. Jorie dropped it on the table with the rest of the mail and only a small twinge of guilt. Whatever it was, it would still be there tomorrow when she had the time and energy to face the inevitable frustration.

Tonight, she admitted, she didn't think there was room in her brain to contemplate anything beyond the still flushed feeling she had when she considered the way Simon had looked at her in those few moments in the alcove.

After her Uncle Bill had officially announced James and Lily's engagement, Jorie had continued the daunting task of introducing Simon to her relatives. All in all, he'd taken it rather well. He'd complimented her great aunts and third and fourth cousins. Her Aunt Lillian had actually seemed to like him. Twice he'd rescued Lily from inevitable embarrassment by heading off her cousin Paul's efforts to turn the party into a political campaign platform. Even Dunstan, who'd tried to interest Simon in his human cloning device, had not seemed to faze him. He'd shaken hands, and smiled, and made general small talk.

And he'd watched her.

With that smoldering, heated look in his eyes, he'd watched her. And each time she'd felt her heart turn over, she'd mentally run through all the reasons that she was not going to get involved with him.

First, Lily was going to marry James. As close as James was to Simon, any relationship Jorie had with him would cause nothing but tension.

Then there was their absolute incompatibility—socially, culturally, and emotionally. He lived in a world she didn't even particularly like. A man of wealth and power, he moved in circles she deliberately avoided.

Not to mention that he seemed like a broken heart looking for a place to happen—what with his devil-take-it personality and an emotional countenance that screamed, "I don't get too involved." James seemed to be the only exception.

Falling for Simon was undeniably a bad idea. If she had any sense at all, she'd walk away before she got too involved. With a groan, Jorie levered herself off the couch and headed for bed. Maybe the argument would sound more convincing in the morning.

Chapter Three

𝄞

JORIE SQUINTED AT THE CLOCK ON HER NIGHT-
stand and pulled the pillow over her head to
shut out the banging noise. One of her neighbors
must be renovating his apartment. The thin walls
of the century-old building muffled very little. Especially at seven A.M. on a Sunday morning.

The banging continued.

It was close.

Too close.

Jorie removed the pillow and tilted her head to
listen. Someone was beating on her door.

With a groan, she tossed the pillow aside. "Go
away," she said, her voice still hoarse from talking
above the noise at Nora's party.

There was a slight pause. She listened as sleep
reached for her once more.

The pounding resumed.

"Ezekiel's wheels," Jorie muttered darkly and reached for her robe. Nobody who knew her well would even call—much less come visit—before nine o'clock in the morning. Whoever was at the door had better have one hell of a reason.

She padded across the floor and looked through the view hole. Simon Grant, looking, she thought irritably, refreshed and alarmingly attractive, was standing on her welcome mat with a determined expression on his face that said he wasn't leaving until she let him in.

Jorie groaned. Not now, she thought. Not when she'd lain awake too long remembering the clean scent of him and the feel of his fingertip on her skin. Not when she could still recall the fine, chiseled line of his lips and the way his dark hair had swept away from his forehead in those oh-so-appealing waves that seemed to beckon her fingers. Not when her body was still on high alert from the sheer energy of being with him. She needed at least a day to recover from the impact.

He knocked again. "Jorie? Let me in."

Jorie tipped her head against the door. "Oh God."

"I know you're in there."

With a feeling of inevitability, she undid the multiple locks.

"Did I wake you?" he asked when she opened the door.

She frowned at him, though she suspected the effect was severely lessened by her half-open eyes. "Do you have any idea what time it is?"

"Around seven." He wore a denim shirt and black trousers, which emphasized the way his broad back tapered to a narrow waist and long legs. He strode past her into the apartment. "Good morning."

"Why don't you come in?" she told the now-empty space outside her door as she stooped to pick up the paper.

"I thought things went well last night."

Jorie shut the door, turned to give him a hard look, and tossed the paper onto her coffee table with last night's mail. Without a word, she made her way past him to the kitchen. If she had to be up this early, she had to have coffee. Vaguely she wondered if her hair was its usual out-of-control morning tangle. That would teach him, she thought smugly, to drop by at an unholy hour. If he didn't want to see her looking like she'd walked in from a tornado, he should call first.

Simon followed her into the kitchen. "I don't think I completely pissed anyone off," he went on. He sounded proud of himself. "Did you?"

She filled her coffeepot with water. Simon paced behind her, full of energy. "Yes."

He stopped pacing. "Yes, what? Yes, I did, or yes, I didn't?"

She measured out two scoops of coffee. "Just

yes," she said, and slid the filter into place. She switched on the coffeemaker.

"I was going to bring coffee," he said, "but I wasn't sure if you were a drinker or not. Then there's the potency issue."

Jorie hesitated as she reached for two mugs. Yes, there certainly was the potency issue. She held up one mug with a questioning look.

He nodded. "I take mine black." Simon was studying her now, that same probing look he often had that made her feel like a bug under a microscope. "What about you?"

"Sugar," she said.

He blinked, then shook his head with a slight laugh. "No. What did you think of the party?"

The coffee began to percolate. Jorie inhaled a deep breath of the bitter aroma. "It was long."

"Hmm." He propped one hip against the counter and studied the picture on her refrigerator. "Are these your parents?"

She couldn't decide whether he was deliberately trying to torture her. He was looking at her with a genuinely curious expression that seemed oddly incongruous with the fact that he'd shown up on her doorstep at seven in the morning. "How did you find me?" she asked him.

"Phone book." He continued to look at the picture, evidently finding it fascinating.

She seriously doubted that he'd made the trip across town to acquaint himself with her life. Yet there was a complete lack of guile on his face, as if it had never occurred to him that she wouldn't be delighted to see him, and immediately make time in her schedule. And he was so damned perky. People had no right to be that perky this early in the morning.

She'd had a roommate like that once. One in a seemingly endless number of housemates, Margo had driven her crazy. This was yet another sign, she warned herself, that she and Simon Grant were completely incompatible. "Oh God," she muttered.

He shot her a curious look. "What?"

"You're a morning person."

"No, I'm not."

Jorie's eyes drifted momentarily shut. "How else do you explain the fact that you're awake and alert at this hour?"

"I stayed up all night."

Her eyes flew open and she frowned at him. "Why?"

Something altered in his expression. His lips turned up slightly at the corner in a half smile. A spark leaped across the banked fire in his eyes as his lids lowered slightly. Her lips parted on a swiftly indrawn breath. "I couldn't sleep," he admitted. "Unfinished business does that to me."

Jorie's hand went to the top button of her pajamas. She fiddled with it, feeling suddenly wide awake as her body went on full alert. "Unfinished business?" The coffeepot's gurgling punctuated the still air.

"Sure." He took a step toward her. "Wouldn't you agree that we have unfinished business?"

She swallowed as a memory of the heated look on his face in the alcove in those few seconds before Lily had interrupted them burned a path across her brain. "I suppose," she said carefully.

"How did you sleep?" he pressed.

Rotten, she thought. "Like a baby." Her throat felt tight.

"Hmm. That doesn't seem fair." His gaze fixed on the button where her fingers were twisting the thread. He closed the distance between them. With the counter right behind her, she had no choice but to bend her head back to look at him. "Not when I stayed up late wondering what our next step was going to be."

"Next step?"

"Lily and James," he clarified. He glanced at the coffeepot. "You really aren't yourself before you've had coffee, are you?"

Jorie sagged against the counter. "Um, no."

Simon noted her discomfort and felt a surge of satisfaction. His instincts hadn't been wrong last night. She'd felt the sexual tension just as surely as he had. He should have guessed that a woman with as much passion and warmth as Jordan Morrison would not have missed the pure chemistry of those few moments in the alcove. Had Lily not interrupted, he would have kissed her. He'd been curious since meeting her about the fullness of her mouth and the way it would feel against his.

Excessive passion, he noted. He'd been right in that assessment. The passion in Jordan Morrison burned hot and bright. Simon had learned from his mother that excessive passion, when untamed, was destructive. Like a fire left unhindered, it could destroy everything in its path. Banked, however, tended, guarded, and carefully fed, it provided life-giving warmth and energy. The secret lay in control.

Simon was very good at control. He had a lifetime of practice to assure him that he could keep his desire for Jorie in check. Instinct told him that she was the kind of woman who tumbled headlong into relationships, freely giving away parts of herself with little concern for the emotional risk involved. She'd expect nothing less in return.

The way Simon saw it, he had two choices. He could walk away from her without risking the chance of tasting the forbidden fruit. Or he could ensure that, at all costs, he stayed firmly in control of their relationship. The former seemed cowardly, and the latter, though risky, was far preferable to the idea of never again experiencing the lavish warmth he felt in her presence. He was strong enough, he'd assured himself. He'd weathered plenty of storms before and come out victorious. He could do it again.

Looking at her now, with her eyes still smudged from sleep, her tangled hair in glorious disarray, he suppressed the inner voice that told him she could easily become an addiction and moved to press his advantage. He'd waited too long to taste her. He'd waited too long to feel her warmth. He could get close enough to the fire without getting burned.

Her eyes were watching him warily. The coffeepot continued to gurgle, filling the tense silence with its jarringly cheery sound. Simon placed one hand on her shoulder and leaned closer to her. "Would it surprise you," he said softly, "to know that I couldn't get you out of my head? The way you looked coming down those stairs last night . . ." She took a swift breath and lowered her gaze to his mouth. Simon touched the base of her throat. "I kept remembering the sound in your voice when you said my name."

She tensed. "Simon—"

Satisfaction roared through him at the slightly breathless whisper. "Like that," he assured her. "It's a little rough. A little husky. It makes me wonder what it sounds like when you're drowning in passion."

"Oh God." Her eyes drifted shut.

He touched a curl where it lay against her throat. It curled around his finger and hugged it close in a silken embrace. He could feel her pulse leap. "Do you know that I'm fascinated by your hair?"

"It's wild," she protested.

It certainly was, he mused. Her dark, red hair, and the way his body was responding to the flush of peach that had stained her cheeks. "That's why it fascinates me."

"This is probably not a good idea," she said softly.

He tipped his head closer. She was right there, he admitted, but he no longer cared. He had to taste her. His lips hovered inches from hers. "You're probably right."

"We're totally incompatible."

He nodded, his gaze fixed on her mouth. "I couldn't agree more."

"Simon—"

"I'm going to kiss you now, Jordan."

With a soft sigh, she slid her arms around his neck. "Thank God. I was afraid you were going to make me beg."

His lips covered hers. She was warm and inviting and every bit as intoxicating as he'd suspected. Jorie leaned against his hard length and wended her fingers into his hair. Her nails slid over his scalp, making him tingle. Simon molded her against him, pressing her supple frame to him, gliding his hands over her curves, searching for her secrets. She felt soft, in stark contrast to women he'd known who seemed to possess an unnatural number of hard angles. He tipped his head and deepened the kiss, absorbing her small exclamation with a muffled curse of desire.

He slid one hand inside the opening of her robe. The heat of her body seeped through her pajama top and tempted his fingers to explore further. She pushed up on her tiptoes with a slight moan. The move fully aligned her body with his.

Simon eased his mouth off hers, sucking lightly at her lower lip, then trailed a line of kisses along her jawbone. "I love your freckles," he muttered as his lips found the spot just beneath her ear. "Like fairy dust."

"Kiss me again," she told him, clinging to his head. "I want—"

He didn't let her finish. He pressed his mouth to hers, learning every inch, every curve and line of her lips. "You taste good," he muttered against her mouth. "Sweet."

She tipped her head back beneath the pressure of his mouth. He moved his hand up to cup her breast in his warm palm. "So soft," he whispered. "I want to touch you."

Jorie moaned softly. The sound warned him that he was dangerously close to the edge. Summoning his self-control, he reluctantly lifted his head. She swayed slightly.

She dropped her head to his shoulder. For long seconds the only sounds in the room were the gurgling of the coffeepot and the harsh sound of their breathing. She pressed her ear to his chest where he knew his heart beat a steady rhythm. Beneath his hands, he could feel hers pounding in double time.

Simon's hands wandered up and down the length of her back, stroking and soothing, warming her already overheated flesh. "Still think this was a bad idea?" he asked, dropping a light kiss on the top of her head.

Hard to say, she thought, when she was reveling in the indescribable feeling of being pressed against him. "Um—"

"Me either."

Jorie pressed a kiss to the side of his neck. Simon tipped her head back so he could meet her gaze. His eyes were sparkling. The banked fire she'd seen in them last night now burned brightly. He traced a finger down the line of her cheek. "You're incredible." He rubbed the corner of her mouth with his fingertip. "Absolutely indescribable." He pressed his thumb to the base of her throat where her pulse beat rapidly. "And I want to take you to bed."

She drew a steadying breath and said, "I need some coffee." She pulled away from him to pour. After liberally lacing hers with sugar, she sat at the oak table and gave him a wary look. "I'm not trying to be flaky," she assured him. "I'm just not sure how to respond to that statement."

Simon raised his eyebrows and took a long drink of his coffee. "As far as I know, there are three usual answers. Yes. No. And maybe later."

He'd expected her to laugh. Instead a worried frown creased her forehead. "Sorry. I haven't quite gotten past the fact that you came all the way over here at seven in the morning because you want to go to bed with me."

"You find that odd," he stated.

Jorie choked on a sip of coffee. "You could say that."

Interesting, Simon thought. "Why?"

She'd stared at him with an expression that clearly said she thought he'd lost his mind. "Why?"

He nodded. "Why would you find that odd?"

Her coffee cup hit the table with a loud *plunk*. "Okay," she said slowly. "First, there's the fact that you hardly know me."

"I know you well enough to know that I'm attracted to you."

She ignored that. "Second, there's the fact that I hardly know *you*."

"But you're attracted to me as well."

"Third," she said, building up steam, "I'm just not the kind of woman that men stay up all night and pace the floor over. Especially not men like you."

"What do you know about men like me?"

"I know that you like your life orderly and controllable." She indicated her apartment with a broad sweep of her hand. "Look around you, Simon. I'm not the orderly and controllable type."

He watched her over the rim of his cup. She had a point there, but he'd already crossed that bridge in his mind. "I've accepted that. I can deal with it."

She sputtered. He was fairly certain he'd never seen a woman sputter before. "You are impossible," Jorie muttered.

"And what makes you think men don't stay up all night over you?"

"It's not like I have some self-esteem crisis," she countered. "I'm a reasonably attractive, healthy, extremely intelligent, talented woman. I'm just not a"—she seemed to search for the word—"a siren."

Simon's eyebrows lifted. "A siren?"

"You know, they lured Jason and the Argonauts to their death."

"Only the Argonauts. Jason strapped himself to the mast and survived." Simon was counting on the same formula working for him.

Jorie gave him a pained look. "Are you always so literal?"

"Yes."

She momentarily closed her eyes, as if searching for a hidden reservoir of patience. He knew that look. He saw it often on the faces of people he worked with. When she opened them again, she looked resolute. "The point is, I'm not one."

"You may be right there," he mused. He'd known a few sirens in his life, and Jorie's utter lack of guile didn't fit the description.

"Men stay up all night over sirens," she informed him.

"You have a lot of firsthand knowledge about this?"

"Are you teasing me?"

"No. I'm dead serious." He usually was.

Jorie stared at him for several long seconds, then stood and dumped the remaining contents of her cup into the sink. "I need a shower."

"I'll wait for you," Simon assured her. The look she gave him said she couldn't decide whether that was good news or bad news.

Simon studied the picture on Jorie's refrigerator as he listened to his longtime friend and private investigator Mark Baine on the other end of his cell phone. "I looked it over yesterday afternoon. There's not a lot there, Mark." In the background, he could hear the water running where Jorie was still in the shower. He'd taken the opportunity to use the phone.

"I know," Mark told him now. "I've got my best guys on this." At Simon's request, Mark had begun a casual investigation into William Benton's business affairs. "All I can tell you is, something's definitely not right with William Benton's books.

Did you see that table comparing the investment income with the profit projections?"

The woman in the picture resembled Nora Benton, but the man had Jorie's coloring and build. Though the couple stood in front of a tree that could have been anywhere from Oregon to Zimbabwe, something about the photo suggested that it had been taken overseas. He wasn't sure why. "There's nothing concrete there," he told Mark.

"No, but there is something. We just have to find it."

Simon thought that over. "While you're looking, I'd also like you to find out if Howard is asking any questions." Howard Wells, James's uncle and vice president of Wells Enterprises, had openly challenged the terms of his brother's will. Though Simon had won the battle in court, Howard had tried, several times, to persuade James to exclude him from key business decisions.

"You suspicious?" Mark asked.

"I'm always suspicious of Howard. He took the news of James's engagement better than I thought."

"Hmm. I think I know who to check with on that. I've got a guy who knows a girl who's dating a fella, kind of thing."

"Just be discreet."

"Hell, Simon, I'm always discreet."

"I know. That's why I hired you." Simon wiped

a hand over his face. "Just remember that the wedding's around the corner. If you're going to find something, I need you to find it soon."

"Do you really think this girl is trying to take James for a ride?"

He thought that over. There was a purity about Lily, something that said she wouldn't even know how to perpetrate a scam, much less concoct one. The way she looked at James, the way she talked about him, all pointed to a young lady deeply in love and utterly guileless. "I think Lily may not have any idea how desperate her father's business situation is," he said carefully.

"But the way she met him—"

"I know. It raised my suspicions, too." James had been in Europe at a well-publicized business symposium. Lily was attending the same symposium with a group of fellow students from Harvard. She'd met James when an apparent reservations error booked her into his room. The six hours it took for the hotel to find appropriate accommodations for her had been all she and James needed to decide they were meant to be.

"Too damned coincidental if you ask me."

"I don't think she orchestrated her relationship with James," Simon told him, "but I'm not ready to rule out her parents' motives."

"Do you think she cares for him?"

"If she's not in love with him, she's an Academy Award–quality actress." Simon leaned against the kitchen counter and looked at the eclectic decor in Jorie's kitchen. It suited her personality. Warm, varied, and homey, with a range of international touches and children's art. The walls were a warm pumpkin color that reminded him of the dress she'd worn last night.

"Hmm." Mark said thoughtfully. "James is just so vulnerable. Hell, Simon, I know he's an adult, but I have trouble remembering that he's not that fifteen-year-old kid who walked into a board meeting and took control of his dad's company from his uncle."

"So do I."

"Whatever Benton's up to, I hope for Lily's sake that she doesn't have a clue."

"So do I," Simon said again.

"I've got a guy checking a few things for me. I should know something more in a couple of days."

Simon was studying the painting over her table. It had a Picasso-like quality that should have seemed incongruous in the room filled with antique furniture and handmade accents. But Jorie made it work. It came as no surprise. "Keep me informed," he told Mark, "as soon as you know anything."

"Will do. Tell James I said hi."

"I will. Thanks, Mark."

"Sure, Simon. Talk to you soon."

Simon slipped his phone into the back pocket of

his trousers. The water in Jorie's shower had stopped running. To take his mind off the image of her naked and wet, he walked to the table to examine the painting. He replayed what he'd seen in Mark's report in his mind as he studied the sweeping strokes of brightly colored paint. After reviewing the information yesterday afternoon, he'd felt more strongly than ever that he was going to make sure that James Wells was as safe and protected as a baby kangaroo in its mother's pouch.

He heard the buzz of a hair dryer and pictured Jorie standing at her door with her hair tousled and gloriously sexy. How in the world, he'd mused, had she managed to look messy and appealing at the same time?

Sirens, Simon thought with a shake of his head. At least this wouldn't be boring.

"I'm telling you, James, he likes her." Lily leaned against the deck railing outside the second story of the Benton home and studied her fiancé. Last night's party, by all accounts, had been a huge success. And Lily found the obvious connection between her cousin and James's former guardian absolutely fascinating. She'd been attempting to persuade James of it for the better part of last night and this morning.

He wrapped his arms around her. "Babe, I've

known Simon my whole life. He does not fall for women like normal guys do."

"Jorie's not a normal woman."

"You can say that again."

Lily poked him in the ribs. "That's not what I meant."

"I like her," James insisted. "A lot. She's just—"

"Quirky."

"Yeah. Simon is not into quirky. He's the most unquirky person I know."

"Opposites attract."

"They also annoy the hell out of each other."

"You didn't see it, James," Lily insisted. "The way he was looking at her when I saw them in the alcove." She shook her head. "It was hot. Really, really hot."

"I can't picture it," James told her. "Not Simon."

"Is he dating someone now?"

"Simon doesn't date. He"—James considered it for a moment—"he schedules."

"Huh?"

"If he likes you, you get a lot of time on his calendar."

"How much time do you get?"

He grinned. "I have unlimited access."

Lily laughed at that. "Well, he's bound to have had some affairs since you've known him. I mean, he's a very sexy man."

"Oh?"

"Don't get jealous," she chided. "He's just, you know, dynamic. I can picture him with a super-model hanging on his arm."

"As far as I know, the women Simon has been involved with are the business barracuda types. There was this one. What was her name? It was something weird." James frowned for a second, then snapped his fingers. "Daphne DuMonde."

Lily scrunched her nose. "Sounds like she's a stripper."

James laughed. "Actually, she was this really bitchy merger and acquisitions attorney for a company we ended up buying."

"Simon liked her?"

"I don't think so. I think Simon thought that dating her was good for business."

"James."

He held up his hands in defense. "That's what I'm trying to tell you. Simon's not a regular guy."

"Come on. He's bound to have had at least one steady woman since you've known him."

"Once," James admitted. "He was engaged."

Lily gloated. "See. What was she like?"

"Pretty. Sophisticated. Her parents knew my parents' parents. That kind of thing. She was sort of a professionally trained wife, you know."

Lily frowned. "Sounds boring to me."

"I think Simon liked her because she was predictable. He doesn't like surprises."

"Which is why he doesn't like me," she said thoughtfully.

"He likes you," James protested.

"Maybe. But he doesn't like you and me together."

James hugged her. "He'll get used to it, Lil. I swear he will. It's just that he thinks we're being impulsive."

"And Simon is never impulsive," she guessed.

"Exactly."

She squeezed him tight. "James, if he really cuts off your access to Wells Enterprises—"

"He won't," James assured her.

"But if he does—"

James tipped her slightly away from him. "Would you stop worrying about that? Simon will come around. And if he doesn't, well, then I've got enough of a nest egg that I can start over if I have to. I have my mother's money, too, you know."

"I'm not worried about the money," Lily insisted. "You love Simon."

"Yes."

"I couldn't stand it if I came between you."

"The only way that's going to happen is if Simon lets it," James said firmly.

"I don't mind signing a prenuptial agreement, you know."

"*I* mind," James insisted. "We don't need one."

"But that's my point. It doesn't matter anyway, and I don't think—"

He covered her lips with his fingers. "Subject closed. We're not having one. I won't walk into marriage with you thinking I don't trust you. Besides, once we're married, everything I have is yours. I'm going to mean that when I say it. If you take it all from me," he said with a lopsided grin, "well, it was yours anyway."

Her eyes turned slightly watery. "Honey," he protested, "that was a joke."

Lily hesitated, then nodded. James lowered his hand. She lightly kissed his cheek. "I'm sorry."

"Did it ever occur to you," he quipped, "that maybe I'm after *your* money?"

That made her laugh. "Yeah, sure."

"You never know. If Simon cuts me off, maybe I'd enjoy being a kept man."

"Like prisoners enjoy torture."

James shook his head. "Baby, please. Lighten up. I promise you this isn't that serious."

"I'm trying to believe you," she assured him. "It's just that Simon is so determined. I have to tell you, James, he intimidates me."

"Which is why I'm telling you that Jorie is not his type of woman. I just can't picture the two of them together."

Lily smiled slightly as she adjusted his collar. "You couldn't picture us, either."

"Because you were gorgeous, and I was a geek."

She gave his shirt a playful yank. "Stop. I fell madly in love with you, didn't I? You can't possibly be a geek."

James straightened his glasses. "All I'm saying is, Simon is a law unto himself. He has a lot of women, but there aren't women who have him. Jorie's like a nester or something. She makes homes for people as a hobby, for crying out loud. She just isn't his type. At all."

Lily drummed her fingers on his shoulder. "I think you're wrong."

"I know him better than you."

"But you're not a woman."

"Thank God," he muttered. "Women have the most complicated lives."

Lily rolled her eyes at him. "What I meant was, you wouldn't pick up on something like this. It's subtle."

"Then it's definitely got nothing to do with Simon. There's nothing subtle about Simon."

Lily considered that for a moment. "Why didn't he get married?" she asked him.

"Huh?"

"You said he was engaged once. Why didn't he marry her?"

"Oh." He shrugged. "I don't know. He didn't say anything about it for a long time, and when I asked him one day, he just said that they decided they had different goals. He didn't seem real torn up about it."

"So he wasn't in love with her."

"Honey—"

"I know. I know," she said. "You think Simon doesn't fall in love."

"He doesn't."

Lily's expression turned knowing. "Well, I think, James Wells, that you're about to be proven perfectly wrong."

"No way."

"Bet you?"

He grinned at her. "Bet me what?"

She smiled as she glanced over his shoulder into the music room of her parents' home. Most people thought Jorie gave her heart easily, but Lily knew her better than almost anyone. To the world, Jorie presented a slightly enigmatic, openly friendly, simple façade. She was a caring friend with seemingly boundless energy to commit to lost causes. Lily had seen Jorie involved in one relationship after another where she'd taken on a lonely, shy guy, given him some self-esteem, and eventually paired him off with a woman more his type. Jorie had been a bridesmaid in over sixteen weddings that Lily knew of. But Lily had seen a side of Jorie that most people rarely, if ever, got to see. She'd seen Jorie play the piano. She'd heard the incredible emotion pour from her fingers as she spun magic with her instrument. Jorie was a woman of amazing passion. When she finally found a man worthy of her heart, she'd give it completely and utterly. And Lily had the unshakable feeling that Simon Grant had finally met his match.

If she had any honor at all, she'd let poor James off the hook from the sucker bet he was about to make. He didn't stand a chance.

"Bet me what?" he asked again.

She grinned at him. He'd just have to learn the hard way. "Loser does the dishes at our house for the first month we're married."

"Deal," he assured her.

Lily looked smug. "Then what are you doing this morning at eleven?"

He looked suspicious. "Why?"

"Because I know where Jorie will be. We'll go see her and you can find out for yourself."

Chapter Four

𝄞

SIMON EASED INTO THE PEW NEXT TO JORIE. SHE caught the smug look Lavonia Jackson threw her from the choir loft and cringed. She'd never hear the end of this.

After he'd sent her world teetering off its axis that morning, she'd retreated to the shower where she'd taken herself firmly in hand. Either she was or she wasn't going to have an affair with him. It was that simple.

It would be a lot simpler, she'd thought, if she was the kind of woman who could boil it down to the issue of sex. Did she want to make love with Simon? That question had brought a smug smile to her face while she'd shampooed her hair. What woman wouldn't?

But Jorie knew herself well. And she knew that

making the decision to have an affair with Simon meant much more than welcoming him into her bed. She'd be asking him into her life—which had far greater consequences. She'd already accepted that she was starting to fall for him. Had she doubted it at all, last night's conversation had settled the matter.

She just hadn't counted on Simon falling for her.

"Oh Jorie, you hypocrite," she'd whispered to her reflection in the foggy mirror. For all her lectures to the people who came through her office about following dreams and choosing their destiny, she'd been running scared. It had taken years for her to put her heart back together after her parents had broken it. She'd guarded it carefully for years, avoiding relationships that asked her to feel too much or care too deeply. Only Lily, who'd come to her with the unconditional devotion and loyalty of a child, had access to it.

It was more than Simon wanted. She knew that. He wouldn't desire anything as messy and obligating as her heart. She had an absolute conviction, however, that if she kept it to herself this time, something inside her would die. She'd never again have the chance to feel that heart-pumping exhilaration she felt with him, that top-of-the-roller-coaster feeling that had made her aware of every hair on her head and every inch of her skin. She was shocked into the realization that she'd been slowly dying for years. It explained what she felt had been missing in her music. Though no one else had noticed it, Jorie had felt her passion dying.

In her music and in her life.

Simon was offering her the chance to reach for the brass ring, devil take the consequences, and rediscover the sheer joy of being alive. And though she knew the aftermath would leave her reeling, a part of her demanded that she take it. Maybe, she'd thought with a slight smile, *he* was the siren in this equation. She certainly seemed unable to resist the call that was luring her to certain doom.

She had dressed in a green crinkled skirt and matching cotton sweater and walked into the kitchen to find Simon right where she'd left him.

"It's Sunday morning," she'd informed him, having found some of her equilibrium. "I go to church on Sunday mornings."

That hadn't seemed to faze him. He'd asked if he could tag along.

Jorie had stared at him a full ten seconds before agreeing. He'd insisted on driving, despite her advocacy for the T and protests about parking problems. He'd driven his black sports car that morning—an ever-rarer privilege, he'd explained. He relied on Joe almost exclusively during the week and looked forward to the few times when he had an excuse to venture outside his normal routes.

Jorie had given him directions to the church,

then lapsed into silence as she thought about the events of last night and this morning. One of the things she appreciated about Simon was his comfort with silence. He obviously felt no need to fill it up with chatter. Simon had located a parking spot two blocks from the church and adroitly maneuvered into it. She'd been attending this church for six months and had yet to see an open parking spot that close to the door. The early arrivers took the prime spots. Strangers were left with whatever they could find. That's why Jorie took the "T."

It shouldn't have surprised her, she'd thought irritably. Simon seemed like the kind of man who simply willed the world to turn his way. She'd led the way to the two-hundred-year-old brick building where the sound of gospel music already spilled into the street.

They'd walked through the massive oak doors, and Jorie immediately realized the consequences of bringing him with her. The sanctuary of the Shiloh Christian Church was hot, crowded, and alive with energy. Huge stained-glass windows covered the walls, casting a multicolor glow across the polished wooden pews. Ladies' hats in a range of bright colors and styles, bedecked with ribbons, feathers, and jewels, bobbed on the heads of the mostly female congregation like the lobster buoys on the Massachusetts Bay. A large robe-clad choir was warming up on stage under the dynamic direction of their leader. The bare wood floors seemed to amplify the music, which in turn caused the congregants to talk louder in order to be heard. The preacher, whose ecumenical robes were a mix of bright primary colors, was giving instructions to two young boys in white robes, while several deacons in dark suits encouraged the occupants of each row to slide closer together to make room for latecomers.

Clarence Hodges, one of the older deacons, saw Jorie and Simon near the door. His eyes twinkled beneath bushy white eyebrows as he hurried down the aisle to greet them. Clarence, with his usual flair for fashion, wore a royal blue suit with a wide ribbon stripe and matching bright blue snakeskin shoes. "Well, well, well," he said as he kissed Jorie's cheek in friendly greeting. "This is a welcome surprise."

"I come here every Sunday," she told Clarence, deliberately missing his point.

He elbowed her with a slight grin. "But not with company." He extended a hand to Simon. "Clarence Hodges."

Simon shook his hand. "Simon Grant."

"You a friend of Jorie's?"

"Yes," Simon assured him.

"A good friend?" Clarence persisted.

"Clarence," Jorie warned.

He chuckled. "Can't blame an old man for looking out for you," he told Jorie. "That's what old men do."

"That," she concurred, "and gossip about other people's business."

Clarence laughed. "Keeps me young." He tipped his head toward the front. "There's some room down there. Second pew."

As Jorie had made her way down the aisle, she'd sensed the speculation brewing around her. She'd stopped and greeted several people, though some streak of stubbornness had kept her from introducing Simon. He'd seemed oblivious to the curious looks he'd received, although he'd pressed his hand to the small of Jorie's back in an unmistakable claim of possession. If the knowing look Jorie received from Iris Hodges, Clarence's amiable and engaging wife, was any indication, the action did not go unnoticed. A large, imposing woman, Iris gave Simon a shrewd once-over, then nodded appreciatively at Jorie.

By the time Jorie found their seats in the second pew from the front, the choir had completed its warm-up. She slid into the pew, with Simon easing in behind her.

Darius glanced over the top of the piano, mouth open, and gave Jorie an incredulous look. His wide-eyed stare was curtailed when his mother snapped her fingers at him, causing him to fumble with the hymnal as he settled back on the bench. Lavonia then glanced down from the choir loft and spotted Jorie and Simon. The look she gave Jorie spoke volumes.

Simon took his seat, draped one arm across the back of the pew so his hand rested on Jorie's shoulder, and settled in beside her. She didn't think she imagined the whispering that went on behind them.

They were a half hour into the service before Jorie started to unwind enough to enjoy herself. Around her, the congregation participated joyfully in the pace and style of worship. Darius was playing well, a confirmation that her lessons were not wasted. She closed her eyes and hummed softly as the choir began one of her favorite hymns. She could feel Simon's thigh brushing hers as he patted his foot in rhythm. She smiled slightly as she wondered what he was thinking. However he'd planned to spend his Sunday morning, it hadn't been like this.

The music director turned to stand the congregation. With exclamations of praise and thanksgiving, people rose to their feet and started to sing along with the choir. The pace of the music accelerated with the volume level. Hands clapped. Voices rang. Jorie took a deep breath and let the familiar setting soothe her. Pleasant memories of her childhood and the welcoming atmosphere of the congregation always gave her a sense of peace.

A slight commotion from the aisle drew her attention. Simon moved closer to her, and Jorie glanced past the family on the end of their pew to see James and Lily easing into their row to stand next to Simon. James looked uneasy. Lily waved briefly at Jorie. Jorie raised her eyebrows as she looked at her cousin. Lily, to her knowledge, had not attended a church service since her christening. Whatever inspired her to make the trip into the city with James to visit this particular church on this particular Sunday morning was almost definitely part of a grand scheme.

Nearly everything Lily did was part of a grand scheme. Her cousin smiled at her and mouthed, *We'll talk later. You bet we will*, Jorie thought as the song ended. "Glory," the woman behind them shouted. Simon shot Jorie a dry look as they took their seats. The preacher moved into the pulpit, and Jorie settled back against the pew with smug satisfaction. The message would probably last at least an hour. Whatever Lily and James were up to, she doubted they'd intended to immerse themselves quite this thoroughly in her life today. As for Simon, he was just going to have to accept that this was part of the bargain.

"Amen!" The congregation said almost as one when Andrew Tipton completed his dynamic sermon.

Simon gave his watch a quick, incredulous glance. It was difficult to believe the man had been speaking for nearly an hour. His charisma had held his audience enthralled for the delivery of the message on the consequences of arrogance. Several times Simon had found himself nodding agreement. He'd understood why the man's preaching inspired the calls of "Preach it, brother" and "Amen, pastor" that came regularly from the large congregation.

Darius moved back to the piano bench to play the postlude as the service began to break up. Simon looked at James. "This is a surprise."

"Lily wanted to come," James said, pushing his glasses up the bridge of his nose.

Simon studied him through narrowed eyes. He was nervous. James always fiddled with his glasses when he was nervous. Lily beamed at Simon. "Good morning. Nice service, wasn't it?" She evidently didn't expect him to reply because she looked past him at Jorie. "Hi."

Jorie gave Lily a shrewd look. "This *is* a surprise."

"Yes, well, James and I were talking this morning, and we just decided to come hear Darius play. I haven't heard him since that day I came to see you at the office."

The expression on Jorie's face said she wasn't buying it, but she smiled at James. "Not what you expected, was it?"

He shot a quick glance at Simon. "Um, no, not exactly."

"Lily should have warned—" Jorie was interrupted by a hand on her shoulder. She turned to smile at Iris Hodges. "Oh, Iris. I wanted to introduce you to my cousin Lily."

"Well now," Iris said with a curious glance at Lily. "So you're the young Miss Lily that's been causing all that worry."

Lily smiled engagingly. "I'm afraid so."

"I'm Iris Hodges. It's nice to meet you."

Lily shook the woman's extended hand. "Nice to meet you, too."

Iris looked at Jorie. "You all are staying for lunch, aren't you? We're having dinner on the grounds this afternoon."

Simon wondered if Jorie noticed the small crowd of matrons they'd begun to draw. She seemed to consider Iris's offer, then shook her head. "We can't. I didn't bring anything."

One of the women standing behind Jorie laughed. "Lord, child, don't let that stop you. We've got enough food to feed Pharaoh's army."

A third woman looped a hand through the bend of Simon's arm. "You can't be leaving now," she told Jorie. "We've got to have a chance to interrogate your young man."

Lavonia Jackson had shucked her choir robe and was now hurrying toward them. "Don't you dare leave," she instructed. She gave Lily a quick hug. "Nice to see you again, Lily."

"Hello, Lavonia."

"You must be James," Lavonia said, turning to the young man. "I'm pleased to meet you." She greeted him with a warm hug and a kiss on the cheek that left a smear of pink lipstick on his jawline. He seemed a little stunned by the overtly friendly gesture, but accepted it in good stride. Lavonia looked at Jorie. "You're all staying, and that's that. I've got more than enough food for just me and Darius."

The trio of older ladies agreed. Darius, who had finished his postlude and made a beeline in their direction, added his vote. "You've got to stay, Jorie," he insisted. "We're going to have singing later. You can play if you want."

She smiled at Darius, a secret, knowing kind of smile that Simon found simultaneously intriguing and worrisome. When she looked at Simon, there was a definite sparkle in her eyes. "What are your lunch plans?" she asked him.

A woman of excessive passion, Simon remembered, and infinite surprises. He watched as Jorie played the harmonica while Clarence Hodges picked a banjo to a toe-tapping arrangement of "Amazing Grace" on the small stage on the back porch of the church.

The church's well-kept cemetery had served as the backdrop for the overladen tables of food where the congregation had gathered for Sunday dinner on the grounds. There had indeed been enough food to serve a small army. The dessert table had been particularly noteworthy. James had polished off one piece each of five different pies. When everyone had wandered through the impressive lines, small groups began to segregate. Two of the deacons had engaged Simon in a game of horseshoes near the edge of the property. From his vantage point, he had watched as a bevy of older women surrounded Lily and James. James had fiddled with his tie most of the afternoon.

Jorie had sat with Lavonia and another group of women near the picnic tables. The children had seemed drawn to her, constantly approaching her with a picked daisy or a colored picture. Simon had watched her marvel over each offering, engaging the child in conversation about the gift. He could understand why she was so good at her job. She had a way of communicating with children that had to assist her in promoting her agency's mission.

For his part, Simon had found the company and the setting charming and nostalgic. Several times he'd caught Jorie watching him as if weighing his reaction. She'd stopped him during his second trip to the dessert table.

"Personally," she'd said, "I like those." She had pointed out a tray full of chocolate and coconut cookies. "But they're lethal."

Simon had slid a piece of pecan pie onto his plate. "I'm a pecan man myself."

"Do you have any idea how many calories are in a piece of that stuff?"

He'd shrugged. "I worked it off playing horse-shoes."

"Which you won, I noted."

"Surprised?" he'd asked her.

She had laughed softly and shaken her head. "Not really. I imagine you're good at just about everything you do."

"Everything," he'd assured her with a pointed look, thinking there were a few skills he'd like the opportunity to demonstrate.

Her blush told him she'd gotten the message. "Simon," she'd said, "I just wanted you to know how much I appreciate what you've done today. No one would imagine that you haven't enjoyed yourself. I'm sure this wasn't what you had in mind this morning."

"You could say that," he'd quipped.

"No, I meant—"

"I know what you meant," he'd said quietly. "And for your information, I have enjoyed myself. It's not an act."

"Well, thank you even more, then."

"You didn't think I would, did you?"

She'd glanced around at the large crowd. "This doesn't seem like your cup of tea"—she'd looked at his plate—"or slice of pie."

"Actually," Simon had told her, "this brings back fond memories." At her surprised look, he'd nodded. "After we moved to the Wells estate, my mother would leave me with the other resident maid when she dated. Sometimes she didn't make it home on Saturday nights." That happened more often than not, but Harriet Jefferson had never complained when Simon's mother failed to retrieve him. Instead she'd made him dress in his best clothes and dragged him off to church on Sunday mornings. Harriet had probably figured that the only chance Simon had for decent moral instruction would come on those Sunday mornings when his mother was too hung over to make it home. "When that happened I went to church with Harriet," he had told Jorie, indicating his pie. "This is a lot like I remember."

She'd given him a look that was simultaneously curious and admiring as she rose on her tiptoes to kiss his cheek. "I don't care what they say, Simon. You're a nice man."

"Don't let it get around," he'd warned her.

But their time alone was short-lived. Soon she'd been cajoled into making her way to the stage where Clarence Hodges was tuning his banjo. Simon had joined James and Lily near the edge of the porch. When Jorie had accepted the diachronic harmonica from Clarence, James had given Lily a surprised look. "Berklee," Lily explained. "Jorie studied performance piano for her major, but she plays just about everything. She's amazing with that harmonica. You'll see."

"Does your mother know about this?" James had asked.

Lily had laughed. "Are you kidding? Lord, she'd die."

Simon had taken the opportunity to look at the crowd who'd gathered for the impromptu concert. Jorie tuned the harmonica to the banjo as she joked with Clarence. Clearly these people loved her. They had opened their hearts and their lives to her and accepted her as one of their own.

As he listened to her accompany Clarence, Simon knew why. She invested in them. All that passion he sensed in her flowed freely out of her into the lives of the people she loved.

And, Simon decided, he couldn't wait to be on the receiving end.

Jorie hummed softly, feeling content and at peace as Simon navigated his way to her apartment through the streets of downtown Boston. She could see his reflection in her window, so she studied the angles of his face. Noble, she decided. He had a noble face. The word suited him so much better than something bland like *handsome*.

"You're quiet," he said softly.

"Hmm." She gave him a slight smile. "I'm unwinding."

"Is this your usual post-gig state?"

She had to think about that. "I think so. Yes."

He shot her a quick look. "You don't know?"

"I'm usually alone after I play," she explained. "I never really thought about it before."

He nodded thoughtfully. "I see." He took the sharp turn on Charles Street to cut through Boston Common. "You're very good, by the way. I had no idea you were so musically, er, diverse."

Jorie laughed. "Most people don't expect a classical pianist to play blues harmonica, I suppose, but it's really not that different." She wiggled her fingers. "It's still a fingering skill."

"Lily says you picked that up in college."

"Yeah. I had a friend who played piano in a jazz band. She did a lot of club gigs, and I'd go with her when I wasn't holed up in the practice room."

"Do you like jazz?"

"It's complex," she said. "From a musical perspective, it fascinates me. But I didn't really fall in love with it until she took me to Sticky Mike's."

"The blues bar?"

"You know it?" she asked, surprised. The overcrowded, smoke-filled bar didn't seem like Simon's kind of place.

"Of it. Never been there." He stopped at a light and turned to look at her. "That's where you discovered harmonica?"

"Yes. Cosmo Joe and his jazz ensemble were playing that night. They're a New Orleans blues combo. Cosmo is considered the Louis Armstrong of the harmonica."

"I can see why you were impressed," he said. The light changed, and Simon put the car in gear as he eased forward.

"*Impressed* isn't the word," she told him with a slight laugh. "*Infatuated* is more like it. I'd never played anything but keyboards. You may find this hard to believe, but my Aunt Nora wasn't exactly openminded about music lessons."

That made him laugh. "I'll bet."

"I borrowed a guitar once when I was about fifteen. Nora went berserk. She gave me this lecture about how much my piano lessons were costing, and that if I wasn't going to take it seriously, she was going to stop paying for the best teacher in the city." She remembered the argument with a hint of a smile. "I think she secretly thought I was going to sell all my possessions, buy a van, and move to California to live in a commune."

"Did you give up the guitar?"

"Heck no," she told him. "I just didn't bring it home anymore."

Simon chuckled. "I'll bet you drove that woman crazy."

"Absolutely," she concurred. "When Lily was younger, she worried that I was going to corrupt her. Nora does not approve of impulsiveness."

"So you're saying she wouldn't have been necessarily pleased that Lily and James went to church with you today?"

"You could say that," she quipped. "Did you ever get out of James why they were really there?"

He shook his head. "Something about a bet with Lily."

"I think they're matchmaking," she told him.

The corner of his mouth twitched. "Me too. I guess they figure if we're together, I'll quit arguing with them about getting married too fast. I'm sure James thinks you'll have a positive influence on me."

"Don't be so cynical," she chided. "They're young and they're in love. It's natural for them to think everyone else should be similarly euphoric."

"That may be true for Lily, but I know James. He's trying to get away with something."

"Oh, I didn't say Lily wasn't scheming. I just don't think that's her only motivation."

Simon negotiated through a couple of tight turns, then found the street for her apartment. "We may have to circle the block five or six times to find a space."

"Don't say I didn't warn you."

"Nobody likes a smart-ass, Jorie," he said softly.

At the dry quip, she leaned back in her seat with a slight smile. "I've never been deeply concerned about public opinion."

That made him laugh. "I don't doubt it." He slowed as he approached a possible spot, then saw the fire hydrant and moved on. "Which brings us back to how you learned to play the harmonica."

"Oh. I fell in love with Cosmo Joe."

"You don't say."

"Um hmm. It was my first experience with an older man."

"How much older?" he probed. He found a parking space and maneuvered into it.

"Fifty or so years," she said with a chuckle. "I think Cosmo was seventy-two when I met him." She could still picture his round face and wide, partially toothless grin. Cosmo had been a great friend to her at a time when she'd desperately needed one. She'd been in her third year of college and was trying to find her way. Still angry at her parents for what she perceived as their abandonment, and feeling the need to rebel against Nora's autocracy, she'd stopped finding pleasure or fulfillment in her music studies.

Until that time she'd always used music as her retreat. Because it had been the one interest she had that Nora was willing to support, she'd been able to study with excellent teachers throughout high school. By her senior year, she had won several prestigious competitions, and when the Berklee College of Music offered her a full scholarship, Jorie had seen it as a gift from God.

But after three years of the pressure and rigid practice schedule, playing had begun to lose its joy for her. She'd begun to feel trapped. Cosmo had opened her eyes to the joy of creating music instead of merely playing it. With his cantankerous ways and sharp wit, he'd taught her so much more than a skill. He'd taught her to seize life instead of merely living it. He'd taught her that taking chances always made life richer—even if you got burned. She glanced at Simon. "He had a gold tooth," she told him, tapping her right incisor. "Right here. And he was a brilliant musician."

He switched off the ignition and turned toward her, draping one arm across the back of the seat so his hand rested on her shoulder. He traced the line of her jaw with his index finger. "He must have been," he concurred. "You wouldn't have settled for less."

"No," she agreed. "I don't settle." She covered his hand with hers and lowered it slowly from her face. "I'm an all-or-nothing kind of woman."

Simon studied her for long seconds, his expression probing and intense. "Are you trying to tell me something?"

"I thought about what you said this morning," she told him quietly.

He took a long breath. "I imagine you have. I handled that badly. I shouldn't have rushed you."

She didn't argue with him. "I'm not the kind of person who has casual affairs."

He cupped her head in his hand and leaned closer. "Believe it or not, neither am I. I don't generally proposition a woman that soon after meeting her." Dipping his head, he pressed a kiss to her throat. "There's just something about us that feels right to me. I want you."

Jorie tipped her head back with a slight moan. "I need some time—" She sucked in a sharp breath when he pressed his mouth to her ear and blew a hot, moist stream of air into the shell. "I don't know you . . ."

He nipped her earlobe with his teeth. "I understand," he said, and the buzz of his lips against her ear sent shivers down her spine. "I'll give you all the time you need." His lopsided grin made her heart skip a beat. "Although I'm not going to promise you I won't try to accelerate your timetable."

Chapter Five

{ "So." LAVONIA JACKSON DROPPED INTO THE
{ battered chair by Jorie's desk and pinned her
with a shrewd look. "Tell me about last night."

Jorie glanced up from the file she was studying
and looked at her friend in amusement. "It's Monday morning, Lavonia." Something she was all
too aware of after a night filled with erotic dreams
and unfulfilled longings. "I've only had one cup
of coffee. Aren't you going to cut me a break?"

"No way. I have"—she glanced at her watch—
"an hour and ten minutes before I have to be at
work. Darius is at school, and I am *dying* to know
what happened after you left yesterday."

Jorie picked up her mug and took a long sip. "I
went home."

"With or without Simon?"

"He took me home."

"Did he stay?" Lavonia asked bluntly.

"No, he didn't."

Lavonia crossed her legs and leaned back in the chair. "You're going to have to do better than that. You owe me. I fed that man. Twice."

"That was Darius's idea."

"Um hmm. I didn't see you complaining."

Jorie laughed. "All right, all right. You're not going to relent, are you?"

"No way. I have no life, so I'm stuck living through other people. You're the only person I know with rich relatives—"

"They're not rich—"

"They're richer than me," Lavonia pointed out, "God save them. I've always heard that being disgustingly wealthy makes you miserable. I'd like to give it a try, I think."

"Lavonia—"

"But since that's obviously *not* in the cards, I have to get the dirt from you." She propped one elbow on the corner of Jorie's overladen desk. "Tell me everything," she prompted again. "I'd have to be blind not to know what that man had on his mind. And what inquiring minds want to know is, how in the world did you drag him with you to church yesterday?"

"I didn't have to drag," Jorie told her. She picked up a pencil and spun it between her fingers. "He came by yesterday morning. I told him I

was going to Shiloh, and he asked to tag along."
She waved her mug in Lavonia's direction. "Do
you want coffee, by the way?"

"You're not going to deter me," Lavonia assured her. "Did he have any idea what he'd gotten
himself into?"

"Actually yes." Jorie told Lavonia what Simon
had said about his childhood.

Her friend's expression turned thoughtful.
"There's more to that story, I think."

"I'm sure there is. It's not the first thing he's
said about his mother that makes me think there
were some serious problems there. I'm sure it has
something to do with why he's so reserved."

"Probably. What about his dad?"

"Never knew him. And James's father and
grandfather seemed to have played a bigger role
in his life than his own mother."

"That would explain why he's so committed to
James," Lavonia mused.

"He loves James," Jorie concurred. "Simon
knows how influential James's family was in his
life. He credits Peter Wells for helping him succeed. When Peter died, I'm sure Simon felt responsible for ensuring that James had the same
type of influence."

"James is nice," Lavonia said. "Good manners."

"Um. He is nice. And he's good to Lily."

"Still think their marriage is a bad idea?"

"I still think Simon's right and that they could

afford to wait a little while, sure. Lily should graduate from college first. They're so young."

Lavonia shook her head slightly. "Which is why you'll have trouble convincing them of anything. My mama always said that you should hire a young person while they still know everything. The older they get, the less they know."

Jorie laughed. "Between Lily's conviction that James walks on water, and James's utter belief that he's the most fortunate man alive because Lily condescended to love him—they're almost unbearable."

"He seems like a nerd to me. I sort of expected Lily to go for the athletic type."

"Oh, he's not a nerd," Jorie assured her. "He's a geek."

"There's a difference?"

"Sure. Geeks are sexy. It's a new trend. Or so Darius says."

Lavonia's eyes sparkled as she gave Jorie a pointed look. "That must be what you saw in Kevin Riley."

Jorie ignored that. Kevin Riley was one of the child advocate lawyers her agency frequently called in for advice. He was dedicated, competent, compassionate, and he'd made no secret of his attraction to Jorie. She'd dated him casually for a couple of years, but despite frequent attempts to convince herself that Kevin was a perfect match, Jorie had been unable to make herself fall in love with him. The warm, comfortable feeling she felt with Kevin was nothing like the hair-raising exhilaration of being with Simon Grant. She was beginning to understand why passion had started wars and brought down empires.

"James is astronomically intelligent," she told Lavonia. "Not-of-this-planet intelligent. Lily says his IQ is off the charts. No surprise that he had trouble in school. Poor thing was probably bored out of his mind."

"If he hadn't come from money, he'd have been one of the kids in this program."

"Uh huh. He's as brilliant with a computer keyboard as Darius is with a piano. Terminally misunderstood by a system that can't cope with his brain. But his family life was good. Not dysfunctional like a lot of kids from his social strata."

"I liked him," Lavonia assured her. "And he does seem mad about Lily."

"He is." Jorie put the pencil down with a sigh. "I think they'll be good for each other. I just think they need some time to explore each other's values and expectations. Lily isn't going to be happy if James expects her to be a typical social wife. She doesn't want the kind of life her mother has had."

"Can you blame her?"

"Not at all."

"So is Simon still determined to stop the wedding?

"Maybe just delay it a little," Jorie told her with

a slight smile. "It's like I told you yesterday. He was very well behaved at the party Saturday night. No major disasters. He hasn't wielded any threats lately."

Lavonia was watching her closely. "And?"

Jorie felt her face turn warm. "And—he asked me to have an affair with him."

"I knew it." She nodded. "Lord, girl, that man is pure sex appeal."

"You noticed," Jorie said, tongue in cheek.

"Honey, *every*body noticed. My phone rang off the hook last night. You are the hottest topic at Shiloh."

"Gossip is a sin."

"It ain't gossip," Lavonia assured her. "Just pure observation. Clarence wants to ask the poor man what his intentions are."

Jorie laughed. "I'm sure he does."

Lavonia's expression turned serious as she patted Jorie's hand. "Are you absolutely sure you want to get involved with this man?"

Lavonia knew her well, and the same razor-sharp instinct that helped her survive as a single parent with no college education and no extended family to help support her told her that Simon Grant wasn't the kind of man who gave his heart away. "He's . . . difficult," Jorie admitted. "Sometimes I'm not even sure I like him. But I can't say I dislike him, either. I admire him. He's overcome a lot in his life. And I'd be lying if I said I wasn't attracted to him." She thought about it for a minute. "He bothers me."

"Oh Lord, I knew it."

"I don't mean he bothers me in a bad way."

"I know what you meant. Jorie, when it comes to men, I've been fascinated, infatuated, enchanted, charmed, annoyed, irritated, and revolted. I have *never* been bothered except by the ones that have the impact of a nuclear bomb."

Jorie laughed. "Simon isn't what I'd call the nuclear bomb type."

"No?"

"Uh uh. More like a smart bomb. Deadly accurate and extremely efficient."

"Lord, girl, you picked one heck of a challenge this time."

"I'm not going to fall for him," Jorie assured her. "I'm too smart for that."

Lavonia studied her through narrowed eyes. "Then you told him no?"

"Well, no."

"Jorie—"

She held up a hand. "I know what I'm doing," Jorie assured her friend. "I know the rules."

"Yes, well, in my experience, men like Simon play by their own set. Promise me you'll take care."

"I swear."

Her friend hesitated, then nodded. "If he breaks your heart, though, I'll beat the crud out of him."

"I'm sure you will." Jorie leaned back in her chair. "If it comes to that, I'll bring the ice cream and the picture if you'll supply the dartboard."

"Deal." Lavonia seemed satisfied. "I'll corner him later, when I know you're okay."

Jorie laughed. "I always feel safe in your hands, Lavonia."

She nodded briefly as she stood. "And as much as I'd like to continue this conversation, I've got to get to work. You still coming Friday night?"

"Of course. We've only got three weeks until the fund-raiser. Darius and I need the practice."

"Okay. We'll see you then."

"Thanks, Lavonia."

"Anytime." Lavonia pointed to the door. "And you have a visitor. I'll talk to you later."

Jorie turned to find James standing in the middle of the cluttered office, looking lost. "James, what in the world brings you here?"

Across town, on the tenth floor of Wells Enterprises in downtown Boston, Simon's assistant announced into the intercom, "Lily Benton's here to see you."

His eyebrows lifted. "Send her in."

Lily entered his office through the frosted-glass door. She looked fresh, he thought, as she usually did when he saw her. Simon stood and rounded the desk. "Lily. This is a surprise."

She grinned at him. "I don't doubt it."

Clad in jeans and a Harvard sweatshirt, she looked as young and guileless as she had yesterday at church—far too innocent to be involved in the increasingly incriminating evidence that was beginning to accumulate against her father. But looks, Simon knew, could be deceiving. Deliberately, he pushed aside the memory of his phone call that morning from Mark Baine. "You here to see James today?" He indicated a stuffed leather chair with a sweep of his hand.

"No." She took the chair and waited for him to sit across from her. "I'm here to see you."

Simon didn't comment. Lily crossed her legs and gave him a pointed look. "I actually decided to do this yesterday while I was listening to that sermon."

"I'm sure Reverend Tipton would be glad to hear that," he quipped.

"It was what he said about pride and how we let it get in the way of relating to other people."

She had an intent look on her face that intrigued him. He had no idea where she was going with this conversation, but something told him that she wasn't going to be deterred. "The way I see it," Lily continued, "you and I have two choices. We can either learn to get along, or we can make each other and James miserable. Since we're pretty much stuck with each other for the rest of our lives, I don't see any reason why we can't decide that we both love James, and we both want what's best for him."

No wonder, Simon thought, that James liked her. Poised, charming, and self-confident, she had spirit. Her willingness to fight for James warmed him. "Granted."

"And if I don't sign a prenuptial agreement, you're not going to let James marry me."

"James can do whatever he likes. He's an adult."

"But you can take away his company."

"No," Simon said carefully. "I can't. I can limit his influence in the way decisions at his company are made."

She pursed her lips. "Limit my influence, you mean?"

"If you want to see it that way. When James's father died, he charged me with two things: helping James make it to twenty-one with his fortune intact, and keeping Wells Enterprises healthy and well for the future. I succeeded at the first. I'm not going to fail at the second."

She seemed to think that over. "And if I sign a prenuptial agreement, you can ensure that I don't take half of James's stock if we divorce."

"It's a standard agreement in situations like yours." Simon carefully chose his next words. "I never intended for you to take that personally."

"You can see why I did."

"I can see that you thought it had something to do with you," he conceded. "I assure you it didn't. I would have asked for it no matter whom James wanted to marry. It's my job to protect his interests."

"I can appreciate that."

"And with the two of you moving so fast—"

"James and I didn't see the point in waiting."

Simon accepted that with a slight shrug. "Still, you don't know each other well."

"I know everything about James I need to know," she said with a dismissive wave of her hand. "I'm in love with him. I'm going to be with him for the rest of my life. I want to have children with him and grow old with him and build a future with him. The rest is details."

Had life ever been that simple? Simon mused. "Maybe."

Lily exhaled a frustrated sigh. "What if I agree to sign the agreement?"

"I'd be reassured," he told her.

"And you'd let James maintain controlling interest in Wells?"

"I would."

"Even though those things never hold up in court?"

This one would, Simon thought. "It's a symbol," he told Lily. "It's your way of proving to James that you want him—not his company."

She looked stunned for a moment, then burst

out laughing. "Of *course* I don't want his company," she assured him. "What the hell would I do with a computer business?"

That made Simon smile. "I wonder the same thing myself sometimes," he admitted. "But I'm talking about his net worth, not his business interests."

Lily nodded. "I know. And if you ever doubted it, I'm sure James's dad would be very pleased with the job you've done. Really. James loves you. And I appreciate that you're looking out for him."

"I'm glad you realize that."

"But here's the thing, Simon. I want you to like me. I *want* to like you. I mean, I have visions of the three of us on holidays. Like Christmas morning and Thanksgiving. You'd come over and play with our kids. I'd know your favorite meals, and you'd know my favorite colors. I'd be able to find the perfect little birthday gift for you because we would have been talking about some story in your past and I'd see something that reminded me of it. You could call me to find out why James is being such a pill at the office. You know, that kind of thing." She pursed her lips. "Like family."

She would have grown up like that, he realized. Despite her mother's emotional remoteness, Lily had been surrounded by a large extended family full of character and warmth. Even he had trouble believing that Nora Benton had been cold *all* the time. Lily was a warm and loving girl who would naturally want a family-oriented home life. She had no idea that the image of home, for him, evoked memories of Christmas mornings spent alone while his mother slept off a hangover, or Thanksgivings when he'd climbed the tree outside the Wells living room and watched longingly. Nor could she know how he'd felt that Christmas Eve when Peter had insisted that Simon join them. Peter's girlfriend was visiting for the Christmas holidays, and several of his friends were there for the informal party. Peter's mother had prepared small gifts for each of her son's friends, and though she hadn't known he was coming, had somehow managed to have one of the gaily wrapped bundles for Simon. He'd carried the tissue-wrapped gift home like the rarest of treasures, tucking it safely beneath the pine branch he'd cut from the estate and stuck in a pot in his room. The next morning, while his mother slept in, he'd opened the package to find a delicate glass ball with his name written in gold paint. At ten years old, he thought it was the most beautiful thing he'd ever seen. The memory crowded in on him now, threatening to throw open the doors of the inner room where he kept those feelings tightly locked away. When he felt the door rattle, he took a moment to clamp it firmly shut.

If Lily noticed his inner turmoil, she said nothing. Instead she continued painting her vision of the future. "I want to know you'll be in our future,

Simon," she told him. "And frankly I'm thinking that's not going to happen unless you and I bury the hatchet."

"I'm not at war with you," he told her quietly, his voice sounded slightly husky.

"Well, I've been at war with you."

"Oh?"

"Sure. I kind of wanted James to choose between us. I'm a little embarrassed to admit that, but I figured it out finally." She took a deep breath and gave him a sheepish look. "It makes me feel like a self-absorbed twit."

Simon felt on secure ground once again. "It shouldn't," he told her. "It's perfectly natural."

"Well, thanks for that, anyway. Still, it feels selfish, and I don't like that. So I've decided I'm going to take you at your word that this isn't about me at all. I don't want you to think I'm not willing to marry James without his money, and I don't want him to think that, either. So I'll sign whatever you want. It's a moot point anyway. James is stuck with me for life, so whether I sign it or not is immaterial. I was just being proud."

He should have felt a certain satisfaction at that, but Lily had a way of making him feel like a bully. "I appreciate that."

"But you have to do something for me."

He raised an eyebrow. "What can I possibly do for you?"

"You have to at least act like you're happy for James."

"What makes you think I'm not?"

She laughed again. "Maybe you're just not particularly demonstrative, I don't know, but you didn't exactly look like you were having the time of your life on Saturday night at the engagement party."

"I don't like parties."

She seemed to absorb that with undue glee. "Really?"

"Really."

"You seemed relaxed enough yesterday."

He shrugged. "Different environment. Different crowd."

Lily's smile had a secretive, womanly look he didn't like. He'd seen that look. It almost always preceded a disaster in his life. She seemed to have reached some conclusion he was almost certain he wasn't going to like. She drummed her fingers on the arm of her chair. "That's very interesting, Simon."

"I'm glad you think so."

"So, when can you have the papers ready?"

"It'll take a week or so. Have you told James?"

"Not yet. I wanted your promise first."

"That I'll be happy for James? Granted."

She shook her head. "You're not going to get off that easy."

"What did you have in mind?"

"Tomorrow night, James and I are having dinner at Rialtos at the St. Charles."

"In Cambridge?"

"Yes. We're considering having the reception there." She paused. "I'd really like it if you came with us."

A smile tugged at the corner of his mouth. "I'd think the last thing you'd want is a chaperone," he told her.

"I'm not asking you to go as a chaperone," Lily insisted. "I'm asking you to go as the family and best friend of the groom." Lily leaned forward and covered his hand with hers. "Because you're happy for him." She hesitated. "Please."

Simon studied the pleading look in her wide blue eyes with the very cynical realization that James had no idea what he was getting himself into. He didn't think there was a man alive who could resist that look. "What time do you want me to meet you?" he asked.

Lily beamed at him. "Our reservation is at seven. Thank you, Simon."

Jorie cradled the phone against her ear as she shuffled the papers on her desk. "He just left," she told Simon. Her phone had rung seconds after James had left her office. Her heart had skipped a beat when Simon's low voice had greeted her on the other end. He'd called. Just as he'd said. Simon struck her as the kind of man who always kept his word. She'd greeted him, then told him that James had come by to see her.

"Really," Simon said thoughtfully.

"Um hmm. You'll never believe what he wanted."

"He wants you to have dinner with him and Lily at Rialtos tomorrow night," Simon said.

Jorie frowned. "How did you know that?"

"Because I just had a visit from Lily. I got the same invitation."

Jorie laughed. "Oh. So they *are* matchmaking."

"They are definitely matchmaking," he concurred. "Although I'll give her points for negotiating. She was very smooth."

"James needs some work." Jorie swept a pile of old phone messages into the trash.

"Did he play with his tie a lot?"

"The whole time."

"He does that when he's nervous."

"I've noticed." She scanned a fax for pertinent information before sliding it into a file.

"So what did you tell him?" he probed.

"I told him I'd let him know." She leaned back in her chair and twirled the phone cord around her finger. "Things are a little crazy here right now."

"Oh?"

"Um hmm. I have that fund-raiser coming up in a few weeks. It's my biggest event of the year, and I'm struggling to stay afloat. We've had a couple of major projects make the news lately, so that on top of everything else has me hopping."

"Anybody helping you?"

Jorie laughed. "Are you kidding? We're a nonprofit group. We have one employee for every three jobs."

"I see."

When he didn't elaborate, she prodded him. "Did you want something?"

"I need to bring you this check from the Wells Foundation. I thought I'd come by tomorrow afternoon. You can ride with me to Cambridge."

Jorie smiled. "Simon, etiquette demands that a gentleman ask a lady for a date."

"I never claimed to be a gentleman," he shot back.

"You have a point there."

"So do you want a ride?"

At least, she mused, she'd never have to worry about trying to read his mind. Characteristically blunt and to the point, he evaded small talk and formalities in favor of the direct approach. Fortunately the idea of being swept off her feet had never appealed to her. "Thank you," she told him. "I'd love one."

Chapter Six

𝄞

} "I DON'T KNOW," NORA MUSED. "IT'S NOT WHAT
I had in mind."

Jorie leaned back in the velvet-upholstered chair at the Bridal Boutique with a weary sigh. Lily had begged her to accompany them to the exclusive shop where she was trying on another round of gowns in search of the perfect dress. She'd agreed to meet them for an extended lunch hour on Tuesday. Though Lily had understood Jorie's tighter than usual schedule with Art-Is-In's biggest fund-raiser of the year just weeks away, Nora had found the time restraint irritating.

Which probably explained why, thus far, her aunt had approved of nothing, and Lily, like most brides, knew only that she wanted to look breathtaking when she walked down the aisle. "What do you think, Lily?" Jorie asked.

Lily was critically studying her reflection in the mirror. She tugged at the flounce at the neckline. "I've decided I hate ruffles. This is the third dress we've tried with ruffles and I hate them."

Jorie tended to agree. Lily was a graceful young lady, charming and poised. The ruffles looked too girlish on her.

Nora frowned. "Lots of brides have ruffles, Lily. They look young and innocent."

Lily scrunched her nose. "Which is probably why I don't like them." She attempted to smooth the flounces at her bodice. "I look like a moron."

There was another woman in the store trying on dresses. Jorie had estimated her age to be around thirty or so, and judging from the size of the engagement ring on her finger and the array of gowns she'd tried on, her wedding would be a no-expense-spared event. The woman glanced at Lily with a slight smile. "First wedding, hon?"

"Well, yeah," Lily said. "My last, too. I'm not planning to do this again."

The woman laughed. It had a brittle, tinny sound to it that seemed in stark contrast to her flawless blond hair and photo-quality beauty. "I thought that my first time down the aisle, too," she assured Lily. "It wasn't until the third wedding when I realized I was starting to make a habit of this."

Lily's eyes widened. "How many times have you been married?"

The woman studied her reflection in the mirror, narrowed her eyes at something, and then shook her head to the saleswoman. "I don't like the waistline," she said. "I'm going to try the Vera Wang." The clerk sighed and unzipped the back of the dress. The woman looked at Lily. "This is my sixth," she said. "Seven if you count the one that got away." She held the partially unzipped dress up with one hand and extended the other. "I'm Christina Bainbridge."

Lily took her hand. "Lily Benton."

"Lily is marrying James Wells," Nora interjected. "The young man who runs Wells Enterprises."

Christina's gaze, Jorie noted, dropped momentarily to the ring on Lily's left hand. "You don't say."

Lily smiled at her. "I met him in Paris. We're getting married this summer."

"What does Simon think about that?" Christina drawled.

"You know Simon?" Lily asked.

"Oh yes," she answered. "We're old friends."

Lily laughed. "Then you know exactly what he thinks. James is too young, and I'm a flake who doesn't know her own mind."

Nora clucked her tongue in disapproval. "Lillian. Really."

"It's true, Mother," Lily told her.

"That sounds like Simon," Christina said. Jorie didn't think she imagined the bitter note in the woman's voice.

"I think he's starting to come around, though," Lily assured her. She glanced at Jorie. "Don't you?"

Nora snorted derisively as she eased out of her chair. "That man's never going to come around. He's ill-tempered and obstinate." She fiddled with the ruffles at Lily's neckline, then shook her head. "I'm going to find our sales clerk. We need the next round of dresses."

When Nora left, Christina gave Lily a pat on the shoulder. "All I can tell you, honey, is enjoy every minute of this. Because I guarantee you, there's no wedding like the first." She glanced over her shoulder at the sales clerk. "Is the Wang ready?"

"Yes, ma'am."

Christina looked at Lily again. "Nice meeting you," she said. "When you see Simon, tell him I said hello."

Simon punched the lighted button on his intercom. "Yes, Kym?"

"You in the mood for Howard Wells?"

At the mention of James's uncle, Simon frowned. Howard rarely communicated with Simon. When he did, it inevitably led to an argument. "Why?" he asked, suspicious.

"He's here," the young woman announced.

With a weary sigh, Simon made a mental note to talk to his human resources manager again. The ongoing hunt for an assistant who could stand to work for him had taken several bad turns lately. The young woman, with her unnaturally red hair and outlandish leather dress, now seated in his outer office was intelligent enough, he'd give her that. And to her credit, Howard tended to bring out the worst in people. "Let him in," he said softly.

Howard, looking as oily and wheedling as usual, breezed into his office. He dropped into one of the upholstered chairs. "Really, Simon, where *do* you find these people? What happened to Maria?"

"Maria left to marry one of our accountants." He rounded the desk, keeping a wary eye on Howard. "That was seven assistants ago."

He studied his manicured nails. "Really? Having a little trouble keeping the help around?"

Simon propped one hip on the edge of his desk. "No more than usual. What do you want, Howard?"

Howard gave him a shrewd look. "Direct as usual."

"I'm assuming this isn't a social call."

"No reason for that, is there?"

None at all, Simon concurred. Howard had treated him like a mortal enemy since the afternoon when Peter's will had named Simon as James's guardian.

"I had an interesting conversation with a friend of mine in mergers this morning," Howard said. "Seems someone's been asking some questions lately about William Benton."

"Really. What kind of questions?"

"I don't know." Howard's eyes narrowed. "I thought maybe you could tell me."

"I don't have the slightest idea."

Howard glared at him. "You don't say?"

"Was that all you wanted to know?"

Howard stirred in the chair. "Damn you, Grant. I want to know if you're having Benton investigated."

"Why?"

"Because no matter what role my brother gave you in James's life, he's my nephew. I'm concerned."

Simon suppressed a harsh laugh. As far as he knew, Howard's only concern for James was the controlling interest he held in Wells Enterprises stock. "That's touching, Howard. I'll make sure James knows." He pinned him with a narrow look. "He missed you at his engagement party."

"I was tied up."

"So was I," Simon said. "I changed my plans."

"Don't be sanctimonious, you bastard. I want to know why you're trying to prevent James's marriage to the Benton girl."

"I'm not."

"That's not what I heard."

"Then you heard wrong."

Howard drummed his fingers on the arm of the chair. "Is it your intention to completely cut me out of my nephew's life?"

"Spare me the histrionics, Howard. You aren't interested in James's life. You know it, and so do I. The only thing you're interested in is his bankroll."

The other man visibly balked. "Really, Simon, it wouldn't kill you to indulge in a little goodwill every now and then. You don't have to play the bastard all the time."

An image of Sunday afternoon on the lawn of Jorie's church floated through his memory. He'd had no trouble then, and had in fact actually enjoyed himself. It was only in the stuffy, artificial world filled with men like Howard Wells where he felt suffocated. "I'll take that under advisement," he said sarcastically. "But I'm a busy man, and if this visit doesn't have a purpose, I'd like to wrap it up."

He glowered at him. "You still claim you aren't investigating William Benton?"

Simon crossed his arms over his chest. "You shouldn't believe everything you hear, Howard."

Howard ignored that. "I suppose you've considered the benefit a merger with Benton Electronics would have for us?"

"Actually I haven't given it a second thought."

"Oh come on. You and I both know that Wells Enterprises has had its eye on the Benton manufacturing arm for years. Never mind that William Benton wouldn't give a prospective buyer the time of day."

"That might have been true five or six years ago, Howard, but not anymore. Benton has fallen behind to the Pacific Rim manufacturers. I don't think he's particularly useful to us anymore."

"Maybe he's not the ripest plum on the tree anymore, but hell, we could still cut our production costs. In this market it would be a huge boon to our stock and our business."

"Maybe."

"Definitely." Howard levered out of the chair. "I'm relieved to know the rumors are false. I can't believe you'd jeopardize James's future by mucking up a potential merger with Benton."

"I'll do whatever is necessary to protect him. You, of all people, should know that by now."

Howard studied him a minute. "If I didn't know better, I'd think that was a threat."

"You can take it that way if you want."

He pulled open the door. "You really are a bastard, aren't you, Grant?"

"I'd advise you not to forget it, either."

Howard huffed an outraged breath as he stormed out of the office. The frosted-glass door was still partially open when Simon heard Kym's voice. "Don't let the door hit you on the way out, toots."

Simon shook his head and rounded his desk again. He really had to have a talk with his human resources manager. He reached for the phone. First, though, he wanted Mark Baine to step up his look into Howard's possible connections with William Benton. Any visit from Howard left a bad taste in his mouth, but this one was fouler than most.

Simon made his way through the clutter and apparent chaos of Art-Is-In until he found Jorie's cubicle in the back of the overcrowded office suite. She was on the phone and waved him to have a seat in the battered chair next to her desk. She looked good, he noted. Fresh. Dressed in a simple cotton dress with ridiculously oversized earrings and a necklace that hung well below her waist, Jorie managed to look eccentric and elegant at the same time.

Jorie wrapped up her conversation and hung up the phone. "Hi," she told him.

"Hi. You look tired."

Amusement twinkled in her eyes. "Thanks. So do you."

Simon frowned. "I was making an observation, not passing judgment."

"I know." She reached for the monstrous bag

she called her purse. "No offense taken. I am tired, actually. I don't doubt that it shows." She tossed a few items into her inbox. "How bad's the traffic tonight?"

"Not too bad. We'll get there in plenty of time." He retrieved the envelope from his inside jacket pocket and extended it to her. "Here's your check."

Jorie took it with a slight sigh. "You have no idea how much this means. The timing—" She shrugged. "Let's just say my boss is pretty sure you're an angel."

"Hardly."

"I told him that," she assured him. "He didn't believe me."

"I consider it money well spent."

She swiveled in her chair to open the small safe behind her desk. "We'll get you all the tax stuff after our fund-raiser. We hire a firm to do all that for us once a year. It's just easier to keep up with."

"No problem."

She shot him an amused look over her shoulder as she opened the safe. "So what did James think of his company's generosity?"

"The Wells Foundation exists to be the charitable arm of Wells Enterprises. James is pleased he was able to help."

With a deft turn, she secured the check in the safe. "Well, I don't know if he believes in eternal rewards, but if I have anything to say about it, he just earned a big one."

Somehow Simon could picture her standing before the throne of the Almighty making demands. The image suited her. And it wouldn't surprise him to find out that the Almighty conceded.

"That's an awfully odd expression you have, Simon. What are you thinking?"

He smiled slightly as he stood. "We should get going if we want to miss the traffic."

She hesitated for a brief moment before she slung her purse over her shoulder and switched off her desk lamp. "I still think it would be easier to take the T," she said.

"I'm sure you do," he conceded, thinking the Almighty probably didn't stand a chance.

"Oh, by the way, Simon," Lily mentioned later that evening. "We met a friend of yours today."

"Oh?"

She nodded, fork and knife poised above her plate. "Christina somebody or other." She looked at Jorie. "What did she say her name was?"

James choked. "Christina Bainbridge?"

"Yeah," Lily assured him. "That's it." She returned her attention to Simon. "She's, um, interesting."

James shot Simon a wide-eyed look. Simon nodded thoughtfully. "Yes, I suppose she is." He glanced at Jorie. "You met her, too?"

"Lily was trying on dresses." She was studying her grilled chicken salad with undue interest.

"Who is she?" Lily asked. "And why the heck has she been married a gazillion times?"

"Christina is easily bored," Simon stated flatly. From the corner of his eye, he saw James giving Lily a pointed look. "As a matter of fact, I believe she found me boring."

"Oh shit," James muttered.

Lily frowned at him. "What in the world is the matter with you?"

Simon came to his rescue. "James is concerned that I'm going to be upset because you met Christina."

"Don't you like her?"

"Actually," he assured Lily, "no. Not very much."

Her eyebrows lowered in puzzlement. "She seemed to know you pretty well. When I told her I was marrying James, she asked how you were taking it." Lily's light laugh was musical. "I told her you weren't taking it well at all, but that you were kind of starting to get over it."

"Lily—" James warned.

"What James is trying to tell you," Simon said smoothly, "is that Christina Bainbridge is my ex-fiancée."

Lily dropped her fork with a loud clatter. Jorie gave him a sharp look. "*That's* the woman who said you were boring?"

"The same."

"Ezekiel's wheels, I knew I didn't like her."

Lily was watching him, fascinated. "You were number seven that got away."

"I was what?" Simon asked.

"The seventh husband. She said she was getting married for the sixth time, and it would be seven except that one got away. It was you."

"That's interesting."

"Geez, Simon, what *were* you thinking?" Lily shook her head. "I mean that woman is a first-class hag."

James groaned. Simon clapped him on the back. "I assure you, James, I am not suffering any lingering heartache over Christina Bainbridge."

Lily seemed undaunted. "Didn't anyone ever tell you that women who look like that might be beautiful when they're young, but when they hit forty"—she let out a low whistle—"you'd better look out. All that sun and bleach, she'll look rode hard and put up wet."

Jorie choked on a slight laugh. Simon glanced at her briefly, then looked at Lily. "That's an interesting thought."

"Sure," Lily told him. "It's starting to show already. She's beginning to look kind of pruny."

"Geez, Lily," James protested.

"Well, she is." Lily glanced at Jorie. "Isn't she?"

Simon shot Jorie a dry look. She stabbed a piece of chicken, hard. "I can't say that I noticed."

"Oh come on," Lily protested. "Those lines around her eyes. And her upper lip." She shook her head. "Consider yourself lucky, Simon. In a few years you'd be waking up in the morning, taking one look at her, and thinking what in the hell have you gotten yourself into."

"I doubt it would have lasted that long," he assured her.

That made Lily frown. "What?"

"As it turned out," he explained to Lily, "she had an interesting definition of fidelity."

"She cheated on you?" Lily sounded horrified.

"With one of the accountants at Wells Enterprises."

Lily frowned sharply. "Eeew."

Simon nodded. "My thoughts exactly. So what did Christina have to say to you today?"

"Oh, just some wedding stuff. Nothing serious. Definitely nothing important. I was trying on gowns. I'm having trouble finding one."

Beside him, he heard Jorie exhale a long sigh. He shot her a quick look. "Lily," she said, her expression slightly pained, "you've tried on three dozen at least. You're going to have to pick one soon."

"I know, I know. I just want it to be perfect."

James reached for her hand. "I'm sure you'll look wonderful, honey, no matter what dress you buy."

She seemed to melt at his compliment, then

tipped her head toward the small jazz combo at the end of the room. "Let's dance, James," she suggested. "Do you realize we haven't since that night—"

"In Paris," James finished. He rose and extended his hand. "I'd love to."

Lily slid gracefully from her seat and followed him onto the small dance floor.

Simon watched them a moment, then looked at Jorie. "You look perplexed," he told her.

"I'm trying to picture you with Christina Bainbridge," she admitted.

Simon shrugged. "That was a different time in my life. I was younger, less sure of who I was and what I wanted. She seemed like she'd make a good partner."

"Were you in love with her?"

He considered that, as he often had in the past. "I'm not sure. I thought I was, I guess. I didn't have the best role model for healthy adult relationships when I was a child. I'm not sure I really knew what love was."

Jorie twirled her fork between her fingers. "Do you now?" she asked quietly.

He sensed danger in the question. "I know what it's not. It's not the hollow feeling I felt when I was with Christina." His eyes narrowed as he remembered their parting arguments. "It's definitely not the relief I felt when the relationship ended."

"But the affair—"

"Believe it or not, Christina's affair isn't the only reason I terminated our engagement."

"There was more?" she asked, wide-eyed.

"Hmm. She made it very clear that she wasn't comfortable with the role James had in my life. He was only eighteen at the time, but Christina thought I should no longer feel obligated toward him. She wanted me to leave Wells Enterprises and start my own practice."

Her face registered a momentary outrage, and then she laughed. "Are you serious?"

"Completely," he said grimly. "You find that amusing?"

"I find it amusing that anyone could be stupid enough to think you'd go for that. Good grief, Simon, what *were* you thinking when you got engaged to that woman?"

Puzzled and intrigued by her reaction, he watched her curiously. "That I was thirty-three, and it was time for me to get married."

"Is there a calendar for that kind of thing?" she prompted. "See, I always thought you were supposed to wait until the right person came along. I didn't know there was a deadline." Her eyes twinkled at him. "I guess I'd better get busy."

Her teasing chafed. Simon stoically pushed aside the sting and watched her through narrowed eyes. "Don't tell me you've never gotten involved in a bad relationship?"

"Oh Lord, scads of them." She leaned back in

her chair. "I have a very bad habit of taking on lost causes and trying to salvage their lives."

He lifted an eyebrow. "You don't say."

"I've married off at least a dozen men I once dated to different friends of mine who were much better suited for them." Her grin turned self-effacing. "I guess you could say I'm like a personal dating service, premarital counselor, self-esteem guru, and shrink all wrapped up in one."

He considered this. "So the men you've dated," he said carefully. "What are they generally like?"

"Easy to manage." At his expression, she laughed. "I don't normally get involved in relationships I can't control."

"I know the feeling." He gave her a close look. "Ever get your heart broken?"

"By a boyfriend? Only once. I was young and stupid, and I thought all my friends were wrong when they said he was a creep."

"Friends are usually right in cases like that."

"So I learned." She shook her head. "But love is blind, you know. And I had trouble believing that Mason wasn't the answer to all my prayers."

"How old were you?"

"Eighteen. I was a college freshman. He was a senior. I was so lonely. I had just moved out of my aunt and uncle's house, and I was trying to figure out who I was. Mason made me feel . . . wanted."

"But?"

"But what he wanted was someone naïve

enough to cook his meals and clean his apartment. I was just as good as the next attention-starved freshman."

"Who ended the relationship?"

"I did. I wised up after a couple of months, but it still hurt. Every time I saw him on campus with another girl, I felt a little wounded. But by the end of my sophomore year I realized that I'd never been in love with Mason, I'd just been in love with the way he made me feel. I liked feeling needed."

"Like Lily needed you?"

She frowned slightly. "I suppose. When you're twelve and your parents send you away to live, no matter how good and logical their reasons are, it still feels like they don't want you around."

"I can imagine."

"Can you?"

"Sure. I spent most of my childhood foisted on willing strangers who felt a greater sense of responsibility for my well-being than my mother did. That tends to have a shaping effect."

"About your mother—"

He shook his head. "Not here, and not now." He leaned closer to her and lightly covered her hand. "I'll tell you later." The ease of the admission surprised him. He rarely discussed his relationship with his mother with anyone, yet Jorie seemed to make even the thorniest conversations more bearable.

Jorie's eyes widened slightly, and she dropped her gaze to his hand. "Simon—"

He tightened his fingers and gently rubbed the back of her thumb with his own. "James and Lily will be back soon," he said softly. "I'd rather not get into it."

"I understand. I wasn't pressuring you."

"I know. It's one of the things about you that fascinates me. You don't seem to mind my privacy. Or my secrets."

"I'm nothing like Christina Bainbridge," she told him.

"Thank God."

Jorie propped her chin on one hand and regarded him somberly. "She's sophisticated," she said carefully. "I can see why you wanted a partner like that."

He gave her a close look. "Can you?"

"Sure." She shrugged. "I'm sure she seemed like a wise choice."

He thought that over. At the time that had probably been true. He'd been prone to choose lovers based on an imaginary list of criteria that included life goals and temperament. "I suppose she did."

"If she hadn't challenged you about James—"

"She still would have had an affair."

"Probably," Jorie mused.

He leaned close to her. "My tastes have gotten much more sophisticated, I assure you." He reached up and twined a curl around his index finger. "I have discovered that I find eccentricity and unpredictability extremely sexy."

A slight smile played at the corner of her mouth. "I suppose that's a good thing."

"Most definitely."

Chapter Seven

🎼

"SO DID SHE FIND A DRESS?" LAVONIA ASKED Jorie Friday night as she put a bowl of mashed potatoes down on the table.

Jorie munched on a carrot. "I don't know. Right now she's considering this off-the-shoulder thing. I don't like it, but Nora is wild about it." She glanced at Simon, who at Lavonia's request was looking over her lease agreement. Lavonia's landlord was threatening to raise her rent for the second time that year. At the new rate the small apartment would eat up nearly two-thirds of Lavonia's monthly income. When Lavonia had called Jorie Wednesday morning in tears, Jorie had recommended reviewing the lease. If Lavonia could hold off the rate hike, she'd have time to look for a new place. To her surprise, Lavonia had asked for Simon's number. "He's a lawyer," Lavonia had explained. "And a friend. I've fed that man. He owes me."

After the previous evening's dinner with Lily and James, Jorie had found her mind wandering to the look Simon had given her at the table. With the imprint of his Sunday morning kiss still on her brain, and the way her hands trembled when she remembered the hot rush of desire she'd felt in his arms, she'd found herself feeling flustered and warm for the rest of the evening and the ride to her apartment. Simon had told her again how much he'd enjoyed himself on Sunday, but he'd not pursued the issue of his proposition. Evidently he was taking her at her word when she'd told him she needed time.

He was, however, doing his level best to keep her heated, on edge, and slightly off balance. He touched her whenever he had the chance. He looked at her through desire-deepened eyes. And he watched her when she moved around the room. So far she was winning the battle to resist his seemingly irresistible charm, but it was getting harder by the day.

Worse, her friends and family seemed intent on taking the matter out of her hands. She'd reluctantly surrendered his number so Lavonia could solicit his help, with a sinking feeling that she was losing the war to avoid falling for him.

Simon had evidently complied. He'd called

Jorie to tell her that he'd be joining her for her Friday evening with Lavonia and Darius.

Looking at him now, she felt her blood heat a little. He looked sexy and lawyerly. His wire-framed glasses sat near the end of his nose as he pored over the agreement. How was it possible, she mused, for him to look scholarly and sexy at the same time? She found herself unexpectedly irritated by the sudden tug of attraction she felt to him. She forced the thought aside with some effort as she glanced at the papers in his hand. "How's it going?" she asked him.

He frowned. "I think this was written by the same lawyer who drafted the Nuremberg indictment." He glanced up from the papers. "It's a little severe."

Lavonia made a disgusted noise and began chopping radishes with a vengeance. "I'm not surprised. They figure poor people ain't going to kick up any kind of fuss that matters for nothing. So they just push us around." She brought the knife down on the cutting board with a loud *thwack*.

Darius was spreading frosting on a yellow sheet cake. "Don't worry, Mama. Simon'll fix it."

Simon had risen to icon status in Darius's mind. Not only did he have his own driver, but he was buying the child a piano. Lavonia shook her head. "Hardly matters. If it's not this, it'll be something else."

Jorie winced at the comment. She often won-

dered how Lavonia managed to remain so generally positive when life had dealt her so few good
hands. She'd noticed in the last few weeks,
though, that her friend's characteristic optimism
was waning. A rash of crimes in the neighborhood, a quickly worsening job situation, and now
the crisis over her lease agreement had Lavonia
feeling beaten down and defeated. "We'll find
someplace else, Lavonia," Jorie said softly.

"Not on my income." Lavonia wiped the
radishes into the salad with a brush of her hand.
She looked at Darius. "Please go get the paper out
of the box."

He waved the spatula. "But I'm not done."

"You can finish later." She tilted her head toward the door. "I want the paper."

"Is this your way of saying you're going to talk
about adult stuff and you don't want me to hear
it?"

"It's my way of saying I asked you to get the paper, and I expect you to do what you're told. Act
like you've got some training."

He narrowed his gaze. "Are you gonna talk
about sex? 'Cause I already know most of it."

Lavonia raised the spoon she was holding.
"Then you know that I brought you into this
world, and I can take you out again if you don't
do as I say."

He rolled his eyes but put down the spatula.
"Yes, ma'am."

When Darius left the room, Lavonia looked at Jorie. "You're going to have to face the fact that not every story has a silver lining, Jorie. Sometimes the ending's just plain sad."

"It's not that grim, Lavonia," Simon assured her. He pushed the papers aside. "There are a couple of things you can consider."

"Am I going to be able to keep this place?"

"Have you ever been late making a rent payment?"

"Not yet. I thought I wasn't going to make it that month Darius was sick and I missed so much work, but my tax refund came earlier than I expected."

Simon nodded thoughtfully. "Then you can stay here. At least for a year."

She breathed a sigh of relief. "He can't raise the rent?"

"The contract says every twelve months unless you make a late payment. If you miss a payment, the owner can hike your rate. If you can afford what you're currently paying, you can stay."

Lavonia dropped into a chair and buried her head in her hands. "Oh thank God."

Simon folded his hands across his stomach. "I think you're going to need to consider some options, though. There's no doubt he'll hike it when the next cycle rolls around."

She sighed. "I don't know what options. I can barely afford what I'm paying now." She looked at Simon. "This isn't the greatest place in the world, but it's relatively safe. I don't want to move us somewhere that we have to worry about crime all the time."

"I understand," Simon assured her.

"It's hard when the only work I can get is retail." She shook her head. "Sometimes I wonder if Darius even hears me when I tell him how important it is for him to finish high school. Our lives would be different if I'd stuck with it."

Jorie saw the intent look on Simon's face. He appeared to be calculating something as complicated as the solution to pi. "Simon—?"

Darius chose that moment to return with the paper. "Hey, guess what?"

Simon looked at him. "What?"

He held up the paper. "Some guy in Boston got arrested yesterday for screwing up some company's stock. He looks like Frankenstein."

With a frown, Simon held out his hand. "Let me see."

Darius handed him the paper. Simon scanned the article, his expression dark. "Anyone you know?" Jorie asked him.

He pursed his lips as he studied the piece. "Bronson VanMetre."

The name rang a bell. "Why do I know that name?"

Simon raised his gaze to hers. "He's a financier

and investor who makes most of his money buying out larger companies and breaking up the
pieces." He paused. "Recently he entered into negotiations with Benton Electronics."

Lavonia's forehead creased. "Your uncle's company?" she asked Jorie.

"Yes." Jorie turned to Simon. "Uncle Bill's not
mentioned in that article, is he?"

"No." He turned to the continuation. "But if
your uncle was counting on that deal, he's got serious problems."

"Hmm." Jorie reached for a carrot stick. "I
never heard him mention it, but then, until Lily
got engaged, I hadn't seen a lot of my aunt and
uncle lately."

Simon folded the newspaper and set it on the
table. "I'm sure if there's trouble, you'll hear about
it soon enough," he said carefully.

"If your uncle has legal problems, I wonder if
it'll affect Lily's wedding," Lavonia mused.
"Nothing spoils a wedding like a bunch of bad
publicity and mean reporters."

Darius frowned. "Lily and James are still gonna
get married, aren't they?" he probed.

"It certainly looks that way," Simon drawled.

Jorie gave him a dry look. "You're starting to
sound resolved."

He shrugged. "Maybe you're winning me
over."

"Good thing. Lily asked me to play at the wedding. I never played a wedding before," Darius said.

"If Lily doesn't decide on a dress soon, you may not get to play this one," Jorie told him. She grinned at Simon. "You, by the way, behaved impressively well at dinner the other night. You actually managed to look semi-interested in the entire conversation."

"I was interested," he said, his expression suspiciously serious.

"Since when do men find discussions about bridal satin and tulle interesting?"

"I was interested to see how long James could tolerate that without losing it."

That made her laugh. "No wonder you and Christina Bainbridge didn't make it down the aisle. I'm guessing that her conversational skills are a little, um, egocentric."

"A little."

Darius, who had returned to his cake, waved an icing-laden spatula in Simon's direction. "You were gonna get married once?"

"Once," Simon said. "I learned my lesson."

Jorie laughed. "That's what James was talking about."

"James?"

"Um hmm. When he came to see me Monday, I asked how he was holding up with all this wedding planning. He said you gave him some excellent advice."

"I did?"

She flashed him a brief smile. "Sure. He said you told him to beg for her attention a lot. It seems to work. I think Lily finds it flattering. I guess you learned that from your financée."

"That's always effective with me," Lavonia agreed. "Nothing like a begging man to melt my heart."

Darius had finished icing the cake and was now licking the spatula. "So if I beg enough, can I get Sega Genesis?"

"No." His mother ruffled his hair. "I said begging men, not begging little boys looking for excuses not to do their homework."

Disgruntled, he dropped the spatula in the sink. "It was worth a shot anyway."

"Definitely," Simon agreed.

"Don't encourage him," Lavonia warned. "He's plenty conniving as it is."

"I am not," Darius insisted.

"Do you know what *conniving* means?" his mother challenged him.

"No," Darius admitted. "But I can tell by the way you said it that it ain't good."

"Isn't good," she corrected.

"Yeah, that."

Lavonia rolled her eyes and looked at Jorie

again. "So here's what I want to know. What's she going to do about finding a dress? Lord, the child only has a couple of months. Doesn't she know the thing has to be fitted?"

Jorie laughed. "I don't know, but I guarantee, whatever she picks, James is going to know more about it than he wants to."

Darius scrunched his nose. "I'm not ever getting married. Not if I have to learn about some stupid dress."

"Just pick a woman who's low maintenance," Simon recommended.

"I hate to break this to you," Lavonia said, "but there's no such thing as a low-maintenance woman who's planning a wedding."

"That's probably true," Jorie added. "I've been a bridesmaid more times than I can count. I've never been in a wedding that didn't cause major family conflict. It just goes with the territory."

Darius snorted. "That's why I ain't having one."

"Tell me that again in five or six years when you start noticing girls," his mother challenged. She stood and wiped her hands on her apron. "I think dinner is just about done," she announced. She looked at Darius. "I want you to set the table and put ice in the glasses. I'm going to take Jorie to the back room and show her those clothes I told her you'd outgrown."

"Yes, Mama."

"We'll be right back," Lavonia told Simon as she prodded Jorie's shoulder.

Darius watched the two women leave, then joined Simon at the table. "What's up, dude?" he asked.

Simon leaned back in his chair. "I've got an angle I'm working," he confided.

Darius's grin was lopsided. "Yeah. With Jorie."

"You think I got a thing for her?"

"Hah. You are sorry, man. You got it written all over your face."

Simon nodded, thoughtful. "Yes. I suppose I do."

"But I'm telling you right now, you ain't doing it right."

"You don't think so?"

He shook his head. "No way. You gotta, you know"—he waved his hands in front of him— "work it a little. Girls love that."

"I've heard that."

"They like you to say stuff to 'em like, 'You lookin' good, mama' and 'I want to get me some o' dat.'"

"You have a lot of experience with this kind of thing?" Simon asked.

"Sure." Darius examined his fingernails. "I've had a couple of women."

Simon suppressed a smile. "A couple?"

"Yeah. I got one at school and one at church. Gotta keep my bases covered, you know."

"Naturally."

"So in my experience, chicks dig it when a guy has a cool car—"

"Which you don't."

"Duh. I'm eight. I'm talking about you. You got that limo you ride in *and* the car you drove on Sunday. That was phat."

"Which is a good thing, I'm assuming."

"Yeah. Phat is good. Like sick, you know."

"Okay, so I've got the car. What else?"

Darius nodded. "Clothes. You gotta dress sharp." He gave Simon a once-over. "You do okay. A little vanilla, but overall, okay. Besides, I think Jorie likes vanilla."

"No kidding?"

"Yeah. She's got this dude Kevin she hangs out with sometimes. Man, that boy is just too solid white. No rhythm. No moves. No style."

"No car?"

Darius grunted in disgust. "A station wagon. Can you believe that?"

"Pretty incredible," Simon concurred, making a mental note to gather more information about the wagon-driving Kevin. If Jorie wouldn't tell him, he was fairly certain he could get Lily to talk.

"And believe me, if she'd hang with this Kevin

guy, I'm thinking she ain't exactly repulsed by vanilla."

"So my clothes are okay?"

"For Jorie they are. If you wanted some style-conscious chick, you might have to dude it up a little."

Simon had a mental image of the way Christina Bainbridge would have responded to that suggestion. "All right, got it. Clothes and a car. Anything else?"

"Well, see, that's the hang in all this. You got the first two covered. It's your act that needs some work."

"My act." Simon nodded as he considered this. "What's wrong with my act?"

Darius slid out of his chair. "First there's the way you walk." He took several striding steps across the linoleum. "It's like you're always going somewhere. You gotta take your time. Give the woman a chance to admire you." He demonstrated a well-practiced strut.

Simon had to swallow a laugh. "I see."

"Chicks gotta check you out. They want to look at the package."

"That's what the clothes are for."

"Yeah." His grin broadened. "Now you're getting it."

"Anything besides the walk?" Simon asked.

Darius returned to the table. "It's the way you

talk. You always talk like a lawyer—whether you're lawyering or not."

"Like a lawyer." Simon stroked his chin. "What do you mean?"

"Big words, which Jorie probably likes. She's smart, you know."

"I've noticed."

"But you're too serious. You want a woman to get soft on you, you gotta be smoother." Darius leaned over the table and stared into Simon's eyes. "You gotta flatter her some. Tell her she's a fine-looking woman. Tell her she's got style, and you like it."

"Tell her she's phat?"

Darius's mouth dropped open. "Are you crazy?"

"I thought phat was good."

Darius shook his head. "Phat *is* good, but only a dude with a death wish would tell a woman she looked *fat*." He cocked his head to one side. "I think you might be hopeless."

"Yeah? I think maybe Jorie likes me."

"Oh, she likes you," Darius agreed. "I can tell you that for sure. But if you want to get very far with her, you're gonna have to work for it. She ain't the kind of woman who comes cheap."

Simon nodded thoughtfully. "You may have a point there."

"Jorie needs a hero, you know. Some guy who just blows her socks off." Darius nodded. "You might be him, but you're going to have to work it. The next couple of weeks are, like, *it*."

Jorie and Lavonia reentered the kitchen. "It for what?" Jorie asked.

Darius gave Simon a knowing look. Simon glanced at Jorie. "It's a guy thing," he explained. "You two ready to eat? I'm starved."

She hesitated, looking at him curiously. "A guy thing?"

"Let it be, Jorie," Lavonia told her. "You'll never get it out of them."

When they were seated at the table and Lavonia had said grace, she passed Jorie the bowl of mashed potatoes. "So," she said, "the weather's supposed to turn bad tonight, I heard. There's a storm coming in."

"Lots of rain," Darius concurred. "I heard it on the radio." He gave Simon a narrow look. "Rain can be a good thing."

"You two planning anything for the weekend?"

Jorie choked on a swallow of iced tea. "Why do you ask?"

Lavonia gave her a curious look. "Just wouldn't want you to get rained out."

Simon was watching Jorie, his expression thoughtful. "Actually," he said carefully, "I do have some plans. I'm pretty sure the rain's not going to be a problem."

Lavonia waved a hand toward the window. "All I know is, if it rains too hard, the ceiling in that back room is going to leak again. Darius and I spent the last thunderstorm we had mopping up the water."

"You should get that fixed," Simon said, his gaze on Jorie.

Lavonia laughed. "I've told the super five times. He looks at it every now and then and tells me he can't find nothing wrong."

"But Mama," Darius pointed out, "that's the room where you want to put my piano."

She nodded. "I know, baby. We'll work out something."

Darius turned to Simon. "You said Jorie bailed you out at James and Lily's party."

Simon nodded. "Yes. She did."

"That means you owe me one piano. Like you said."

"Yes, it does."

"When are we going to get it?"

"As soon as you tell me what kind you want."

Chapter Eight

𝄞

❳ THE FOLLOWING AFTERNOON JORIE STOOD ON
the sidewalk outside the Wells Enterprises office building for several minutes, staring at the
glass and steel monolith with apprehension. It
seemed to represent all the logical reasons that she
shouldn't take this step with Simon. His world
and her world were on completely separate rota-
tions.

If she'd ever doubted that, she'd seen it clearly
the moment she'd met Christina Bainbridge. After
last night's dinner with Lavonia and Darius, Jorie
had spent most of the night trying to picture Simon with the other woman. Physically they were
well matched. Her blond hair and fair skin would
have looked striking with his darker coloring. She

was tall, as was he, and shared his sophistication and casual elegance.

But she'd seemed brittle to Jorie. With her six husbands and obvious wealth, Christina Bainbridge struck Jorie as one of what she called the impoverished wealthy. She had enough money to cover her every need, perhaps even her every whim, yet she had none of the things that mattered in life.

And while Simon had patiently and methodically gone over Lavonia's lease agreement with her after dinner, Jorie had watched him, imagining how Christina would have reacted had Simon told her how he planned to spend his evening.

Not well, she guessed.

That image of Christina's stark disapproval had worked its way into her mind, and somewhere in the deep parts of the night as she lay in her bed, it had been that image that had helped her make up her mind to take an irrevocable step with Simon Grant. Since she'd met him, sheer instinct for self-preservation had helped her guard her heart.

Until she'd met Christina Bainbridge.

Then she'd begun to see that she wasn't the only one on the precipice of a life of untaken chances and missed opportunities. Simon, too, in his effort to control his world and minimize his risk, had nearly married a woman like Christina Bainbridge.

She'd first seen that slightly vulnerable look on

his face the night of Lily and James's engagement party. Under no circumstances, common sense told her, could she afford to fall in love with him. But she could offer him something no woman ever had—the assurance that there were some people in the world who gave of themselves and expected nothing in return. His mother had failed him. Christina had failed him. Jorie's heart twisted at the idea that Simon would spend the rest of his life behind a shield of emotional reserve. No desire of her own could have swayed her to take this step, but hell would freeze before she'd allow Simon to walk out of her life thinking that all the world had for him were women like Christina Bainbridge. If she were careful, very, *very* careful, she stood a chance of walking away from this with her heart intact.

She'd called his cell phone that morning and asked to see him. He hadn't seemed surprised. He'd told her he'd be working that afternoon, and suggested he could come and pick her up. Jorie had wanted to meet him, to see him in his own environment, to absorb the impact of what she was about to do.

Taking a deep breath, she pushed open the door to the office building. This saving lives business, she had learned, was best done head on and directly. Any other approach merely wasted time in reaching the inevitable.

* * *

Simon stared out the window of his office at Wells Enterprises. He could see Mark Baine's reflection in the glass. "How do you think this business with VanMetre is going to affect Benton?"

"Hard to say," Mark told him. "I'm guessing, though, that Benton was counting on that merger. He's in desperate need of cash flow."

That didn't surprise Simon. He'd asked Mark Baine to meet him at the office today after reading last night's article about VanMetre. Uppermost in his mind was his recent visit from Howard Wells. Something in this deal smelled rotten, and Simon was determined to know what it was. "Did I tell you that Lily's agreed to sign a prenuptial agreement?" She, at least, seemed thus far to be completely innocent about her father's questionable financial status.

Mark snorted. "Too bad they aren't worth the paper they're written on."

Simon thrust his hands in his trouser pockets. Too bad, he mused, though he'd make sure this one protected James as much as possible. Still, the increasingly suspicious appearance of Benton's business practices worried him. If William were counting on James to bail him out, the financial impact would be enormous. Worse, if Benton Electronics became embroiled in a legal scandal, Wells Enterprises could go down with it. "I'm going to need some proof, Mark. James isn't going to listen to anything until I can show him hard facts." He turned and faced his friend. "What did you find out about Howard? Has he got ties to VanMetre?"

"Well, here's the thing. Howard apparently has been in contact with VanMetre since last year. Remember when VanMetre's trouble started with the SEC."

Simon frowned. "He was negotiating a merger for a U.S. firm with a German conglomerate. It went sour."

"And the stock took a nosedive," Mark said. "VanMetre was rumored to have his hands all over that."

"He was acquitted of wrongdoing."

"Through legal maneuvering. The guy is guilty as hell."

"And Howard's involved with him?"

"Howard's practically in bed with him, he's so involved."

"And you think Howard's investments in Delitron are linked to VanMetre as well?"

"I was looking over the numbers, comparing some figures. Last year Howard cashed out stock options on four different companies just a few days before the stock nosedived."

"And?"

"And all four went south right after VanMetre announced he was taking them over."

"Could be innocent," Simon pointed out. "Howard knows the market. He's savvy enough to read the stock trends."

"Could be," Mark concurred, "but then consider that Cornwell is VanMetre's broker of choice, and that VanMetre testified in Cornwell's defense at his trial last year."

Simon thought that over. He'd suspected for years that Howard's investment successes weren't entirely on the square. As long as he stayed out of James's affairs, Simon didn't especially care. Now, though, he had a terrible feeling that he simply wasn't seeing something that should be clearly evident. "How long," he asked Mark, "until you can prove some of this?"

"One week, maybe. Two at the most."

Simon nodded, thoughtful. "Good."

A light on the corner of his phone indicated that security had signed someone in to see him. Jorie, he thought with satisfaction. She'd come to him. The idea held far greater appeal than he'd imagined. He looked at Mark. "All right, Mark. Just keep an eye on this VanMetre business and keep me informed."

"Will do." Mark stood and reached for the notebook on Simon's desk. "Anything else you need me to look into? You okay with the girl, or you want some background?"

Simon had considered asking Mark to investigate Lily's personal background, but had decided against it. James might forgive him for delving into William Benton's finances, but not for digging up Lily's past. "Not yet," he told Mark. "Just get me what you can on Benton and Howard." Through the frosted-glass door to his outer office, he saw the shadow of the elevator doors glide open. "I've got a visitor."

Mark glanced over his shoulder. "Expecting someone?"

"Yes."

Jorie pushed open the door and stuck her head in. "It's me. Security said you'd already told them to buzz me up." She looked at Mark. "Am I interrupting?"

"I was just leaving," Mark assured her. He tucked the notebook into his back pocket.

"Are you sure? I can wait out here."

"No, ma'am." He glanced at Simon. "I'll get back to you on this as soon as I can."

"Thanks, Mark."

Mark turned to go, then stopped to extend his hand to Jorie. "I'm Mark."

She shook his hand. "Jordan Morrison. Nice to meet you."

Her name registered with Mark, Simon noted. He looked over his shoulder to give Simon a quizzical look. "Nice meeting you, too," he told Jorie. He let himself out of the office.

The glass door swished shut behind him, leaving a tense silence in its wake. Jorie looked breathtaking, he thought, though there was nothing particularly spectacular about her Berklee T-shirt and faded jeans. The fabric looked well-washed and butter-soft. His fingers itched to touch it. One of the things he found most sexy about Jorie was the way she always looked soft. Soft angles, soft hair, soft clothes, like he could just sink into her and forget all the harsh edges of life. "Hello," he told her.

She gave him a slight smile. "Hi."

"I was glad to hear from you this morning."

Her eyes twinkled. She took the opportunity to glance around his office. "Nice digs." Simon didn't know how to respond to that, so he simply waited. Anticipation was making his palms tingle. He'd watched her last night at Lavonia's, wanting her, as he always did these days. The sting of desire had grown sharper lately, more compelling. He wasn't sure how much more time he could give her before he stepped up his efforts to win her. Recently he'd found himself thinking about her at the most inconvenient times. His determination to control the surge of passion was waning. Soon, he knew, he'd reach the point of no return.

Jorie shoved her hands into the back pockets of her jeans. "I, um, was surprised you were in the office today."

"It's not unusual." He decided not to mention that he'd worked almost every Saturday and Sunday of his life since the day Peter Wells died. Somehow he'd feel ashamed to admit that to her.

"I know how that is," she was saying. "When we're in the middle of a big project at work, the hours get kind of crazy."

"I'm sure."

Silence again. Simon could hear his pulse hammering in his head. Jorie studied him a moment, then walked across the wide Oriental carpet to round his desk. "Simon?"

"Yes?" His fingers clenched to keep from reaching for her.

Jorie laid one hand on his shoulder. Her fingers scorched him through his cotton shirt. He felt the muscle tighten beneath her touch. "About that proposition of yours?" Her voice had dropped to a husky whisper.

"Yes?"

"Remember I told you I thought I needed a little time."

"Yes."

She met his gaze, her eyes a clear, steady blue filled with hope and something else he dared not name. "I think now is the time."

He hesitated, not sure he'd heard her correctly. "Did you say now?"

Jorie nodded, her eyes bright. "Yes. I said now."

"Be sure," he told her. He wouldn't walk away from her again. "Be absolutely sure."

Jorie nodded. "I am. I was thinking—"

Simon didn't give her a chance to complete the thought. He pulled her into his arms for a long, thorough kiss. Jorie wound her arms around his shoulder and clutched him to her. She made a tiny little mewling sound in the back of her throat that drove him wild. Simon explored and plundered her mouth, seeking every secret and every mystery. She flowed into him, as he'd known she would, soft and giving and unfailingly warm.

He tore his lips from hers, ran them across her jaw to her earlobe. "I want you, Jorie."

Her finger trembled as she stroked the side of his face. "That's probably a good thing," she whispered. "I've never felt like this. I'm—"

"Burning?" he prompted.

She pressed her hips against his with a slight swivel that sent his libido to the moon. "Really hot," she confessed. "My skin is so sensitive."

Simon worked one hand beneath the hem of her T-shirt and she gasped, dropping her head back. "I ache."

He knew the feeling. He stroked the velvet softness of her stomach. "So do I," he assured her. His gaze flicked to the leather sofa. Somehow he couldn't bring himself to have his first time with her on the sofa in his office. He wanted her in his home, in his bed, surrounded by his possessions and the evidence of his life. He respected Jorie more than any woman he'd ever known, and he owed her more than a quick tumble on a leather couch.

She ran her hands down his back with a soft sigh. "Simon, I—I should probably tell you—"

He shook his head and covered her mouth with his fingers. "Not here," he said. "I want to take you home."

Jorie hesitated, then nodded. Simon took her hand as he reached for his keys.

They didn't speak on the short ride to his downtown apartment. He kept Jorie's hand tucked firmly in his, stroking the back of her thumb with his own. She stared out the window. Simon had to concentrate on driving at a reasonable speed. He stopped at a red light and felt his adrenaline rise another notch. The ride to his apartment had never taken so long.

Jorie's fingers tightened on his when the light changed. His only other indication that she shared his urgency was the sound of her slightly too fast breathing and the hammering of the pulse in her wrist. He pressed his thumb to the spot and raised her hand to his lips. Her fingers trembled. He kissed them lightly.

He turned into the gated parking garage of his apartment complex and entered his key code. Jorie squirmed slightly in the seat beside him. He pulled into his parking space and switched off the ignition. Turning to her, he leaned across the console and kissed her deeply. She sighed against his mouth. "Welcome to my home," he said as he raised his head.

She gave him a tremulous smile as she turned to open her door. Simon led her to the elevator. As the doors slid shut and the elevator began its ascent, he turned her into his arms. "Jorie," he said, stroking the back of her head as he reached deep inside for the formidable control he'd relied on for years. "I don't want to shock you with how much I want you."

She shook her head against his shoulder. "You won't."

"Right now I'm having a hell of a time not taking you right here in the elevator."

"I know," she whispered.

Simon took a shuddering breath. "But I don't want to rush you." He managed a half smile. "I don't want to have to rush," he clarified. Jorie didn't respond. He ran a hand down her back and shot a quick glance at the elevator's indicator lights. Ten floors to go. "When we get upstairs Joe'll be there," he told her.

Jorie lifted her head to meet his gaze. "Does Joe live with you?"

"Downstairs. He's doing some work for me today in the office at my apartment. If you want to take a minute for yourself, I'll tell him to go."

She blushed gorgeously. "Simon—"

He studied her, entranced. "Are you embarrassed?"

"He'll know why we're there."

"Probably."

She wiped a hand through her slightly mussed hair. "I'm a little new at this kind of thing," she confessed.

The admission sent satisfaction roaring through him. He'd suspected from his conversations and observations that Jorie's experience with men was somewhat limited. He felt a little barbaric and arcane for liking that so much, but there was something fresh about her that he was beginning to find addictive. "Joe won't embarrass you," he assured her.

"I didn't think he would. It's just—it's the middle of the afternoon, Simon." She chuckled, a little self-deprecating sound he found intoxicating. "Missionaries' daughters don't go home with men for illicit rendezvous in the middle of the afternoon."

"Are you telling me you're a prude?" he teased.

"My father is a Methodist minister," she told him, a definite sparkle in her eyes. "Of course I'm a prude."

Simon laughed, finding the experience oddly exhilarating. He'd never had a lover he laughed with. Jorie had brought that to his life, showing him how much he needed it. "We'll have to work on that," he said as the elevator reached his floor.

The doors slid open, and Simon led her down the short hall to the door of his apartment. He shoved his key in the lock, then eased Jorie against the outside wall. Slowly he kissed her again, taking his time to enjoy the simple pleasure of her scent and her presence in his environment. He put his mouth against her neck and inhaled deeply. The citrusy, slightly tangy scent she wore contrasted so starkly with the overly florid perfume of women he'd known that he wondered how he could have overlooked it before. "You smell wonderful," he told her.

She moaned and tipped her head to one side. Simon trailed his lips down her throat. "What is that scent?" he pressed.

Jorie gasped when he thrust his tongue into her ear. "Essen . . ." She moaned softly. "Essen Little's Organic Lemon Spritzer."

Simon smiled. He should have known. She was not the designer fragrance type. Hers was odd, a little quirky, and incredibly sexy, just like the woman who wore it. "I like it," he told her. "It's sexy."

She laughed slightly. "I never thought of it that way."

He raised his head and captured her gaze. "I'm hoping by the time we're through, you'll see a lot of things a new way." He dropped a light kiss at the nape of her neck. "Joe's in my study." He kissed the curve of her shoulder. "Make yourself at home. I'll be right back."

*   *   *

Simon switched off the private phone line in his study.

Joe gathered a stack of papers and gave him a knowing look. He'd taken the word that he was done for the evening in his usual stride. "So," Joe asked him. "You want me to pick you up at the regular time tomorrow morning?"

Through the doorway, Simon saw Jorie curiously studying a painting in his living room. Joe generally took Simon into the office on Sunday mornings. Last week Simon had been with Jorie. This week, he thought with a slight smile, he intended to be again. She certainly was shaking up his well-ordered world, and so far he had no complaints. He looked at Joe and said, "I'll call you."

Simon waited until he heard the door click behind Joe before joining Jorie where she was still studying the painting. It was a watercolor painting of a woman and a young boy, but unlike many watercolors, it had a depth of tone that was unusual. The woman was seated on a blanket spread on a verdant lawn. The boy lay with his head in her lap, listening while she read him a book. Simon had chosen the dark gray wall in his living room to hang the painting for two reasons: the dark backdrop emphasized the painting's rich palette, and he could see it from his study. He wrapped his arms around her from behind. "It doesn't seem like my style, does it?" he asked her.

Jorie leaned back against him. "It's very good," she observed.

"But you're surprised?"

"It's—pretty. If I'd speculated on your art preferences I would have guessed dramatic or decorator. This is a very original piece."

"I've always liked it."

"Who's the artist?"

Simon released her and slid his hands into his pockets. "My mother." At Jorie's surprised look, he nodded. "She always wanted to paint. Watercolors were her favorite medium."

"She was very talented," she told him. "Did she work commercially?"

"Between cleaning jobs, you mean?" He couldn't keep the bitter note out of his voice.

Jorie's forehead creased. "Simon—"

"Sorry," he said roughly. "I didn't mean to sound harsh. Those are old memories. I like to keep them in the past where they belong."

Jorie studied him a moment before sliding her hand into his. "They are part of what make you who you are, Simon. The good and the bad."

"Is that the way you look at it?"

"I try to," she said. "I don't always succeed, but I try." She smiled slightly. " 'A joyful heart is good medicine, but a broken spirit dries up the bones.' Proverbs 17, verse 22. My father used to quote that a lot."

He thought that over. "Before or after he shipped you off to live in Boston?"

"Both," she told him. Her smile was slightly wistful. "I won't lie to you and tell you I haven't had my differences with my parents. For a long time I resented them for sending me to live with my aunt and uncle." She rubbed her hands together slightly. "But I grew older. I let things go." She gave him a close look. "I began to understand that sometimes parents have to make difficult choices."

"I don't want to give you the impression that I'm ashamed of my past. That's not true."

"I know."

"I've always kept it to myself."

"I understand that." Her expression told him that she did. He felt no pressure from her. She was interested in his life because she was interested in him, not because of some macabre fascination with listening to him dredge up the often painful memories.

"This isn't the way I planned to spend my afternoon," he said finally.

Jorie stepped into his arms and hugged him. It was comforting and consoling. He couldn't remember a time when he'd held a woman, or been held by a woman, when the only impetus in the act had been to offer solace. He crushed her to him with a slight groan. Jorie hugged him closer.

"You'll tell me when you're ready," she assured him. "I just wanted you to know I'm here for you." She tilted her head toward the kitchen. "Whatever that is in your oven, it smells fabulous. And I missed lunch."

Chapter Nine

𝄞

Jorie tucked her bare feet beneath her on the sofa and tipped her head back. The keen edge of want she'd experienced at Simon's office had ebbed slightly, subsiding to a banked fire that licked at the edges of her conscience. She and Simon had exchanged stories about Lily and James during lunch. The light banter had chased away the lingering shadows in his gaze.

He'd joined her there on the sofa, where he'd gathered her into his arms and began nuzzling her neck. Through the large window, the view of the tree-strewn grounds of Boston Common was breathtaking. "If I were you," she told him, shivering slightly when he found her earlobe and worried it with his teeth, "I'd never want to leave here." She indicated the view with a wave of her hand. "That window in my living room is the only one in my apartment. It overlooks an air-conditioning unit on the building next door."

Simon's long legs were stretched out in front of him. His fingers danced a light rhythm at the nape of her neck. "The view is one of the reasons I chose this place."

Her gaze strayed to the painting. How much of the pastoral setting, she wondered, evoked memories of his childhood at Peter Wells's home?

His fingers wended through her unruly curls, caressing and rubbing her scalp. She felt goose bumps spread down her spine. "Jordan?" he said softly.

She liked the way he said her name. She looked at him. "Yes?"

He applied a gentle pressure to the back of her neck, easing her against him. "I told you I didn't want to talk about the painting."

"Yes." She sucked in a sharp breath when he lifted a hand to cup her breast. Her cotton T-shirt and the lace of her bra provided no barrier from the warmth of his hand.

"I don't want to talk about the view, either." He rubbed his thumb in a tight circle on the tip of her breast.

"Oh." She placed one hand on his chest where she could feel his heart beat. "What do you want to talk about?"

A slight smile played at the corner of his mouth.

"I don't want to talk about anything." He slid his hand down her arm, bringing her closer. "Although I would like to hear you tell me *now* again."

Jorie took a deep breath and looked into his compelling eyes. The fire burned there, now, reaching out to her, sending shivers of desire down her spine. She wet her lips with the tip of her tongue. "Now, Simon," she said softly. "I'm ready."

"I'm glad."

"I think you should know—"

He covered her mouth with his fingers and gently stroked her top lip. "I'll learn the secrets as we go along," he assured her. "Just tell me yes or no."

Something inside her melted and flowed white-hot. "Yes. Oh yes," she said softly.

With a light oath, he covered her mouth with his own as he lifted her slightly so she lay across his lap. "Kiss me, Jorie," he told her. "Kiss me like your life depended on it."

She wrapped an arm around his neck. Beneath her hand, his body was warm and solid. She worked the buttons of his crisp cotton shirt, eager to feel his smooth skin while his mouth continued to weave a heady spell around her.

Simon licked the crease between her lips until she opened her mouth to him. He slipped his tongue inside to taste and tease and promise of things to come. One large hand eased beneath the hem of her cotton T-shirt where he toyed with her satin camisole. Heat seeped through the thin satin.

Jorie parted his shirt, then tugged his T-shirt free of his waistband. When she lightly scored his chest with her fingernails, he groaned and cupped her breast in his large, hot hand. "Simon," she gasped.

He flicked his thumb over the aching tip. "You're beautiful. Warm. So warm." Tilting his head, he kissed her deeply.

She moaned and pressed herself against his hand.

"Jorie," he whispered. "I want you." He eased one leg between her knees. "I want you."

At his fevered whisper, her heart skipped a beat. Her body clenched in anticipation. She pressed a heated kiss to his throat. He tasted salty and masculine. She pushed his T-shirt higher, baring his flat stomach. "I want you, too," she told him. "I think I'm on fire."

Simon shifted suddenly on the sofa. He eased her beneath him, covering her with his length. His hand slipped beneath her shirt again, then tugged up her camisole. When he pressed his fingers to her stomach, she shivered, a delightful, breathtaking shiver. Simon slid his mouth along her jawline. "So soft," he muttered. "Beautiful."

How had she ever feared, she wondered, that she'd be nervous and unsure with him? Simon had a way of looking at her, of touching her, that made her feel completely feminine and completely sexy. "It's you," she told him. "You do it to me."

Simon nipped her earlobe. "No, baby," he whispered. "It's us." He bent his head to kiss her again.

A demanding knock on the apartment door arrested his attention. With a soft oath, Simon glared at the door. The pounding continued.

"Simon?" It was James. "Simon, are you in there?"

Simon froze. Jorie struggled for breath. "It's James," she said unnecessarily.

"Simon, I need to talk to you. Something must be wrong with your phone."

Jorie prodded his shoulder. "Go," she whispered.

Simon gave her a hard look. "I have to let him in."

"I know." She prodded him again. "Go."

He rolled off her and pressed a hard kiss to her lips. "We're not through."

"I know," she said again, running a hand through her hair. Jorie eased off the sofa. Simon began buttoning his shirt.

James pounded on the door again. "Oh God, Simon, you have to be home."

"He sounds upset," she said.

He tucked in his shirt with a brief nod. "Something's wrong."

"Maybe I should go—"

Simon wrapped an arm around her waist and pulled her to him for a brief kiss. "No. I don't want you to leave."

"He needs you."

"Then he can talk to me while you're here." Simon released her and headed for the door.

Jorie smoothed her T-shirt, hoping she didn't look freshly ravished, though her lips felt swollen and warm. She tucked a stray curl behind her ear as Simon opened the door to a haggard-looking James.

"Simon." James burst through the door. "God, I've been trying to call you for an hour."

"I was busy," Simon told him.

"But I—" James broke off when he saw Jorie. Wide-eyed, he looked at Simon. "Oh. God. I'm sorry. I'm sorry. I shouldn't have come."

Simon prodded James toward the living room. "What's wrong?"

"I didn't mean to interrupt," James continued. "But when I couldn't get you on the phone—"

Simon nodded and sat on the sofa next to Jorie. "Sit down, James. Tell me what's going on."

James dropped into the wingback chair with a groan. He buried his face in his hands. "Oh God," he muttered again. "I screwed up, Simon. I screwed up everything." He shook his head. "It's over. Lily isn't going to marry me. What am I going to do?"

Jorie frowned. "What are you talking about?"

Simon glanced at her, then looked at James. "What happened?"

"We argued," James told them. He raised his haggard face. His eyes looked bleary. "I don't even know why. We just . . . we were talking about the wedding, and then the next thing I know, she was upset and angry. And then I got angry, and then she walked out." He looked at Jorie. "She wouldn't answer my phone calls. I went by the house, and your uncle said she didn't want to see me. What am I going to do?" He dropped his head into his hands again. "God, what am I going to do?"

Jorie shot Simon a dry look. He was watching James with an expression of concern and bewilderment. Poor man, she thought. He had weathered the storms of James's adolescence, survived the young man's passage to adulthood, and lived through an unimaginable number of crises and catastrophes. But he had no idea how to deal with a broken heart. Simon glanced at her. "It'll be okay," she told him quietly.

"No," James said. "No, it won't. If Lily doesn't marry me . . ."

"We'll work this out," Simon assured him.

Jorie reached for her purse. At Simon's sharp look, she nodded. "I think you two need some time alone."

"I don't want you to leave," he said again.

She gave him a reassuring smile. "Lily is probably trying to call me," she pointed out.

That seemed to strike a chord in James. "You have to talk to her," he said hoarsely. "You have to tell her I love her. You have to tell her I'm sorry. I'm so damned sorry." He bolted out of the chair and headed for the bathroom. "I need a tissue."

"James—" Simon said

"It's okay," Jorie told Simon. "It's mostly melodrama. It's part of young love."

Simon swore softly. "What did I do to deserve this?"

With a slight smile, Jorie straightened his collar. "Just try to be sympathetic. Let him talk it out."

Simon hesitated. "Please stay."

"I can't. He needs you."

"And I need you."

She shivered. "I know. I need you, too."

Simon muttered a dark curse as he tipped his head and kissed her. Hard. "God, Jorie, I'm burning up."

"I know," she assured him.

"I'll never sleep tonight."

"Me either."

"Can I call you?"

"Yes. If I'm not home, I'll be at Lily's."

He stared into her eyes, searching. "If I can, I'll come to you tonight."

She nodded. "We'll talk later. Take care of James."

* * *

Jorie handed Lily the box of tissues. "Here, sweetie."

Lily mopped her eyes. "Oh God, Jorie, it was just awful."

"I know." Jorie had barely unlocked the door to her apartment when the phone had rung. A teary Lily had begged Jorie to let her come over. Not wanting the girl to drive in her current emotional state, Jorie had called a cab and made the trip across town to her uncle's home.

Her aunt had let her in. "Jordan," Nora had said. "Lily called you, I suppose."

"Yes. Is she upstairs?"

"I tried to talk to her. She won't tell me what happened."

"I saw James," Jorie told her. She ignored Nora's questioning look. "They had an argument. I think it's just nerves about the wedding."

Nora had made a disapproving noise in the back of her throat. Jorie had heard that noise a thousand times in the past, but never directed toward Lily. "She thinks with her heart," Nora said. "I've always known it was going to hurt her."

Jorie had felt the usual rush of sorrow for her aunt. In Nora's struggle to insulate herself from any type of uncertainty or pain, she'd also sacrificed her ability to feel joy. "Everything's going to be all right," Jorie had assured her aunt.

"She's too emotional," Nora snapped. "Maybe you can reason with her."

Jorie felt the implied accusation that Lily's emotional side mirrored Jorie's heart-first way of life. Refusing to take the bait, she'd moved to make her way up the stairs. "I'm going up to see her."

She'd found her cousin in her bedroom, stretched across the canopied bed, sobbing into the stuffed rabbit she'd had since childhood. When Jorie sat on the bed next to her, Lily had turned to her with a broken sob and thrown herself into her arms.

Now Jorie handed her cousin a box of tissues and waited while Lily struggled for control. "Do you want to tell me what happened?" Jorie said.

"It's going to sound silly now," Lily admitted. "But it wasn't what we fought about—" She choked on a sob.

"I know." Jorie rubbed her shoulder. "It's okay, sweetie. It's going to be okay."

Across town, James tore off his glasses and tossed them on the coffee table in Simon's apartment. "I swear, Simon, I have no idea how it even started. She was talking about the wedding." James choked out a harsh laugh. "Which is all we ever talk about lately."

Simon folded his hands across his chest and studied his young friend. James reminded him so much of Peter. Like his father, he was emotional and passionate. He felt things deeply, and when he'd given his heart to Lily, he'd given it completely.

James wiped a hand over his face. "I didn't mean to sound impatient. I swear I didn't."

Lily hiccupped. "He . . . we were talking about the wedding." She wiped her eyes and delicately blew her nose. "I've been trying to keep him involved, you know. He doesn't have a mother, or anyone to make him feel like he's got some say in everything. I didn't want to just spring it all on him."

Jorie was beginning to get a very clear picture of what had transpired. "That's very kind of you," Jorie said gently.

"But lately he's been resisting even discussing things." Lily waved the tissue in a gesture of frustration. "At first I thought he was just trying to let me know that he'd be happy with whatever I picked, but then today I saw that I was about to make an awful mistake." She gasped on a broken sob. "James doesn't want to marry me, Jorie."

"Start at the beginning," Simon prompted James. "Tell me exactly what you two talked about."

James flopped back in the chair. "I took her to

Biba for lunch. We've been so busy lately, I just wanted to have some time alone with her at a nice place. We got a table, and Lily started telling me about this florist she'd talked to."

Lily's eyes filled with tears as she continued. "So, this morning," she told Jorie, "I went with Mother to meet with the florist. We're using Geraldo's, over on Commerce."

"Your mother likes him."

"Yes. And he talked about several things I wanted to consider. I don't just want flowers, Jorie. I wanted my wedding to be the most memorable and special event of my life."

"That's perfectly understandable."

"So Geraldo suggested these dramatic-looking bouquets with trailing ivy and white orchids and violets. And they were really pretty and really fresh-looking. Since I was considering those purple bridesmaid gowns, I liked the violets."

"Sounds nice," Jorie concurred.

"But I thought maybe James might want something more traditional. It's his wedding, too," she insisted.

"She was telling me about these flowers," James was explaining to Simon. "I don't know, some kind of thing with ivy and"—he manipulated the air in front of him, showing Simon the basic shape of the bouquet—"orchids or something. To tell you the truth, I wasn't paying much attention."

Which had, no doubt, Simon thought dryly, been his first mistake. "Women don't like that," he said.

"She didn't know," James insisted. "I was looking right at her. I was just thinking about how pretty she is and how much I like her eyes." He dropped his head back against the chair. "That's when she asked me what I thought."

"I explained everything to him," Lily told Jorie. "I described what Geraldo had told us, and then I asked him what he thought."

Jorie stifled a groan. She could well imagine where the conversation had gone from there. "What did he say?" she prompted.

Lily burst into tears again as she shredded her tissue. "He said he didn't care."

"I swear to God, Simon. I don't even know what set her off. She just asked me what I thought about these damned flowers and I told her it didn't matter to me."

Simon winced. "Did you say that exactly?"

James frowned. "I don't know. I guess. I may have told her I didn't care."

"And then I just couldn't shake the fact that he's been more and more distant for the last few days," Lily went on, "and that maybe he didn't care about the flowers because he didn't care whether or not we got married."

James shook his head. "So she just started getting totally upset, and she was crying and all hysterical. And then she wanted to know whether or not I even wanted to get married." James's eyes widened with remembered horror. "Can you believe that?"

"If you said you didn't care, I can," Simon said dryly.

"How could she think that? I just want to be married to her, Simon. I don't care if she wants dandelions."

"And when I asked him that," Lily told Jorie, "he couldn't even answer me." Her lips began to tremble as she fought another sob. "God, Jorie, I love him so much."

"He loves you, too, Lily," Jorie assured her.

"I thought so," Lily said. "And maybe he does, but he's not sure he wants to marry me."

"I don't think that's true."

"You haven't been around him for the last few days. I should have recognized it sooner."

"The next thing I know," James said, "she walked out of the restaurant. By the time I paid the bill, she was already hailing a cab." He rubbed his neck in remembered frustration. "I tried to reason with her. I couldn't believe she was just going to leave like that."

"So I called a cab," Lily said. "And I came home." She dissolved in tears again.

Jorie exhaled a soft sigh and hugged Lily while the girl wept. She murmured comforting words, waiting for the storm to pass.

"I guess I should be grateful. What if"—Lily drew a shuddering breath—"what if I hadn't found out until after I married him?"

"Hell, Simon," James muttered. "What am I going to do?"

Simon considered the irony of what he was about to say, but as opposed as he was to the haste of James's wedding, he didn't want James's heart broken, either. "Right now," he said as he levered himself off the sofa, "you're going to relax and try to put this out of your mind for a while."

"I can't."

"You're going to have to. There's no way Lily is going to talk to you about this until at least tomorrow morning."

James looked horrified. "Tomorrow? I can't wait until tomorrow."

"A good night's sleep will be good for both of you. You've had a lot of late nights the past week or so. You're exhausted."

"I can't sleep. Not with things like this."

Simon ignored that. "And tomorrow you'll call her and beg her to forgive you."

James looked at him intently. "I've got to make her understand."

"This won't seem so dire in the morning, James. I promise you that."

James shook his head. "I just can't understand how this happened. How could she think I don't love her?"

"It's nerves," Simon said. "She's got a lot invested in planning her wedding, and she's feeling a little overemotional."

"Is she going to get over it?"

"If you avoid saying things like 'It's just a cake,' and 'I don't care what you wear,' then yes." Simon nodded. "She's going to get over it."

"I guess you were right about everything, Jorie. I should have listened to you." Lily clutched the rabbit to her chest, looking young and vulnerable.

Jorie glanced around the room where she had watched Lily grow from childhood, to adolescence, to young adulthood. Here her cousin had poured out her heartaches and shared her dreams. The room was still filled with tiny reminders of each of those phases, from the stuffed rabbit, to the high school letter jacket, to the Harvard University pennant above her desk. Jorie gently stroked Lily's hair. "Lily," she said gently, "just because I think you and James were moving a little fast doesn't mean I think he doesn't love you. James does love you," she assured her. "Very much."

Lily wiped her eyes. "Do you really think so?"

Jorie nodded. "Yes. I really think so."

"Then why—"

Jorie shook her head. "I'm sure it's a misunderstanding. If you get some rest tonight, you can talk to him about it tomorrow."

Lily seemed to hesitate. "I love him, Jorie," she said. "I love him so much."

"I know you do."

"What am I going to do?"

Jorie smoothed Lily's hair back from her tearstreaked face. "I recommend you take some time to settle down a little. James is very upset, too."

Lily frowned. "How do you know?"

"I saw him at Simon's before I came over here."

"You saw him?" Lily's eyes widened. "You were at Simon's?"

"Yes."

Lily sniffled. "What did he say?"

"James? He's upset. He's concerned. He's worried. He's distraught."

"I wasn't sure he'd even care," Lily told her.

"He does. You two can work this out, but not when you're both upset. Just give it a little time. Tomorrow you can discuss things more rationally."

"I *am* being rational," Lily insisted. "If James doesn't feel ready to get married, then I don't think—" She dissolved into tears.

With a weary sigh, Jorie gathered her cousin in her arms again. "It's okay, sweetie. I promise it'll be okay."

Lily took a shaky breath as she fought for control. "Jorie?"

"Hmm?"

"Will you stay here with me tonight?"

Jorie thought of the look in Simon's eyes when she'd left his apartment. He'd had her quivering and heated when James had pounded on the door. Her equilibrium still wasn't entirely restored. With a pang she realized that tonight wasn't going to happen, either. Maybe this was God's way of telling her she was in over her head. Jorie dismissed the thought with a slight smile. She had a terrible habit of ignoring the warning signs life sent her way. She always had. But no matter how urgently she wanted Simon, she couldn't turn her back on her hurting friend. Lily, in many ways, had been a younger sister, and sometimes even a daughter to Jorie. Every impulse she had demanded that she wipe away the tears, heal the hurt, and ease her cousin's pain.

Everything else would have to wait.

"Are they going to survive?" Simon asked Jorie that night, his voice low and deep.

She pulled the covers up to her neck and snuggled into the bed she'd called her own since she'd moved in with her aunt and uncle. In the small room in the Benton home where she'd spent most of her teenage years, only the bed remained of the furniture and decor that had made the room uniquely hers. Nora had painted over the bright green walls with drab beige and replaced the eclectic accents with designer-friendly pieces. "I think so," she told Simon. She'd agreed to stay the night at Lily's request, but was already regretting the decision. She never slept well in this room. When her cell phone rang, she'd been staring at the ceiling, remembering the feel of Simon's mouth against her skin. The jarring digital ring tone of Mozart's Minuet in G had startled her back to the present. "Lily calmed down a little. They'll need to talk it out."

"We won't have to be there for that, will we?" He sounded appalled.

Jorie laughed. "No, I think we're off the hook."

"Thank God. I don't think I can take another round of this."

"How is James?"

"He's not hysterical anymore."

"Did you talk him through it?"

"I gave him two shots of bourbon and told him to sleep it off."

"Simon—"

"That's a joke, Jorie," he said softly.

"Are you teasing me?" she asked.

"Depends on what you mean by that." His tone was blatant suggestion.

Jorie felt her skin flush. "I didn't mean about that," she clarified. "Really, how is he?"

"He's okay. He'll live. I told him to call her tomorrow and do a lot of begging."

"That's probably good advice."

"I also told him that whatever she says about the wedding, he should nod a lot and look fascinated."

Jorie's lips turned into a slight smile. "You're very wise, Simon."

"I remember being engaged." He made a frustrated sound. "It was a miserable experience."

No doubt, she thought, as an image of Christina Bainbridge materialized in her mind. "I'm sure it was."

"I suppose I should be grateful, though, that Christina wanted time to plan a monster wedding. The length of our engagement is what kept me from marrying her."

Jorie chuckled. "My father would tell you that's why the Bible says, 'Blessed is he who waits.'"

"He's probably right." Simon's voice turned serious. "I didn't want you to leave tonight."

"I didn't want to leave. Lily needed me."

"She relies on you."

"Like James relies on you." She rubbed a hand across her stomach where the skin still tingled from the remembered feel of Simon's caress. "I'm sorry I had to go."

"Damn. The last time I felt like this I was sixteen. I'm way too old to resort to cold showers."

"Playing the piano always works for me." She'd spent an hour in Nora's music room.

"I'd get evicted," he stated flatly. "Jorie, let me see you tomorrow."

The slight demand in his tone made her smile. Simon was used to getting his way. No doubt she would drive him crazy, but she didn't have the heart or the desire to deny him tonight. She felt herself slide a little farther down that slope that her head warned her led to ruin, but she dismissed the thought as she pictured the heated look in Simon's green eyes. "All right," she agreed.

"Monday's Memorial Day," he added. "You off?"

Though the offices would be closed, she'd planned to work at least part of the day. With the fund-raiser just a few weeks away, her workload was beginning to pile up. "I'd planned to work," she said.

"Do you have to?"

She thought about it, then made a quick decision. "No."

"Good. I'll pick you up at your apartment around ten." His tone was pure satisfaction. "Pack an overnight bag. We're getting out of town for a while."

Chapter Ten

𝄞

❯ As Simon and Jorie headed out of town the next morning, the sky was gray but not terribly threatening. According to the forecast a pending storm had stalled off the coast, causing ominous cloud cover but no expected rain.

She had opened her apartment door to him and nearly drowned in the fathomless look in his green eyes. Simon had stepped inside, kicked the door shut with his heel, and pulled Jorie into his arms for a kiss filled with all the frustrated hunger of the night before. "I could kill James," he'd finally muttered as he lifted his head.

Jorie's knees had felt weak, so she'd clutched Simon's shoulders until her equilibrium returned. With a slight laugh she said, "I'm sure they didn't do it on purpose."

Simon had kissed her again, briefly. "Let's go," he'd said. "I want to get on the road."

Once they were headed out of town, Simon had broached the subject of James and Lily's wedding plans and his responsibilities. Now Jorie used the opportunity of having him as a captive audience. "I take it you've accepted that there will be a wedding?"

He exhaled a long breath. "After last night? Who knows? That's exactly why I wanted them to wait a while."

"But are you still determined to stop James from getting married?"

"I'm coming around. In any case, I'm smart enough to know you're right. If I push him too hard, he'll ignore me completely."

"Very wise."

"So given his generally bullheaded nature, I'm thinking there's definitely going to be a wedding. Regardless of what I may think, I'm going to have to fulfill some responsibilities on James's behalf."

Jorie nodded. "Okay, then here's the thing, Simon," she said. "There are two schools of thought. You can do what most families of the groom do and foot the bill for the rehearsal dinner."

"Not a problem."

"Or you can be a little more modern about it and get involved."

He shot her a wary look. "Involved? What do you mean, involved?"

"Calm down. It's not like you have to go pick out flowers or something."

"Thank God."

He sounded so serious, Jorie laughed. "I take it Christina Bainbridge didn't solicit your advice on her wedding plans."

The look he gave her spoke volumes. "No. And like James, I didn't give a damn about her wedding plans."

"But you were smart enough not to tell her that."

"I couldn't get a word in edgewise," he drawled. "It was never an issue."

"I'll bet."

"Explain 'involved.' "

"I think both of them would appreciate it if you chose the location for the dinner rather than just telling James to send you a bill."

He thought that over. "How many people are we talking about?"

"At last count, Lily had nine bridesmaids."

"Good God. It's a parade. How long is this wedding going to take?"

"If she does everything she's mentioned, I think we're probably looking at three and a half hours."

He flinched. "Are you serious?"

Jorie laughed. "No. She'll keep it to under an hour, I swear."

"Just tell me this: when this is over, is *Good*

Morning America going to be making comparisons to Charles and Diana?"

"Probably, yes."

Simon groaned. "I'm doomed."

She patted his knee. "I'll get you through it, don't worry. Besides, my relatives are all strange enough to take all the pressure off you. By the time my cousin Dunstan dips his cup in the punch bowl and cousin Edna shows up with a twenty-two-year-old stripper for a date, no one's even going to know you're there."

"That's very comforting." He paused for a moment. "So I have to pick the place. Anything else?"

"You have to be sociable."

"Now you sound like Lily."

"She told you to be sociable?"

"She told me to act like I was happy for James."

Jorie gave him a close look. "Having a hard time with that?"

"Not as much as I was," he said solemnly. "I think she loves him."

"Then that's all that matters, isn't it?" she quipped lightly as she turned to look out the window. *Oh Jorie, you fraud*, she thought. She was glad Simon couldn't see the way her eyes had suddenly teared. She believed that James truly loved her cousin, but the thought of Lily getting married still made her emotional. A part of her recognized the simple pangs of nostalgia for the child she'd loved who'd become an independent young woman. But another part, the part she barely wanted to admit even to herself, was just plain selfish. Lily had always been hers to love. Soon Jorie would no longer have the first place in her cousin's heart.

She dismissed the grim thought with typical resolve. She was happy for Lily. Her cousin had discovered the love of her life. Jorie was thrilled that he turned out to be someone as decent and dependable as James Wells. "Are you going to tell me where we're going now?" she asked, deliberately changing the subject.

"Rockport," he supplied. "I know a place there."

"And?"

"And what?"

She frowned at him. "Is that all you're going to tell me?"

"I thought women liked surprises." There was no expression in his voice.

Jorie studied his profile for a moment as he negotiated his way onto the interstate. "You are very hard to read sometimes, do you know that?"

He exited onto the Fitzgerald Expressway. "I've heard."

"I'm usually good at reading people, but sometimes I just can't figure you out."

"Am I giving you mixed signals?"

"I don't know. You seem—distant."

He pulled his sunglasses off and gave her a probing look. "That's because if I get too close to you for too long I'll turn around and go back to your apartment and we'll never make it out of town."

"Oh." She settled in her seat with a smug smile. "I see."

"You don't have to sound so damned pleased about it, you know. I've been intensely frustrated since last night."

"Can't help it. I've never had a man panting over me before."

"I am *not* panting." He put the sunglasses back on. "But I understand that Kevin Riley pants."

Jorie shot him a surprised look. "Who told you you about Kevin?"

"Actually Darius gave me his name, but I had to pump Lily for information."

She chuckled. "I'll bet they were enlightening."

"Darius said he's vanilla."

"Darius would. That's his definition of anyone who doesn't drive a hot car and wear expensive clothes."

"Something like that," Simon assured her. "So I asked Lily about Kevin."

"And she said?"

"You've dated him for a couple of years."

"I don't think I'd call it dating."

"Not if it's been a couple of years," he drawled.

"What do you mean by that?"

"That any man who'd take that long to get down to business with you is disturbed. Lily says she's pretty sure you didn't sleep with him."

Jorie choked. "I'm glad to know you and Lily have gotten so close."

Simon shrugged. "I was just curious. I wondered what kind of man could hold your attention for that long."

"Kevin's a good friend. He's a child advocate lawyer I work with on occasion. Sometimes we go to fund-raisers together."

"Sounds like a real human dynamo."

She whacked his arm. "He's a very nice guy."

"No wonder Darius thinks he's vanilla." He drummed his fingers on top of the steering wheel. "So did you?"

"Did I what?"

"Sleep with him."

"That's a very personal question."

He shot her a dry look. "We have a very personal relationship."

"Did you sleep with Christina Bainbridge?"

"Yes." He pursed his lips. "It was intense and unsatisfying. I usually left immediately after it was over, and almost always regretted the experience." He glanced at her. "Christina taught me that sex isn't very enjoyable if you don't respect the person you're with."

Jorie wondered if she'd ever reach his level of nonchalance. "Sounds like a great foundation for a marriage," she said sarcastically.

He shrugged. "I had different priorities at that

time in my life. I wised up. You haven't answered my question."

Jorie squirmed a little. "No," she said finally. "I didn't."

Simon seemed to relax beside her. "I see." He flashed her a brief smile. "Probably a good choice. From what Darius said, I'm guessing Kevin isn't all that passionate a lover. He probably didn't even make the advance." A smile played at the corner of his mouth. "The fool," he muttered.

She took a deep breath. "Actually, he did." She ignored the quick downturn of Simon's mouth. "I chose not to sleep with Kevin because he wasn't the man I wanted to be my first lover." She waited for the information to register.

Simon's fingers tightened on the steering wheel for a brief second, then he reached for her hand. He raised it to his lips and gently kissed the back. "Do you know," he asked quietly, "that I find you utterly fascinating?"

"Because I'm a thirty-two-year-old virgin?"

"No, because you told me you weren't willing to settle for Kevin Riley."

"You've never even met the man," she said with a slight smile.

"You've told me everything I need to know." He pressed her hand against his thigh. Beneath her fingers his thigh muscles flexed.

Jorie looked out the window for several minutes, studying the scenery as he drove out of the city and headed toward the coast. Something in the increasingly pastoral view reminded her of the painting in Simon's living room—and the sad look in his eyes when he'd spoken about his mother. Something told her that the secret to deciphering Simon's enigma lay in understanding how the events of his childhood had affected him. She already knew that his mother had disappointed him, that he'd learned early to depend on no one but himself. She'd gone to his office yesterday determined to show him what it meant to be wanted for who he was. That resolve had strengthened when she'd seen the look in his eyes as he'd discussed the painting.

The wounds ran deep and he guarded them carefully. Increasingly, she believed that if fate had brought her into his life for one reason, it was to show him that he didn't need to hide the disappointments of his past from the rest of the world. They made him who he was. They were not to be feared or forgotten. She remembered her mother's letter, which she'd finally found the energy to read that morning. "I got a letter from my mother this week," she told him carefully. She'd worked with enough hurting people to know there was comfort in shared experiences. If she expected Simon to give her his secrets, she had to be willing to reveal a few of her own.

"Oh?"

"Yes. My parents are coming for Lily's wedding." She'd read the news that her parents had decided to come to the States for Lily's wedding with mixed emotions. Her parents had missed her high school graduation because of a problem with their travel visas. They'd been unable to make her senior recitals and college graduation because of a staffing shortage at the mission where they worked. In the twenty years since they'd sent her to live with the Bentons, Jorie had seen her parents eight times.

"How long has it been since you've seen them?"

"Three or four years."

He frowned. "Years?"

"China is very far away, Simon," she said patiently. "It's a little tough to get there from here—or here from there." She'd used the same argument with herself a hundred times in the past. It usually rang hollow.

"Sure, but, damn. Three or four years? Did they see you more often when you were living with the Bentons?"

"No."

He glanced at her. "No?"

"No."

"Now who's being hard to read?"

She gave him a slight smile. "My parents missed a lot of my life," she admitted. "It's hard not to feel bitter about that."

"I know the feeling," he said tightly.

She seized the subtle opening. "Your mother?"

"Hmm. She didn't have what you might call a nurturing nature." Jorie waited. In her experience, memories like these were best waited on and often required long silent moments between revelations. Simon finally rewarded her patience. "My mother was an alcoholic with absolutely no common sense or survival skills," he said. "She got herself pregnant at seventeen by some teacher at her high school. She refused to divulge the guy's name because he promised he'd marry her after she graduated. Within six months of the day she told him she was having his baby, he skipped town."

"Poor girl."

"My grandparents tossed her out of the house. I never met them." He paused again. "I never tried. I never wanted to."

Jorie pressed her lips together and squeezed his thigh. The story unfolding sounded so much like the ones she heard nearly every day at the office. Sadly, despite Simon's emotional poverty as a child, he'd been one of the lucky ones. Somehow his mother had managed to provide a life that gave him an opportunity to break free of her world.

"She started drinking after I was born," he continued. "The responsibility overwhelmed her." He shook his head. "I never understood why my mother didn't simply put me up for adoption."

"That's especially difficult for young girls who have no family," Jorie said gently. "Even though it seems that giving up their baby would make their lives less challenging, they have difficulty surrendering a child to adoption when they have no one else to love."

"I guess." He negotiated around a tractor-trailer and took the exit onto Highway 128 toward Rockport. "Whatever her motivation, she didn't have a lot of options on how to support us. She dropped out of high school to have me. Social services arranged for her first job cleaning office buildings. That would have worked out fairly well except that she'd periodically go on a drinking binge and skip work. I have no idea how many times she got fired."

"How did she end up at the Wells estate?"

"We went through a particularly bad time where she couldn't find work. One of our neighbors called social services on her, and they came and threatened to take me from her if she couldn't present proof of employment by the end of that week." He smiled slightly at the memory. "It scared her to death. We scraped together what little money we had and started scouring thrift stores for something she could conceivably wear to an interview. Her fashion taste didn't exactly inspire confidence in potential employers."

"No one ever taught her how to succeed," Jorie

said simply. "After a while, a lot of women in her position just become self-defeating. We see it a lot."

"We had nine dollars and some change," he said. "That was supposed to get us through her next paycheck." He grimaced. "In case you didn't know, nine dollars doesn't go very far in this city. Not even then."

Jorie studied his profile. The angles of his face looked harsh and pronounced. "I'm sure."

"Your father would probably have something to say about this being divine intervention, but I stumbled into a funeral parlor one day because their landlord was evicting them. I'd seen enough evictions to know what it meant when somebody's stuff was being hauled out to the curb. You can get most anything there really cheap, and if you're fast enough, free.

"They had clothes," he went on. "The kind they use on corpses when the family doesn't provide anything. I found a dress in her size. It was blue. Dark blue. They had shoes that matched." He looked at Jorie. "I went to the drugstore and splurged on a pair of ninety-nine-cent pantyhose."

Jorie could picture a small, dark-haired, green-eyed boy diligently searching through the discarded clothes for something, anything that would keep his world from falling apart. The image made her heart clench. "The interview outfit?" she pressed.

"Yeah. She cleaned up and put that dress on."
He shook his head. "I never remembered my
mother looking as soft as she did that day. Without her usual makeup and loud clothes, she was a
very pretty woman."

Jorie watched and waited as he visibly wrestled
with the memories. She wondered how often he'd
replayed this in his mind, much less how many
times he'd actually shared it with anyone. A note
in his voice would occasionally turn raw.

"She took herself down to the unemployment
office," he went on, "and started scouring the list-
ings. Wells's employment agency had listed the
position and indicated that it included room and
board."

"A dream come true."

"A godsend," Simon clarified. "We were going
to get thrown out of our apartment by the end of
the next week."

"So she applied for the job?"

"She had the lady at the unemployment office
call and make the appointment for her. We stayed
up most of that night rehearsing what she was going to say when they asked about her experience. I
went with her to the agency. I told her I didn't
want to be stuck at home, but I wasn't sure she'd
actually make it to the door."

Jorie didn't need to ask what he'd done about
school. Like most kids in his position, education

was low on the priority list when simply surviving had become such a struggle.

"She completed the interview and the guy told us he'd call and let us know." Simon glanced at her. "Our phone had been shut off for a week."

"No number," she guessed.

"I walked eight blocks every morning for the next three days to check and see if my mother had gotten that job. Frankly, I think the agent just got tired of seeing me. The day he told me she was hired, we hitchhiked out to the Wells estate. She worked there until she got liver cancer."

Jorie nodded, thoughtfully. "Mr. Wells must have been a good employer."

"Living on the estate made it easier on her. She still struggled with alcohol, but she didn't have to deal with transportation and rent. Her uniforms were provided, and usually the lady who ran the kitchen and did all the ordering would slip her some food when things got tight."

"When did she paint?" Jorie asked gently.

He frowned. "Off and on. I used to buy her watercolors with the money I made doing odd jobs around the place. She'd paint in spurts, then not at all for long periods of time."

"How old were you when she painted the picture in your living room?"

"Fifteen. Sixteen, maybe." He paused as he pulled into the left lane to pass a delivery truck.

"I've always thought it was one of her best."

"Is it a painting of you and her?"

He looked at her in surprise. "No one's ever asked that."

"Then no one's looked at it closely. Is it?"

"More or less. I was ten or eleven the one and only time we attended the annual staff picnic the Wellses held at the estate. My mother was in one of her better phases. For the first time in my life, I felt like a normal kid with a normal mother doing normal family things."

Jorie gave his leg a gentle squeeze. "For what it's worth, I'll let you in on a secret. There's no such thing as a normal family."

"I've heard that," he mused.

"You've met most of mine. They're . . . unique."

"I like them," he assured her. "Except maybe Nora."

Jorie sighed heavily. "My aunt is the unhappiest person I've ever met."

"How did that happen?" he asked.

Jorie studied the increasingly craggy rock formations that lined the road as they neared the coast. "She and my mother didn't have any other siblings. My grandfather was an archeologist, and he took his family with him on most of his digs."

"Is he still living?"

"No." She shook her head. "He contracted some type of viral fungus on a dig in Egypt when my mother was ten or eleven years old. He died nine months later. My grandmother brought my mother and my aunt back to the States after he died. They lived with relatives." She shot him a slight smile. "It's a family tradition."

He nodded, thoughtful. "What about your grandmother?" he pressed. "Still living?"

"She died a couple of years ago. She was living in a nursing home outside Chicago near my cousin Mildred. I wanted her to be closer to me, but she'd lived with Mildred for so long, we decided it would traumatize her to move this far. Mildred took excellent care of her."

"What did Nora have to say about the fact that somebody else cared for her mother?"

"We didn't discuss it," Jorie said curtly. "Nora made it clear that my input wasn't welcome."

He pursed his lips slightly. "Sounds like Nora."

Jorie felt the familiar pang of pity that always accompanied thoughts of her aunt. "I think Nora's the first person I've ever known who spends her entire life regretting her choices."

"William?"

"Yes. When my mother married my father, Nora was already engaged to Uncle Bill. Evidently she was appalled that my mother would choose to marry a minister with a calling to the foreign mission field." Jorie turned slightly in the seat to face him. "It took me a long time to understand this," she told him, "but I guess Nora has different memories of their childhood than my mother. My mother seemed to thrive on the transience of moving from dig site to dig site. Nora's different. It was hard for her."

"And she never wanted to live that way again."

"Too much risk," Jorie agreed. "Uncle Bill was safe, but she didn't love him. Maybe she thought she could. I don't know, but as time went by, the situation made her bitter."

"What about your mother?"

Jorie took a deep breath. "My mother thrives on the exotic and the unusual. She's very happy in China."

He pinned her with a shrewd look. "But there were times when it felt like she should have wanted to be your mother more than she wanted the thrill of living in a foreign country?"

Jorie nodded. "Yes. There were times."

He tapped one long finger on the top of the steering wheel. "Which is why," he mused, as if working through a complex problem in his head, "you're drawn to kids who need a little nurturing."

"Yes," she said with a slight smile. He would probably never believe that she was drawn to him for the same reason. Though every self-preservation instinct she had warned her that she was about to wade in too deep, she couldn't turn her back on the man with the sad eyes and the lonely spirit. "I suppose it is."

Simon appeared to sink into silent thought as his

car ate up the final miles to Rockport. The terrain altered subtly, and as the craggy rocks and distinctive sea-swept landscapes engulfed them, Jorie pointed to a road sign. "Rockport. Almost there."

Simon covered her hand with his own. His skin was warm. "Almost," he said in a tone that made her pulse leap. He slid her hand closer to the V of his legs so she could feel his hard length.

Jorie felt her pulse leap. "Judging from the way those clouds are darkening," she said with admirable calm when her mouth felt suddenly dry, "that's probably a good thing. Looks like a deluge."

He studied the sky for a moment. "I checked the Weather Channel this morning. It's supposed to hold off until tomorrow."

"Hmm," she said. "We'll see."

"If it doesn't, we'll wait it out in our room and get a late start home tomorrow."

"I already missed church this morning," she said lightly. "People are going to start to talk if we drag in late tomorrow."

"People are already talking."

"You've got a point there. Lavonia tells me you created quite a stir at Shiloh last week."

"I told you that I enjoyed myself."

"I finally got Lily to admit that the reason she and James came to church was to spy on us."

Simon chuckled. "I think James got a little more than he bargained for."

"That's probably true," Jorie told him, "but Lily

should have known exactly what to expect. She's been around me long enough to know I have a penchant for cultural diversity."

"I've actually been meaning to ask you if you speak Chinese," he said.

"I'm fluent in Mandarin. And I can make my way through a conversation in Bai and Amdo, but I can't read and write them."

"Have you kept it up?"

"I minored in Chinese literature."

He gave her an amused look. "Lots of job opportunities for classical pianists with a minor in Chinese literature?"

She laughed. "More than you think, actually. Before I got my job at Art-Is-In, I worked as a translator and cultural trainer for one of the local temp agencies."

"I can see that. Several of Wells Enterprises' largest accounts are Asian."

"The boom in the technology market has forced U.S. companies to adjust to the Asian business culture. It's very different. A lot of companies bring in a consultant to help their employees understand some of the key components of the culture."

Simon negotiated the exit off the highway that would take them into the coastal town of Rockport. "So," he said slowly, "when your parents sent you to the States, how did they choose Nora and William?"

Jorie slid him a surprised glance. She should have known Simon wouldn't let the topic die with her surface explanation of the facts. Simon, she'd learned, was a man who studied people. He learned their strengths and their weaknesses as a way of protecting himself. "My father was an only child," she told him. "His parents died several years before I was born. You met most of the great aunts and uncles and cousins at Lily and James's party."

He smiled slightly. "They're eccentric."

"You could say that," she concurred. "My parents felt that Nora and Uncle Bill were in the best position to give me a stable environment and a decent education."

"What about emotional support?"

Jorie swallowed. She'd wrestled with that same question for years, struggling to understand why her parents hadn't considered the impact their choice would have on her. "There wasn't a perfect solution," she said softly.

"You got hurt."

"Yes," she admitted. "It was difficult."

His jaw had tightened. "You must have been terribly lonely."

"I had Lily to love." And she had thrown herself into the task, lavishing every nurturing instinct she had on her infant cousin. "And I had my music."

"Which Nora encouraged."

"It was maybe the one thing about me Nora and I ever agreed on."

"Didn't she worry about your influence on Lily?"

Jorie laughed lightly. "Absolutely. Nora doesn't believe in taking chances. I, on the other hand, have a really bad habit of never thinking before I act. I probably scare Nora to death."

"I'm sure you do."

"That's why she was so relieved when Lily fell for James. He's so . . . normal."

"Haven't Lily's boyfriends always been rather normal?"

"She hasn't had many," Jorie told him. "Nobody serious. She's far more sensible than her mother thinks. Lily's just the type who knew exactly what she wanted and waited until she found him."

Simon turned down the picturesque street that led into the center of Rockport. "I hope you're right," he said.

"Lily told me she agreed to sign the prenuptial agreement," she told him. "I would think that would reassure you."

He shrugged. "It reassures me that James's money is protected. It does nothing to reassure me about his heart."

Simon, she realized, couldn't imagine any relationship lasting forever. She felt her resolve strengthen. Once in his life, she vowed, he'd know what it meant to be unconditionally desired. She could show him that. "She also told me that James doesn't know yet. You haven't told him."

"It's not my place to tell him. If Lily wants him to know, she'll tell him."

They passed the "Welcome to Rockport" sign, and Simon laced his fingers through hers. "Enough about Lily and James," he said quietly. "Today I've got more important things to think about."

Jorie glanced at the darkening sky. "Good thing," she quipped. "Because from the looks of the weather, we might be cooped up awhile."

Chapter Eleven

𝄞

"SIMON?" JAMES ASKED. "WHERE ARE YOU?" He'd called Simon's cell phone shortly after they'd arrived in Rockport. "I've been trying to call you all morning."

"I'm at Bearskin Neck," Simon told him, glancing at Jorie.

"In Rockport? What the hell are you doing in Rockport?"

"Having a life," Simon told him. "Do you need something?"

"Hell yes, I need something," James said hotly. "Lily told me about your damned prenuptial agreement this morning."

"And you're pissed."

"Yeah, you could say that."

"Sorry."

"I told you I didn't want one."

"And I think you need one." Simon drummed his fingers on the primitive wood table of the Portside Chowder House. "It's a safety precaution, James."

"It's asinine. Damn it, Simon, when are you going to quit treating me like a kid?" James bit out.

"Probably never," Simon confessed. He glanced out the window of the restaurant at the rapidly darkening sky.

James sighed heavily. "I wanted to discuss this with you today, but I guess that's not going to be possible."

"It's not even drafted yet," Simon assured him. "We can discuss it on Tuesday."

"Tuesday? Why Tuesday?"

"Because I'm not coming back until tomorrow."

"You're staying the night? Are you by yourself?"

"I'm an adult, James."

"Yeah, well, so am I. You just don't seem to notice."

Simon rolled his eyes. "Yes, I'm staying the night. And from the way the weather looks here, it's probably a good thing."

James's sigh was pure exasperation. "All right. I guess we'll talk Tuesday."

"Any time. Just let me know."

"Hey, Simon?" James asked before he could hang up.

"Yes?"

"*Are* you alone?"

"That's none of your business, kid. I'll talk to you Tuesday." He ended the call.

Jorie was watching him intently. "Problems?"

"Lily told him about the prenuptial agreement."

"I guess they're speaking again," she quipped.

"Evidently. He's a little miffed at me, but he'll get over it."

"Simon, you've got to let him make his own decisions someday. He's twenty-two years old."

He shrugged. "And naïve as hell. He has no idea what this marriage could do to him."

Jorie's look turned suspicious. "What's that supposed to mean?"

Simon thought of his most recent conversation with Mark Baine and immediately dismissed it. The last thing he wanted to do today was talk about William Benton's grim financial outlook. "It doesn't mean anything," he said. He wiped a hand through his hair. "Today was supposed to be for us. Can we put James and Lily behind us?"

Jorie seemed to hesitate, then managed a slight laugh. "You're right. I guess Lily isn't the only one getting emotional over this wedding."

The waiter brought their bowls of chowder to the table. "You guys need anything else?"

"I don't think so." Simon looked at the window again. The sky had darkened to near black. "Except maybe a lifeboat."

The waiter nodded. "This looks like a bad one. Most of the boats are in already." He propped his tray on his hip. "You two staying here, or passing through?"

Jorie gave Simon a melting look. "We're staying," she said quietly. "At least tonight."

"What did he say?" Lily asked James as he hung up the phone. He'd arrived on her doorstep early that morning with a bouquet of flowers and a well-planned apology that had quickly disintegrated into a nearly incoherent plea for mercy that had completely melted her heart. After she'd calmed down the night before, she'd awakened feeling slightly foolish about her reaction to the argument. It had taken less than ten minutes for her and James to set things right.

They were in his downtown apartment where they'd ordered Chinese takeout and prepared to wait out the incoming storm system. The food was spread before them on a blanket near the large windows at the front of his apartment.

James frowned. "He's in Rockport."

"Rockport? Why?" She waved her chopsticks in the direction of the window. "Didn't he know this system was coming in?"

"I don't know." James looked at her. "This isn't like him. Simon is not what you'd call the impulsive type."

Lily shrugged. "Who knows? Maybe he's with a client."

"I don't think so. And now he won't have time to talk about this until Tuesday."

She patted his arm. "James, look, I didn't tell you about the agreement to make you mad."

"I'm not mad at you, sweetheart."

"And you shouldn't be mad at Simon. He's just trying to protect you. I appreciate that about him."

James shook his head. "That's not the point. Simon has got to quit treating me like a kid."

"It's hard for him," Lily insisted. "Jorie's the same way. She has trouble remembering that I'm not a little girl in pigtails anymore."

James grinned at her. "I'd kind of like to see that."

"In your dreams," she drawled. She plucked a piece of sweet and sour chicken from his plate and fed it to him. "Besides, Jorie always says . . ." She trailed off, her mouth open mid-sentence.

James raised his eyebrows. "What?"

"Oh my God."

"What?"

"*Oh my God.*" Lily glanced at his phone, then at him. "You don't think—" She shook her head. "No. God, it couldn't be."

"You aren't making any sense."

"Jorie was at Simon's last night when you went over there."

"Yes."

"Didn't you wonder why?"

James's expression was slightly abashed. "I was upset. I didn't really think about it."

"Well, she left my house early this morning."

"Yeah, so? She probably didn't want to be around your mother. Who could blame her?"

Lily shook her head. "I don't think so."

"Honey, what are you up to?"

"If I didn't know better, I'd say Jorie and Simon went to Rockport for the weekend."

James's expression turned incredulous. "No. You think?"

"I said, if I didn't know better. Jorie wouldn't. I mean—" She shook her head again. "She just wouldn't."

"Honey, as Simon so adamantly pointed out just now, they're adults."

"No, no, you don't get it. Jorie has never, I mean, I'm not absolutely completely positive, but I'm pretty sure that she hasn't ever . . . She's a virgin."

James's eyes widened slightly. "Oh."

"And Simon . . ."

"It was your idea to get them together."

"Together like dating. God, I didn't think she'd sleep with him."

"Why not?"

"He's not her type at all. I mean, not at all. Jorie goes for what I call search-and-rescue type men."

"Heroic?"

"No, as in they need finding and rescuing."

"Then why the hell did you want to fix her up with Simon?"

"That wasn't my idea," she said. "I just saw the way he looked at her the night of the party. He wants her."

James smirked. "Looks like he got her, too."

"I cannot believe it." She reached for the phone and started dialing Jorie's number. "I just can't." She waited until Jorie's answering machine picked up. "She's not there," she told James.

His expression turned knowing. "Want to try her cell phone?"

Lily stared at the phone in amazement. "I can't believe it," she said again.

"Or you could just try Simon's cell phone. Although"—he glanced at his watch—"if he's doing what I think he's doing, don't expect an answer."

Lily looked at him. "You really think they're together, don't you?"

"Yep." He helped himself to another generous portion of the food.

Lily leaned back on her hands. "Wow."

James's expression turned quizzical. "You're really that surprised?"

"Yeah."

"Is Jorie that much of a prude?"

"She's not a prude. She just knows what she wants. She's . . . I can't explain it. It's just not like her."

"Well, if it's any comfort to you, it's not like Simon, either."

Lily snorted. "Not if that Christina Bainbridge woman was his ex-fiancée. Geez. No wonder he wants me to sign a prenup. I'll bet she was a real piece of work."

"I admit, when you told me you thought he was attracted to Jorie, I couldn't see it, but then I saw them together. There's definitely something there."

She pursed her lips. "Simon wants her all right. His eyes practically smolder when he watches her. Like he's so hot he's going to combust."

James wagged his eyebrows at her. "Yeah, well, I know the feeling."

Lily blushed lightly. "James, you know we decided we'd wait—"

"I know." The look he gave her melted her heart. "And I'm not complaining, but that doesn't mean I don't want it." He leaned over the picnic meal and kissed her lightly. "Really, really bad."

When he raised his head, Lily draped her arms around his neck. "James, Simon won't, I mean, he won't break her heart, will he?" she asked.

"Not on purpose." He smoothed her hair away from her face. "Simon's a good man. He's probably the most honorable person I know."

"I love her, James." •

"I know, babe."

She worried her lower lip between her teeth. "And you really think she's with him?"

"Yeah. I really think so. It fits."

Lily sighed. A rumble of thunder made the lights flicker. "I guess we'll find out soon enough."

Two flashes of lightning lit the room. James tipped his head to nibble at the corner of her mouth. "While we wait, you think we can do something to kill the time?"

Lily giggled when his fingers found a particularly sensitive spot. "There's always Scrabble," she told him.

With a growl, James lowered her on the blanket. "Personally, I'd rather play Twister."

Jorie lit the cluster of tea lights on the small Chippendale table by the door. A loud clap of thunder rattled the windows. The lights flickered several times, but stayed on for the moment. They'd checked into the Peg Leg Inn minutes before the first rain of the storm hit. They were barely settled in their room when the near gale force winds began to rattle the clapboards and pound the driving rain into the windows. Simon had gone downstairs to ask the proprietor for extra candles.

She looked around the charming room with a strange sense of calm. Somehow she thought she ought to be nervous about the fact that she was going to spend her first night with Simon here. She slipped off her shoes and padded across the Oriental carpet to curl up on one of the upholstered love seats near the window. As the storm raged, she watched the torrents of water sheet across the window.

And she admitted to herself that she felt no unease at all. If anything, she felt more at peace with her decision to make love with Simon Grant than she had about any choice she'd made in years. She'd already lost her heart to him. Giving him the rest seemed perfectly natural.

He pushed open the door. Raindrops glistened in his hair, and he carried a brown paper bag.

"You're wet," she said. "How'd you get wet?"

"They were trying to get the storm shutters locked down when I got downstairs." With a swipe of his hand, he brushed the water from his dark hair. "The poor kid who's on duty at the restaurant could barely get them cranked in. I helped her secure them." He moved to the bed, where he started to unpack the bag. He set four thick candles on the nightstand before he shot her a look over his shoulder. "I cleaned the gift store out of junk food," he said, putting several packages of crackers and cookies on the table. "I'm not sure the restaurant will have power tonight." He opened the small drawer and dumped the rest of the contents inside.

He shot her an apologetic smile. "Sorry. I had something a little more elegant planned for dinner tonight."

"I don't mind," she assured him. "I work at a nonprofit agency, remember? I've lived for days on junk food and coffee."

Another clap of thunder sounded and the lights blinked off. The tea lights flickered as a slight draft moved through the room. "That might be it," Simon said. He joined her near the window. "I'm sorry about this. I don't think they expected it to be this bad."

Jorie shook her head. "Don't worry about it. We're safe, and we're dry. That's all that matters." In the candle glow, the angles of his face softened and his hair took on a sheen.

He eased next to her on the love seat. "I asked at the front desk. They don't have a clue when they might get the power back on."

"No generator?"

"Emergency stuff only. We can't watch TV."

A smile tugged at the corner of her mouth. "We could play charades."

He shook his head as he draped an arm around her shoulders. "It's no fun with two people."

"Poker?" she suggested.

Tilting his head closer, he nuzzled her cheek. "Cards? Miss Morrison, you're a missionary's daughter. I'm a little shocked."

"We played cards," she assured him. He eased

her closer with a hand on her shoulder. "Just no dancing."

Simon pressed a kiss to her forehead. "I wasn't thinking of dancing."

"You—" She sucked in a breath when he traced the curve of her upper lip with his tongue. "You had something else in mind?"

"Um hmm." He kissed her briefly. "We've got a long afternoon and all night," he told her. "I might have enough time before morning to learn everything about you I want to know."

"Simon—"

He covered her mouth with his fingers. "I'm aching for you, Jorie. I have been since last night. Hell, I have been since that night at the engagement party."

She kissed his fingers, her eyes shining. Simon rubbed his thumb over her lips. "In case you were wondering," he said softly, "I brought condoms. I didn't know if you'd be protected, so I took care of it."

Jorie wrapped her fingers around his wrist and raised his hand higher so she could kiss the palm. "I think that's the most romantic thing I've ever heard," she murmured.

He studied her, curious. "I wasn't trying to destroy the moment. I just didn't want you to worry."

She pressed his hand to her breast and leaned against him. "I'm completely serious," she assured him. "I find it very romantic that you'd think of something like that, and even more romantic that you'd think to tell me. Thank you."

Simon decided that having a woman understand and appreciate him was quite possibly the greatest aphrodisiac on earth. With a slight groan, he gathered her to him and kissed her deeply, thoroughly, exploring and mapping the curves of her mouth. "Jorie. God, you taste so sweet."

Her fingers went to the buttons of his shirt. "I'm aching, Simon," she whispered, kissing him feverishly. "You make me ache."

He knew the feeling. He swept a hand down the length of her body, aligning her curves to his hard length. She moaned as she finished working open his shirt. Jorie pressed her mouth to his bare chest and took a deep breath. "You smell good," she told him. "So good."

His good intentions to take his time, to savor each touch and each kiss, were quickly eroding beneath her honest desire. Simon grabbed the hem of her top and tugged until she lifted and let him slide it over her head. The sight of her creamy skin confined by the emerald green lace and satin of her bra burned an indelible impression in his brain. "You're beautiful," he told her, lifting a hand to gently trace the full curve of her breast.

Jorie shivered. "I'm glad you think so."

He looked at her curiously. "Don't you think

so?" Thunder crashed outside, punctuating the question.

Jorie jumped, startled, and looked at the window. "The storm is getting worse."

Simon cupped her chin and brought her gaze back to his. "Jorie," he insisted. "Don't you think so?"

She blushed. He found it charming. He found it even more charming that she held his gaze. "When you look at me, I do," she told him.

"I'm very glad." He cupped her breast in his large hand. She was soft and smooth, like the finest silk. Goose bumps rose on her tender flesh. Simon rubbed his thumb over them. He took the tip of her breast between his thumb and forefinger and applied a gentle pressure. "Want to explain why you don't think so when you look at yourself?"

"Not especially."

He teased her with his eyes. "Try again."

"Simon—"

"You don't strike me as the insecure type."

"I'm not."

"But you don't recognize that you're a beautiful woman?"

She tried not to squirm. "Simon—"

His gaze narrowed. "This is making you uncomfortable."

"I guess."

"Why?"

"Are you sure I can't distract you from this conversation?" She rubbed her fingers over his nipples.

"Positive. I'm fascinated." He captured her hand and kissed her fingers. "I'll get distracted later," he promised.

Feeling a little foolish, Jorie glanced toward the window. "I have a very healthy view of myself," she told him. "I'm talented. I'm smart." She offered him a slight smile. "I'd even buy that I look intriguing. But I've seen beautiful women. They're taller than me."

Simon chuckled and bent his head to kiss the shell of her ear. "I can accept that." He placed one hand on her behind and cupped a full breast with the other. "But for the record," he said, levering her so she nearly lay on top of him, "I've never understood the appeal of tall, skinny women." He circled his palm on her breast. "I kind of like something to hold on to."

Jorie gasped and pressed into him. "Make love to me, Simon. Please make love to me."

Rain sluiced down the window as the storm raged outside the window. Beside him, Jorie lay sleeping, one long leg tossed over his thigh, her head pillowed on his chest. He toyed with a strand of her hair as he watched the rain. The storm outside had nothing on the turmoil that had begun roiling in him the moment he'd slipped inside her. It had been delicious.

Passionate.

Hot.

Mind-shattering. She was tight and delicate. She'd waited to take her first lover. She'd waited for him. He found the knowledge almost barbarically satisfying. Modern male that he was, he supposed it shouldn't have meant so much. But there was something about knowing that the incredible passion he'd sensed in her had been kept bottled and perfecting—like a vintage wine—until she had poured it out on him, that was the most powerful aphrodisiac Simon had ever known.

She'd called out his name when she'd climaxed. As long as he lived, he'd never forget the way it had sounded on her lips. His hands were still shaking. His limbs still felt heavy and lethargic. His pulse still hammered a heavier than normal beat.

And he was beginning to suspect that he wasn't going to be able to have a simple, uncomplicated affair with her.

Fool that he was, he'd thought he could assuage the craving that had been building in him since he'd met her. If he made love to her, he'd believed, he could work her out of his system. It had worked in every other relationship he'd ever had. Usually he began feeling anxious a few minutes after the headiness of sex had passed. He'd never yearned for a woman's touch in the moments after. He'd certainly never craved the feel of her skin pressed to his and the soft caress of her fingertips during the aftermath.

That was hard to remember when his arm had pulled her close to his side and his skin had tingled while she stroked it.

"Simon?" She stirred sleepily, and raised herself on an elbow to look at him through drowsy, sexy eyes.

"Hmm?"

"I fell asleep." She sounded surprised.

"Yes."

"What time is it?"

He glanced at the clock. "After four."

"I slept for an hour?"

His lips tilted into a teasing grin. "I guess you were worn out."

"I guess." She glanced at the window. "Rain always does that to me."

He tipped his head to nuzzle her collarbone. "Is that a fact?"

"Yes." The word trailed into a hiss when he pressed a kiss to the upper curve of her breast.

"Hmm," he said, working his way across her breastbone to the other side. "And here I thought it was the three orgasms." Her skin turned a gorgeous blush pink. He smiled and dropped a swift kiss on the tip of one full breast. "Dumb me."

Jorie stifled a muffled laugh and squirmed away from him. "It might have had something to do with that," she admitted, "but I'm thinking I might need more data before I can make a determination."

He gave her a wicked grin. "You don't say?"

She nodded. "Yes. I like to be very scientif— Simon!" She gasped his name when he kissed her intimately. "What are you—"

"Research. Lots and lots of research."

Laughing, she squirmed away from him. She gathered the sheet around her and moved to lean against the headboard. "Hold it right there," she informed him. "You have to give it to me first."

"I'm trying," he protested, reaching for the sheet.

She laughed and held his hand away. "I'm serious."

He rolled to his side so he had an excellent view of the curve of her breasts above the sheet. "Me too."

"I want the speech first," she said. "I'm ready for it."

"What speech?"

She gave him a pained look. "Ezekiel's wheels, Simon, don't you know anything about women?"

He raised an eyebrow. Jorie laughed. "This is the part where you're supposed to tell me it was wonderful. That you've never had it so good . . ."

She was teasing him, he finally realized. Understanding dawned, and Simon levered up on an elbow and kissed her soundly. She needed affirmation. He might be a little new at this lingering after sex thing, but he was smart enough to realize she wanted a little praise. He was glad to give it. "Spectacular," he said against her lips. "Unbelievable."

She wrapped her arms around his neck. "Okay. Better."

With typical dispatch, Simon dismissed the lingering feeling of unease that making love to her might become an addiction. He had the next sixteen or so hours to indulge himself in this incredible woman. By then, surely, this sharp-edged need would ebb. He'd find control again, and then he'd be free to follow this relationship to its logical and neat conclusion.

"Not only the best I've ever had," he told Jorie, "but the best I've ever wanted." He pulled the sheet away with a sharp tug. "Which must be why I want you again."

Jorie curled up on the love seat and watched the rain with a smug smile. After making love with Simon all afternoon and into the evening, she was beginning to understand why people smoked after sex. Even the slight twinges in her body felt decadent. She'd meant what she told him. When he looked at her, he made her feel beautiful and desirable. He had touched her soul as well as her body tonight.

She wrapped the fluffy white robe around her and snuggled into the chair. She felt satisfied—physically as well as emotionally. As she'd suspected, he had made her no promises. This wasn't the gentle, romantic love affair young girls dreamed about. Jorie glanced over her shoulder to where Simon lay sleeping. This particular affair resembled the raging storm outside. It was violent and powerful and consuming, sweeping away everything that stood in its path.

No, there was nothing at all gentle and easy about what she felt for Simon Grant. This was the kind of grand passion that made a woman ignore every lick of common sense, every conventionality, every warning sign, and indulge in the incredible, consuming passion he offered her.

With a slight chuckle, she thought of Lily and James and their awkward, yet evidently effective strategy to maneuver her and Simon together. Lily couldn't have dreamed that Jorie would fall this hard this fast.

Outside, the sharp winds and rain battered the building. Jorie deliberately pushed aside the premonition that it was merely a harbinger of the storm that would follow Simon's presence in her life. She would do well to remember that, she knew. She couldn't hold him. He wasn't the type to be held. Simon didn't express love easily, and she could never demand it from him.

Jorie pushed aside the melancholy thought as she rose from the chair and headed for the shower. She paused at the foot of the bed to study Simon's recumbent form. Relaxed in sleep, with one arm slung across the pillows, his body looked lithe and graceful—in stark contrast to the powerful energy that usually surrounded him. His hair lay in disarray against the white pillowcase. One wave had tumbled over his forehead. Jorie walked to his side of the bed and gently brushed it into place. His face softened slightly at the tender ministration.

With a sudden insight, she realized that Simon had spent his life caring for the people around him. He'd taken care of his mother, himself, and James, yet had never known the luxury of surrendering himself to another person. To teach him that, she decided, the price of giving herself to a man who might never love her was well worth the cost. Simon didn't strike her as the type of man who gave his heart away. He'd given it to James, but there didn't seem to be room for anyone else.

Chapter Twelve

{ TUESDAY MORNING, SIMON ENTERED HIS OFFICE
at Wells Enterprises and suppressed a weary
sigh at the sight of the young man with the long
black hair, earring, and leather jacket seated behind the reception desk. He really had to find time
to talk to his resources manager. Today, however,
he had no intention of letting anything stand in
the way of accomplishing his goal: today he was
going to set the matter of William Benton to rest.

After spending the last two days with Jorie,
he'd come to several conclusions. First, whatever
William Benton's financial problems might or
might not be, Simon planned to determine exactly
what, if anything, James's Uncle Howard had to
do with Benton Electronics. He wanted the matter

resolved, and fast, before he got caught in the middle of something that could turn very ugly. His relationship with Jorie had become too important to him to risk on a manipulative bastard like Howard Wells.

Second, he was going to have to find a way to persuade Jorie to have patience with him. Sometime on the ride home from Rockport, he'd listened to her talking about Darius, his talent, his dreams, and his opportunities, and he'd begun to see just what he'd given up in recent years. Cutting himself off from passion, he'd turned into a man incapable of feeling anything too deeply or connecting too completely with anyone. And when Jorie saw him for what he was, he'd lose her.

He acknowledged the young man behind the desk with a slight nod and pushed open the frosted-glass doors of his office.

Jorie sat behind his desk, her hair limned in the morning sunlight. She was tapping the end of his Mont Blanc pen on her full lips while she studied a notepad on his desk. At his entrance, she looked up and smiled at him. "Good morning, Simon."

"Good morning." He didn't even bother to analyze the sudden tight feeling in his chest. He set his briefcase on the floor and rounded the desk in a few easy strides to lean over the chair and kiss her. "I missed you last night."

With a soft sigh that sent his blood pressure to the moon, she wended her arms around his neck and kissed him back. "I know," she murmured. "I missed you, too."

"I wish you'd stayed." He had tried to persuade her to stay the night at his apartment, but Jorie had demurred, claiming she needed the time at home to get herself ready for the week ahead. With the Art-Is-In fundraiser less than ten days away, her work schedule was going to be crazy. She'd promised to call.

He hadn't been sure she would, he'd realized. The feeling had made him edgy and irritable as he'd accepted that things were getting out of control. He'd never waited for a woman's call in his life.

She finished the kiss and leaned back in his chair. "I wanted to," she said. "But I knew if I didn't get a few things done last night, I'd pay for it this morning."

Simon sat on the edge of the desk and studied her. "I'm glad you stopped by."

"You look surprised," she told him.

He shrugged, not willing to admit that he was. "I know how busy your week is."

"Yeah." She brushed a curl behind her ear and slid the note toward him. "I was on my way to see one of our major donors to pick up a check. I had to come right by here, so I thought I'd stop in and see you." Her grin teased him. "I was a little surprised that you weren't in yet. You seem like an early-to-rise kind of guy to me."

Simon wasn't about to tell her that he'd had a six A.M. breakfast meeting with Mark Baine. Instead he toyed with the edge of her collar. "I got a little worn out this weekend. I was recuperating."

That made her laugh. "Yeah, right. Your, um, receptionist seemed a little ill-informed about your plans."

Simon sighed. "In a town the size of Boston, you'd think it wouldn't be this hard to find competent office help."

"He's new?"

"I've lost count. My personnel manager assures me she's doing her best, but there's a rumor going around that I'm hard to work for."

Her eyes twinkled. "No kidding?"

"No kidding." He glanced at the door. "Either Margaret's got it in for me, or the employment pool is worse than I thought. I don't think this one's going to last through the end of the day."

"Hmm." Jorie looked thoughtful. "He was reading a magazine with leather and whips and some sleazy-looking blond on the cover when I walked in."

"That always makes a wonderful impression on our clients."

Jorie swiveled back and forth in the chair, looking simultaneously playful and sexy. "So I'm guessing your assistant isn't going to be a lot of help in your hunt for an appropriate place for James and Lily's rehearsal dinner."

"Not unless you like biker bars."

She pushed the note toward him. "I wrote down a few things while I was waiting for you." She tapped the note. "I'm pretty busy this week, but we could try to check out a couple. It's peak wedding season, and things start to get booked—" She stopped abruptly when Simon leaned over and kissed her again. "What?" she asked.

"And here I thought you just wanted to see me." He took a deep breath of her unique scent. Organic something or other, she'd told him. It had burned an indelible imprint on his brain during the heated hours of lovemaking they'd shared Sunday night. "By the way," he probed, pressing his thumb to the corner of her mouth, "how are you feeling?"

Her eyes took a moment to focus. He found immense pleasure in that fact. When she finally registered his question, she gave him a sly grin. "Positively delicious. And also positively anxious that if you don't get started on finding a place for that dinner, we might have to check out the biker bars after all."

He would have kissed her again, but behind his shoulder he heard James's voice. "Say, Simon, where did you find—"

James came to a halt three steps inside the office when he spotted Jorie sitting in Simon's chair. She smiled at him slightly and rose to go. "Good morning, James."

"Uh, hi."

She reached for her bag. Simon had given up trying to define the monstrosity as a purse when she'd pulled a change of clothes out of it on Monday morning. "I've got to get going. There's a check waiting for me a couple of buildings down from here."

Simon pressed a hand to her waist. "Can I see you tonight?"

She nodded, thoughtful. "I've got a press conference at four at the Hilton to announce the total dollar amount we're expecting from the weekend. Can you pick me up after?"

"At your office?"

"At the hotel. We can check out a couple of places on that list tonight if you want."

What he wanted was to take her back to his apartment, lay her across his king-sized bed and try and work out the hunger he'd felt since she'd left him yesterday. "No problem," he said calmly. He bent his head closer for a quick buss on her lips. "Should I bring a toothbrush?" he whispered for her ears only.

Her gaze strayed to James. "Simon—"

"Should I?"

She hesitated, then nodded. He gave her a lazy smile and prodded her toward the door. "I'll see you this afternoon."

Jorie gave James a slight wave and told him goodbye as she slung the bag over her shoulder.

Simon watched her breeze her way through the doors before he looked at James. "So, I guess you're here to talk about Lily's prenuptial agreement."

James stared at the door for a moment. When he looked at Simon, his eyes were inquisitive and probing. He looked more and more like his father every day. "Yeah, partially."

Simon raised an eyebrow as he sat behind the desk. "Only partially?"

"I'm also here to talk about Jorie."

"Did you decide that before or after you found her in my office?" Simon leaned back in his chair and picked up the pen Jorie had been tapping on her mouth. He fingered the rounded end with his thumb and index finger.

James sat across from him. "Before," he said. "Lily is concerned."

Simon couldn't repress a sardonic smile. "I had the impression that Lily was completely in favor of my forming a relationship with her cousin."

"That was before you took her to Rockport."

"And now?"

"Lily's just afraid she'll get hurt."

"So we all have that in common. I'm worried for you. Lily's worried for Jorie. Jorie's worried for Lily. I guess I'm the only one nobody's concerned about," he quipped.

"Simon—"

Simon held up his hand. "Look, James. I know

that sometimes you wish I'd act less like your father and your guardian and more like your employee."

"I've never thought of you as my employee."

Simon ignored that. "But I gave your father my word that I'd protect you. As far as the prenuptial agreement is concerned, I'd be breaking that word if I didn't insist on it."

"Lily is not after my money. Her father is loaded."

Simon replayed part of his conversation with Mark Baine in his mind. "Things aren't always what they seem, James."

The young man's gaze turned suspicious. "What do you mean?"

Simon rounded his desk and retrieved his briefcase. He took the seat next to James as he popped open the latches. Pulling the folder he'd received from Mark that morning off the top of the stack, he passed it to James. "Benton Electronics is in trouble."

"What kind of trouble?" James probed as he flipped open the folder.

"I think they're involved in the VanMetre business."

James frowned. "I don't believe it."

"I've had Mark Baine looking into it."

James raised angry eyes to his. "You what?"

"When you met Lily, I asked Mark to check on some things for me."

"You're kidding."

"No. I'm not."

"Hell, Simon, sometimes I cannot believe you."

"I told you when you came back from Paris that I thought you and Lily were rushing things. I wanted to be sure that she was rushing things because she loves you, not because her father is counting on Wells Enterprises to bail out his company."

James slammed the folder shut and tossed it back into Simon's open briefcase. "She loves me. I don't need to look at that crap."

"If it makes you feel any better," Simon said, "I believe she loves you, too." He paused to let that sink in. "Her father's a different story."

James surged out of his chair with an angry curse. "Damn it," he said. "Don't tell me that. Just don't tell me that."

"You have to be protected, James. Your father's legacy is at stake."

"I'm sure it's a misunderstanding," he insisted.

Simon reached for his patience. "There's more."

James's harsh laugh seemed to tear from his chest. "Great. Just great."

"I think Howard is involved."

"Uncle Howard?" James stared at him. "What the hell do you mean he's involved?"

"I have Mark checking on a few things about the VanMetre matter. If Howard is doing what I think he is, then I believe he approached William

Benton about a merger. The two of them recognized the value of a marriage between you and Lily and arranged for you to meet in Paris."

"Oh, for God's sake, Simon. You're making this out to sound like some kind of medieval melodrama. I know Uncle Howard knows Bill Benton. Practically every businessman in Boston knows Bill Benton. I don't find it particularly diabolical that the two discussed me and Lily and thought that the two of us should meet."

"How about the fact that Howard sold forty thousand shares of Delitron stock the day before the bottom dropped out, and that he spent the afternoon before playing golf with Bill Benton and Bronson VanMetre?"

"So?"

"The SEC suspects VanMetre of orchestrating the Delitron cover-up."

"It could be circumstantial."

"The golf game took place a week before you went to Paris." Simon set the briefcase on his desk and leaned back in his chair. "According to his credit card report, Benton didn't purchase Lily's ticket to Paris until the day after Delitron stock collapsed. It was a spur-of-the-moment trip."

James's face was slightly flushed. "I already know that. He told her he'd had an unexpected windfall and wanted to do something nice for her.

She'd been begging to go on the trip for weeks before that."

Simon nodded. "His windfall came from the fat profit he turned selling off his Delitron stock."

"I still don't believe that Howard or Bill conspired against me and Lily. I'm sure this can all be explained."

"Because you don't want to believe it, James."

"Because how in the hell am I supposed to tell my fiancée that I allowed you to investigate her and her father just in case she's been lying to me all this time?"

"It's my job."

"To hell with your job," the young man charged. "I'm sick and tired of living my life in a cocoon. I get to make choices, too, you know."

Cocoons, Simon wanted to tell him, were highly underrated. Safe, protective, and warm, they shielded you from most of the harsh realities of life. "I understand that. I just want you to make informed choices."

"Fine," James said. "You've informed me. Now I want you to cancel the prenuptial agreement and forget it. I'm not letting Lily sign one."

"James—"

"It's my money, damn you. And it's my company. I pay you for advice. You gave it to me. I'm choosing not to heed it."

"I can't let you do that."

James glared at him. "You don't have a choice."

"I've still got control over your financial future until you turn twenty-five. I can stop you in court."

"You'd do that, wouldn't you?"

"To keep you from getting hurt?" Simon's nod was brief. "Yes. I would."

James raked a hand through his sandy brown hair. "You've been opposed to me marrying Lily since the beginning," he charged, "but I never imagined you'd actually try something like this." With a sweep of his hand, he indicated the folder in the briefcase. "What else did you dredge up? News about Lily's sixth-grade boyfriend?"

Simon took a calming breath. Like his father, James tended to react emotionally before he thought all the way through a problem. Simon knew from experience that if he could simply keep James interested, he could get the young man to see reason. "I asked Mark to look at a range of things for me, but since your engagement party, he's been primarily investigating Benton's financial problems."

"If Lily's father has something to do with Van-Metre, she knows nothing about it," James asserted. "I'm sure of that."

"I believe you," Simon admitted.

That seemed to pacify James somewhat. He dropped into the chair again and buried his head in his hands. "I can't believe this." Simon waited. James shook his head before raising it. His eyes looked wounded. The expression tore at Simon's heart. "How am I supposed to tell Lily about this?"

"I'm not sure you have to," Simon said carefully.

James's eyes widened. "Are you kidding? If what you say is true, her father could be indicted."

"Maybe."

"Then of course I have to tell her. I can't let that happen without even warning her. God, Lily will be devastated."

"You don't have anything to tell her yet except some conjecture. At least wait until Mark brings me solid evidence."

"How long?" James asked.

"I've asked him to get me something in the next few days. If Howard is involved, I want to know about it now. I'm going to try to minimize the damage before it happens."

"If Uncle Howard has anything to do with this—" James groaned. "Damn it, Simon. This is supposed to be the happiest time of my life."

"Who says it can't be?"

"With my future father-in-law and my uncle facing possible federal prosecution?"

"When Lily signs the agreement, whatever happens or doesn't happen, you're insulated from it."

James drummed his fingers on the arm of the chair. "And my wife will always know that I didn't trust her enough to marry her without a written contract saying she wasn't after my money."

"I don't think you should look at it that way. Lily volunteered to sign the agreement."

"Because she knew you wanted it. Believe it or not, she likes you. She'd like for you to like her."

"I do."

"You have a hell of a way of showing it." James snorted. "And what about Jorie? Are you sleeping with her so you can get additional information about her uncle?"

Simon's gaze narrowed. "I think you should reconsider that question."

"Why?" James taunted. "Too close to home?"

"Too damned asinine. Not to mention beneath you. You know me better than that."

James surged out of the chair again. "I used to think so, but now, I'm not so sure. How do you think Jorie is going to react to this?"

"I'll tell her when the time is right."

"Maybe I'll tell her," James said.

"Don't push me, James." Simon couldn't keep the hard note out of his voice.

James looked at him angrily. "Why not? This is exactly what you do to me all the time. Only you can't stand it when you're not in control." He paused. "I'm starting to think you and Uncle Howard have a lot in common."

Simon let that pass. "All I'm asking for is three days. If I can't provide you with some concrete evidence by then, I'll ask Mark to drop it."

"And you'll back down on the prenuptial agreement?"

Simon thought that over. "If that's what you want," he finally agreed.

James nodded shortly. "Fine." He headed for the door. As he pulled it open, he looked at Simon. "You'd better pray to God you're right," he said. "Because if I lose Lily over this, I'll never forgive you."

Across town that afternoon, Jorie forced herself to review the financial report once more in preparation for her four P.M. press conference. As she had most of the day, she was having trouble concentrating. Thoughts of Simon continued to crowd in on her. By the time he'd dropped her off last night, she'd felt herself beginning to drown in a sybaritic kind of bliss. Despite her inclination to invite him in, and his very obvious willingness to comply, she'd demurred, needing a little time to get her bearings before she faced him again. Through sheer willpower, she'd managed to write her way through the press releases and reports she needed for today, but had been unable to prevent her dreams from carrying her back to Simon's bed.

He'd been a considerate and passionate lover. With excruciating attention to detail, he'd found each and every one of her secret places and hot spots and driven her to peak after peak of delirium.

But, somehow, something didn't seem right.

During the afternoon and night in the haven of their hotel room in Rockport, isolated from the pressures of their usual environment and the intrusions of life, she'd been unable to identify it. It was only when she saw him that morning in his world, a world where Simon had succeeded despite the odds against him, that she realized what it was. Even when he made love to her, Simon always remained perfectly and completely in control. He had climaxed. She wasn't so naïve not to know that, but only after he'd taken her to the peak four or five times and she'd felt almost limp with the pleasure. By the time Simon's body tightened and convulsed in the throes of passion, she was almost too exhausted to even register the sound of his voice as he called out her name.

She frowned now as she thought about the way he'd reacted when she'd crawled back into bed after her shower. She'd planned to explore him, return the favor he'd visited on her by taking her time learning and mapping his body, but Simon had allowed her only a few brief moments before he'd deftly turned the tables. Then she'd been too caught up in the storm to think about it.

"You look a thousand miles away, Jordan."

Startled, Jorie glanced up from the report to find her Aunt Nora watching her. She wasn't sure if she was more surprised that Nora had apparently sought her company, or that her aunt had deigned to pay her a visit at her office. "Aunt Nora. Hi."

Nora clutched her purse close to her stomach. The gesture seemed defensive. "I'm sure you're surprised to see me."

Jorie scrambled to clear the chair by her desk. "Um, yeah, a little." Her aunt sank onto the chair like collapsing deck rigging. Jorie noted the puffiness of Nora's eyes, though well masked by flawless cosmetics. "Is something wrong?" she asked.

The weak smile on her aunt's lips did little to lessen the severity of her expression. "I suppose I've given you reason to believe that I'd only come find you in the middle of the day if something were wrong."

Jorie frowned. She couldn't remember ever hearing this melancholy tone in her aunt's voice before. She watched her, concerned.

Nora sighed and set her purse down. "I suppose I should get right to the point," she said. "Lily tells me that you're involved with Simon Grant."

"I don't think that's anyone's business but mine, Aunt Nora."

Her aunt raised a groomed eyebrow. "Don't you?"

"No. I'm all grown up. I get to make my own choices."

Nora exhaled a long breath. "Believe it or not, I do know that. I would advise you to be careful with a man like that, however. You and I may not have been close, but I know you have limited experience."

"Thank you for the warning."

"How involved are you?" Nora pressed.

"Aunt Nora—"

She held up her hand. "I'm not asking you this just to be nosy. I have reasons for wanting to know."

"Would you like to share them with me?"

Nora studied her a moment, then flipped open the catch of her purse. "I suppose you've heard about Bronson VanMetre's indictment."

"The Delitron scandal? Yes, I've read the papers."

"Then you know that your uncle's name has come up once or twice in the investigation."

"Something about a merger that didn't go through."

Nora handed her a fax. "I've been asking some questions," she said. "William hasn't been giving me any answers. Yesterday I intercepted this on his fax machine at the house."

Jorie took the piece of paper and scanned it. It was a three-paragraph report to William from one of his accountants indicating that certain unnamed funds had been relocated per William's request. Nothing unusual about that, Jorie knew. As an international business, Benton Electronics often moved assets through different accounts for the sake of currency conversions and overseas payments.

What sent up the flag was the mention of Howard Wells and the information that the accountant had been in touch with James's uncle on another matter William had discussed with him. Jorie frowned. "I didn't know Uncle Bill was doing any business with Wells Enterprises."

"Neither did I," Nora told her. "But I do know that your uncle plays golf with Howard Wells every now and then, and I also know that the last time they played, Bronson VanMetre played with them. It was about the same time that the Delitron stock collapsed." She paused. "A few weeks before Lily went to Paris."

"What are you saying?" Jorie asked.

Nora's lips thinned. "I worked hard to help William get where he is, Jordan. I know you haven't always understood my choices, but I couldn't live like your mother did. I needed security."

"I know that."

"I wanted a decent home and a decent family in a decent neighborhood. I've been a good partner to my husband."

"He would agree."

"If he's involved in this Delitron mess, we could lose everything we've worked for."

"Aunt Nora, you don't think—"

"I don't know," Nora stated flatly. She produced another item from her purse and passed it to Jorie. "But I know that Simon Grant is looking into it."

Jorie held Nora's gaze a moment before she accepted the business card in her aunt's hand. "What is this?"

"It's the name of an investigator I hired when I first got wind of VanMetre's involvement in Delitron. I wanted to know if William was going to be implicated."

"So you had my uncle investigated?" Jorie asked, slightly shocked.

Nora shrugged. "You'd probably be surprised the lengths I'd go to to protect my family." She tapped the card with a manicured fingernail. "I've hired this man before. He's quite reliable."

"What's this got to do with Simon?"

"According to his sources, Simon Grant has been investigating your uncle since James returned from Paris."

"What do you mean, investigating?"

"I'm sure Simon suspects that Lily is after James's money."

Jorie shook her head. "That doesn't make sense. Lily doesn't need James's money."

"In business, things can be deceptive," Nora explained. "Benton Electronics has been in fiscal danger for the past couple of years."

"I had no idea."

"Neither did anyone else," Nora admitted. "William's been able to keep it quiet by shifting assets from our different global interests."

"How much trouble is he in?"

"Enough that losing his shirt on Delitron would have wiped us out."

"Oh, Aunt Nora."

"The cash he got from the Delitron sale gave us a terribly needed infusion. I wanted to believe it was half miracle and half wise investing on William's part."

"But now you don't?"

"I'm not sure." Nora gave her a hard look. "And to be honest, I don't want to know."

"But if something illegal is going on—"

"Then I especially don't want to know," Nora said.

Jorie thought that over and realized it was probably true. In some ways Nora and Simon had a lot in common: both liked to minimize risk in their lives. "But you think Simon knows?"

"I do." Nora picked up her purse. "And I want you to tell him to back off."

"Back off?"

"He's the one stirring federal interest in William's connections to VanMetre. If Simon weren't looking into it, they wouldn't be, either. He's a powerful man, Jorie. When he started asking questions, so did the SEC. If he backs off, then

VanMetre will still probably go down, but William may not have to go with him."

"I can't believe that Simon is responsible for any of this," Jorie protested. He'd never mentioned it, and had certainly never given her reason to think he suspected foul play on her uncle's part.

Nora tapped the business card again. "I thought you might say that. Love is blind. Especially your kind of love."

Jorie looked at her curiously. Nora's nod was short. "You're just like your mother," she said. "You give too much of yourself too fast. You let people hurt you."

"That's what makes you real, Aunt Nora. Being willing to get hurt is what keeps you alive."

A harsh laugh was her aunt's response. "I don't doubt that you think so," she said. "But frankly I'd rather be safe than real."

Jorie felt the same twinge of pity she always experienced when she saw the absolute sadness and bitterness in her aunt's eyes. "I'm sorry," she said.

"I'm not. I don't want your pity, Jordan. Believe it or not, I'm content with my life." Jorie didn't know how to respond to that, so she simply waited. Nora stood and looked down on her. The action seemed slightly ironic to Jorie, who'd felt that her aunt had been looking down on her for most of her life. "I thought you probably wouldn't believe me," Nora stated flatly. "That's why I brought you that card. If you call and tell the investigator that I gave it to you, he'll tell you what he knows."

"What do you want me to do?" Jorie asked.

"Tell Simon Grant that he'd better not cross me." Nora tucked her purse beneath her arm. "I will protect my family." She turned to go. "Goodbye, Jordan. I'll expect to hear from you soon."

"Goodbye, Aunt Nora." Jorie watched her aunt leave with a troubled expression. Somewhere, somehow, there had to be a misunderstanding in all this. She simply couldn't fathom that Simon might have been digging into William Benton's finances and not mentioned it to her. They'd even discussed the VanMetre case during their trip to Rockport. Simon had said nothing about having any knowledge that William might be involved.

She looked at the business card. The only way to clear it up, she supposed, was to call Nora's investigator. Perhaps Mr. Mark Baine could shed some light on this.

Chapter Thirteen

𝄞

SIMON LEANED BACK AGAINST THE DOORFRAME of Ballroom C at the Boston Hilton that afternoon and watched Jorie expertly handle a room full of reporters. He found himself doing that a lot lately—watching her. He found a rare kind of pleasure in it. Studying Jorie in all her environments was like studying a diamond against different backgrounds: she had many facets, all spectacular, all beautiful. When she played the piano, he felt the passion in her. She'd looked poised and, somehow, slightly vulnerable in the vintage dress she'd worn to the engagement party. Against the white cotton sheets, with her hair tousled and her skin flushed, she'd been enchanting and seductive. With one foot tucked beneath her legs, and that definite sparkle in her eyes as she'd teased him in his living room, she'd been irresistibly eccentric. And here, amid the questions and demands of her job, she was the intent children's advocate with a firm control of the room.

Yes, there were many sides to Jordan Morrison. And Simon found all of them fascinating.

She spotted him at the back of the crowd and acknowledged him with a brief nod. Simon jingled his keys in his pocket. He had a perfect evening planned. A perfect evening that he hoped would end in a perfect seduction. Sometime during the day, he'd quit asking himself why he still wanted her so intensely. Instead he'd accepted that this intriguing, multifaceted woman was going to take a while to work out of his system.

"One last question, Ms. Morrison?" a reporter called out.

Jorie shot Simon an apologetic look. "One more."

"Is it true that Art-Is-In accepted a large donation from Wells Enterprises a week ago?"

Instantly alert, Simon identified the reporter who'd asked the question and fixed him with a hard stare. "Yes," Jorie said warily.

The reporter tapped his pen on his notebook. "Then is it just a coincidence that your cousin is engaged to James Wells and that your uncle's business is under fire in the Delitron investigation?"

Jorie collected her notes. "That's two questions," she said with a bright smile. "But yes, for your information, it is a coincidence. There have been no implications about Wells Enterprises in the Delitron matter so far as I know, but I'm in the middle of planning a fund-raiser. I don't get out much." The crowd laughed. Jorie leaned on the lectern. "As far as Wells Enterprises' generous contribution to Art-Is-In, let's just say that Mr. Wells has an appreciation for children and the arts and leave it at that." She glanced at Simon. "I've really got to go. There are complete statements by the door if anyone needs them."

Amid a barrage of questions about possible connections between Wells Enterprises and Benton Electronics, Jorie slipped out the back door. Simon followed her lead by easing out of the room and making his way around to the back. He found Jorie in the service corridor leaning against the bank of elevators. "You okay?" he asked.

She looked at him warily. "I guess. That was unexpected."

"I'm sure it was." He looped his fingers under her elbow and punched the elevator button. "Let me get you out of here."

Jorie clutched her papers closer to her chest. "Simon—about Delitron?"

A warning note sounded in his head. "Yes?"

"You don't think Uncle Bill is involved in anything illegal, do you?"

"I don't know." At least he could answer that honestly. "It looks bad, Jorie."

"I've read the papers," she said.

"Then you know what the investigators think. What do you think?" There was an odd expression in her eyes that he couldn't decipher, a look he hadn't seen before. He probed it, but the enigma eluded him.

"I don't know, either," she admitted. "It's almost impossible to believe that Uncle Bill—I just don't know." She dropped her head against his shoulder. "I don't know," she said again.

Frowning, Simon ushered her into the elevator. "Is something wrong?"

She frowned. "Not that I know of. Maybe that's what's bothering me. It's the idea that something could be wrong and I might not know anything about it."

"You aren't making sense," he said and punched the garage floor button.

"Sorry." She leaned back against the elevator wall. "Where are we going?"

He studied her through narrowed eyes. "I was going to suggest we go pick out Darius's piano, but you don't look up to it. Do you want me to take you home?"

She seemed to think that over. "Yes, I think I do."

The elevator reached the parking garage, and Simon showed her to his car. He'd asked Joe to drive for him tonight, not sure how long the press conference would last and how difficult the traffic would be. He opened the back door for Jorie. "Where to?" Joe asked as she slid into the car.

Simon seated himself beside her. "Home," he said.

"No piano?"

"Not tonight," Simon told him. "Long day."

Joe glanced sympathetically at Jorie in the rearview mirror. "You look tired," he told her.

She smiled at him. "I am a little."

He nodded. "Then lean back and rest. The traffic's rotten. It'll take at least a half an hour to get home."

Jorie followed Joe's advice. She tilted her head back against the leather seats and closed her eyes. Simon couldn't tell if she was resting or ignoring him. Or maybe some of both. The only indication he had that she was aware of his presence in the car was the tight grip she maintained on his hand.

Something was bothering her. And he was willing to bet it had something to do with that question she'd been asked about her uncle's company. He replayed his morning conversation with Mark Baine in his mind. There had been no new information to report about Howard's possible involvement with Benton Electronics, Mark had told him, so Simon had given the investigator until Thursday to come up with answers.

The question was: Why had that reporter been looking into possible connections between Wells

Enterprises and Benton Electronics when an investigator whom Simon had paid to find the same information had been, thus far, unable to produce it? Simon stroked his chin as he thought about it.

"You look a little worried," Joe said from the front seat.

Simon met his gaze in the mirror. "I'm putting together a puzzle," he told Joe. "And so far, I don't like the picture I'm getting."

Thirty minutes later he ushered a still tired Jorie into his apartment. She had opened her eyes when Joe pulled into the apron in front of Simon's building and followed Simon wordlessly into the marble foyer and to the elevator. He unlocked the door of his apartment and prodded her inside. Dropping his keys on the small wooden table by the door, he turned to her. "You want to tell me what's wrong?" he said, trying to keep his impatience at bay.

Jorie descended the two steps to his sunken living room, where she looked at the picture on his wall. Simon shoved his hands in his pockets and waited. After long, excruciating seconds, she turned to him and held out her hand. "Please make love to me, Simon," she said softly. "I feel like I waited forever."

He didn't need a second invitation. In three easy strides, he closed the distance between them and pulled her into his arms. Simon lowered his mouth to hers and took a long, drenching kiss. He was starved for her, he realized, with a sudden, edgy feeling that he might not be able to control himself. Jorie's hands were already at his fly. She jerked open his belt and lowered his zipper with alarming speed. Simon sucked in a sharp breath as her fingers brushed past the quickly growing bulge at his groin. "Jorie—"

She rose on tiptoe and covered his mouth. Simon pressed a large hand to the curve of her breast. Jorie's fingers went to the buttons of his shirt and tugged and pulled at them. One popped free and pinged against the wall. The shirt fell away beneath her hands. She shoved it off his shoulders, jerking sharply until the cuffs slid free of his wrists. With a flick of her wrist, the shirt sailed across the room.

Simon found the zipper at the back of her dress and lowered it. Jorie was already tugging on the hem of his T-shirt. He had no idea why she was feeling so frantic, but was fast approaching the point where he cared. He had to slow her down. "Jorie—" He gasped when she pressed her mouth to his flat male nipple. "Baby—"

She swirled the peak with her tongue. His fingers twisted into her hair. Desire was spiking in him now, causing his pulse to hammer and his blood pressure to rise. He pushed her dress past her shoulders. It slid down, catching momentarily on her full breasts. It was undeniably the sexiest sight Simon had ever seen. Her jade green satin and lace bra looked exotic and rare against the peach hue of her so-soft skin. Her breasts swelled over the lace, and pushed against the satin, tormenting him. Simon's mouth went dry when the dress slipped to her feet revealing matching panties and thigh-high stockings. Jorie kicked the dress aside and reached for him. She pressed her warm body to his, urging him down to the carpet.

Simon dropped to his knees before they could buckle. Jorie pushed him back on the carpet and moved on top of him. "I want you, Simon," were the last words he remembered hearing her say before he lost his mind.

Jorie stretched, wincing at the slight rug burn on her knees. She smiled a wicked little smile as she glanced at Simon, who slept peacefully next to her on the thick carpet of his living room. She'd ravished him. She wasn't quite sure when she'd decided to do it, but she'd looked at the picture his mother had painted, turned to find him watching her with that slightly worried expression, and suddenly decided that she needed to know she could make him lose control.

Maybe it had been the disturbing conversation she'd had with Mark Baine that afternoon in the wake of Nora's visit. There was something about that man that had bothered her. He had claimed to have evidence that Simon was investigating

William Benton, but had demurred when Jorie asked him to provide her with it. He'd claimed that Simon was determined to prove her Uncle Bill and James's Uncle Howard had arranged for Lily to meet James in order to further talks of a merger between the two firms, but could not give Jorie any convincing reason why the two golfing buddies had kept their plans a secret. Bronson VanMetre's apparent relationship with the two men failed to shed any additional light on the subject.

Jorie had pondered Simon's possible involvement for the better part of the afternoon. But when she'd seen him standing in the back of the room, she'd known absolutely, that even if he were looking into Bill Benton's finances, he was doing it simply to protect James. He certainly had no ulterior motive, and had he known anything, he would have told her that weekend. Simon was many things, and was often mercurial and unpredictable. But he was a man of honor and integrity, and if he suspected Bill Benton of wrongdoing, he was keeping the information to himself only because he didn't have enough evidence to prove it.

Had she doubted him for even a moment, the expression on his face when the reporter had asked her that question about Benton Electronics had chased away whatever lingering suspicions she might have. She turned her head to look at him. Moonlight spilled across the angles of his face, casting long shadows on his features. She gently stroked the errant wave of hair off his forehead. Somehow, she would get to the bottom of Mark Baine's accusations. Tomorrow she'd ask Simon to help her.

For tonight she had an agenda of her own, and she'd taken the first step by seducing him on his living room carpet. He'd lost control with her. And that simple fact gave Jorie hope for the future. If he was willing to surrender even that little bit to her, then they had a chance.

Simon rolled to his side and groaned. His back was killing him. He was cold. And his butt felt raw. Rug burn, he realized, from when Jorie had virtually attacked him earlier. He threw one arm across his eyes. Hell, had he really shouted her name like that when he'd climaxed in a blinding rush of adrenaline and bliss? Had he really lost control so completely that he'd been unable to keep from coming the moment she'd slipped him inside of her? He hadn't been that aroused and that powerless since he'd been a teenager. Careful, methodical, controlled, cautious Simon had completely lost it tonight in the hands of a woman who'd been a virgin until the night before last. She'd seduced him though, as well as any practiced courtesan, and left him wanting more.

He sat up with a groan. He was too damned

old to be sleeping on the carpet. He looked at Jorie. She lay resting peacefully, one hand tucked beneath her cheek, her legs draped at a sexy angle on the dark carpet. She had the look of a Vargas girl, all lush curves and opulent beauty, soft and tender and wanting to be touched. He frowned as he considered that shattering moment when he'd experienced the most blinding orgasm of his life. Unless he'd been so far gone he didn't notice, he was fairly certain he had failed to satisfy her.

Idiot, he told himself. He ran a finger down the length of her arm. Like a fool, he'd given her a glimpse of the untamed side of himself that had always scared him. It was that side that could so easily lose all that he'd worked for. It was that side that had destroyed his mother. It was that passionate, intense side that had scared Christina Bainbridge away and into the arms of another man. During a night of particularly intense sex—he'd never thought of what he and Christina shared physically as making love—she'd seen a true picture of who he was. Though she'd climaxed hard and long and clutched at his shoulders and begged him for more, by morning she'd had a wariness in her eyes that he'd seen more and more frequently in the weeks to come. He'd excited her, but he'd also scared her. Christina had been unable to imagine marrying him when she realized that a man who could feel that deeply and hunger that much would want that kind of passion in return.

And he'd driven her away. As he would Jorie if he wasn't damned careful. She might have been too caught up in the sheer passion of the exchange to have noticed that he'd completely lost control. If he acted now, he might be able to repair the damage.

Gently, Simon kissed Jorie's shoulder. She sighed softly and shifted in her sleep. He began the slow, well-executed strategy of building and stoking a fire in her until she began to moan. He knew the moment she drifted fully awake. His lips were kissing her intimately, and her fingers twined into his hair as she gasped his name. Simon smiled against her tender flesh, surged to his feet and scooped her into his arms. He could continue this better in the comfort of a bed where he would visit such exquisite pleasure on her that she'd soon forget his earlier lapse. He was beginning to feel that his very survival depended on it.

"Where are you taking me?" she asked, her lips against his throat.

"Where you belong," he said as he kicked open the door to his bedroom.

With a soft smile, Jorie wrapped one arm around his neck and pulled his head toward hers for a long, savoring kiss. "I'm glad you realize that," she said with a quiet laugh.

He set her on the bed and removed what was left of her clothes. Jorie pulled back the covers and rolled beneath the navy comforter. "Simon?"

"Hmm?" He yanked off his socks. Jorie had virtually torn the rest of his clothes off earlier. The thought had him grinning smugly as he turned to her.

"I spoke to Mark Baine today."

He went absolutely still. "Oh?"

"Yes." She toyed with the top edge of the sheet. "My aunt gave me his number. I didn't realize until I spoke to him that he was the same Mark I met at your office that day."

Simon felt every nerve in his body go on high alert. "Nora?"

"Yes. She's worried about Uncle Bill and this Delitron business," she said carefully.

"That's why you asked me about it at the hotel tonight."

"That," she said, "and because Nora says that you're responsible for Uncle Bill getting dragged into it."

His insides started to twist into knots. "I have nothing to do with your uncle's business affairs," he said.

She looked vexed. "I know that. I mean, Nora claims that her investigator told her that you were digging up information about Uncle Bill's finances."

"I am," he stated flatly.

"And you didn't tell me." She pulled the sheet a little higher.

"I didn't have anything to tell. Lots of suspicions and no evidence."

"That's what I told Nora."

"But you wondered?"

"No," she said, "not really. You would have told me. Especially before we—before Sunday."

"You have a lot of faith in me."

She shrugged. "Shouldn't I?"

He didn't know how to answer that. He jerked back the covers and slid into bed beside her. "I told James what I suspected this morning. I was waiting for proof before I worried you with it."

"He came to talk to you about the prenuptial agreement," she guessed.

"Yes. I showed him what I've learned so far."

"Is he upset?"

"Furious. He doesn't believe any of it."

Jorie sighed and leaned back against the headboard. "I have to tell you, Simon. I don't, either. I mean, I can believe that Uncle Bill maybe heard from VanMetre that he should dump his Delitron stock, but I'm having trouble buying that he'd have an entire scheme built around it. That's just not like him."

"It's like Howard," Simon said.

"James's uncle? What's he stand to gain from any of this except some jailtime?"

"Control of Wells Enterprises."

"But if he gets sucked into this—"

Simon held up a hand. "Peter left controlling interest of his company to James, but then, Wells Enterprises wasn't nearly the conglomerate that it is now. There are many divisions of the company, and James's interests don't extend to all of them. Howard's smart enough to have ensured that he can sink only one or two parts of the ship. As long as he can keep himself out of trouble, he can get what he's always wanted."

"A bigger piece of the business."

"Yes." Simon stared at the ceiling. "And at some level, I think he'd like to prove to James that I'm not capable of protecting his business interests any longer. Howard always resented Peter for appointing me as James's guardian."

"But if Peter didn't appoint Howard, he must not have trusted him, either."

He rolled his head to the side and looked at her. "Exactly."

Jorie's expression was worried. "What's going to happen with all this, Simon? Is it as serious as it sounds?"

"If your uncle was involved in insider trading on Delitron, then yes, it's serious. He could be indicted."

"Oh God."

"But if all he did was take a stock tip from Van-Metre, that's not really illegal as long as he didn't know how VanMetre procured the information."

"What about Lily and James?"

"As far as James is concerned, if Howard's involved in this, I'll make sure he goes down. James isn't going to take the fall for him or your uncle. If Benton Electronics implodes, I'm going to make damned sure that James is insulated."

"I just can't accept that Uncle Bill would sacrifice his own daughter for this. He's not like that, Simon."

"Just because he saw the advantage of Lily meeting and potentially marrying James, doesn't mean he sacrificed her. Benton Electronics has been in trouble for a while."

"That's what Nora said."

"Your uncle's been trying to stay afloat in a technology market that peaked several years ago. He's looking for options. A merger with Wells is a good one. We actually tried to buy him out several years ago, but he wouldn't sell."

"And now?"

"We don't really need Benton anymore. We've got Asian suppliers who are doing what your uncle does cheaper, faster, and better."

She hesitated for a moment, then nodded. "I understand."

Simon felt slightly light-headed from the wave of relief that washed over him. "You do?"

"Yes. When I spoke to that investigator this afternoon, he couldn't give me any solid answers, either. I was sure that's why you'd kept this to yourself. You're not the type to toss around accusations you can't substantiate."

"Thank you," he said simply.

Jorie glanced at him in surprise. "Did you think I'd jump to conclusions?"

"Most people would in your shoes. I wasn't trying to keep anything from you." He reached for her hand. "I just didn't want to get ahead of myself."

She snuggled down in the bed. "I'm worried about Uncle Bill."

"You should be. He's in a lot of hot water."

"Can anyone help him?"

"If he's smart, he'll help himself by telling the SEC everything he knows about Bronson Van-Metre."

"And Howard Wells?"

"And Howard."

She seemed to think that over. "What are you going to do if Howard gets indicted?"

"Absolutely nothing," he said flatly. "He can hire his own damned attorney."

With a slight laugh, Jorie turned to pillow her head against his chest. She traced a lazy circle on his breastbone with the pad of her index finger. "Have I ever told you that one of the things I admire most about you is how direct you are?"

"Most women find it annoying."

"I'm not most women."

You can say that again, he thought wryly, feeling vaguely as though he'd just escaped a bullet. He turned to Jorie and swept a hand down the lush curve of her body. He wanted her again. Maybe wanted her more than he ever had when he looked in her eyes and saw that expression of absolute faith and trust. He bent his head to kiss her, making a mental note to find out just what Mark Baine had to do with Nora Benton as soon as he came up for air.

Chapter Fourteen

𝄞

❵ SIMON WAS STARTLED AWAKE BY THE TELE-
phone's ring. Jorie slept peacefully beside him,
one arm thrown across his waist. He reached for
the phone and glanced at the clock on his bed
stand. Two A.M. Nothing good happened at two
A.M. He'd learned that as a child when his mother
would call late in the night to tell him she wasn't
going to make it home until morning.

With a sharp frown, he punched the talk button
on the cordless phone. "Hello."

"Simon, it's Lily. I need to talk to Jorie."

Jorie had awakened and was watching him, her
eyes concerned. "What's the matter?"

"Hold on." He handed her the phone. "It's Lily."

Jorie frowned as she accepted the phone. "Lily?
What's wrong?"

Simon watched her in the semidarkness. The glow of the phone's digital display cast an eerie light on her face. She sucked in a sharp breath. "My God." Jorie sat straight up in bed. "My God, when?"

Simon rubbed a hand up her spine. She was trembling, he realized. He sat up and wrapped an arm around her shoulders. "What's going on?" he asked quietly.

Jorie choked on a sob and clutched the phone closer to her ear. "Tell her I'll be there as soon as I can." She turned to Simon. Tears streamed down her face as she thrust the phone in his hands.

"What's wrong?" he asked gently.

"It's Darius," tossing aside the sheet. "He's been shot."

Simon took a seat next to Lily and James in the hospital waiting room. He hated places like this. It reminded him of the sterile environment where he'd watched his mother suffer through the final stages of liver failure.

After Lily's phone call, he'd held a shaking Jorie close while she'd given him the sketchy details of the accident. Lavonia and Darius had been at home that evening. His mother had sent him out for the paper—as was her habit.

While he'd stood on the stoop retrieving the copy of the *Globe*, four members of the local gang drove by, too fast and too loud, and in a random hail of gunfire, had buried two bullets in the child's tender flesh—one in his arm, the other in his abdomen. He was fighting for his life in a Boston hospital.

Simon had immediately risen to dress. Jorie, stunned and shaking, had struggled into her clothes. Her fingers had been trembling so much, he'd had to zip her dress for her. "Do you want to go by your place and get some clothes?" he'd asked. "It's going to be a long night."

"I need to get there," she'd said. "I just need to get there."

Simon had chosen not to argue with her. He could always send Lily to Jorie's apartment to fetch her clothes, he decided. He had nodded and slid his wallet and cell phone into the back pocket of his trousers. Jorie had clung to his arm as he led her through the apartment and down to his car.

He had made the drive to the downtown hospital in record time. Jorie sat with her hands clenched, her face pale, and her body shaking until he'd pulled into the hospital parking lot.

Simon got the information from the admitting nurse, then had led Jorie to the waiting area where Lavonia was pacing, her face anguished. Lavonia had spotted them the moment they stepped off the elevator. With a broken cry, she'd rushed toward Jorie and pulled her into a fierce embrace. Simon had watched the two women as they cried and consoled each other with a tight feeling in his chest. Jorie gave everything she had, he'd realized. And she accepted nothing less than complete surrender in return.

He had given Lavonia's shoulder a reassuring squeeze, then had scanned the occupants of the emergency room and found Lily and James huddled together in the waiting area.

Lily now turned to Simon, her blue eyes fathomless pools of compassion. "I'm so glad you were with her," Lily told Simon. "God, this is awful."

Simon glanced at Lavonia and Jorie, who still stood huddled together near the elevator. Reverend Tipton had joined them, now, evidently arriving shortly after Simon. "How did you hear about this?" Simon asked Lily.

"Lavonia called looking for Jorie after they got Darius here and into surgery," Lily said. Her face was tear-streaked and red. "When she couldn't reach her at home, she kept trying until midnight, then she tried my house." She laced her fingers through James's. "I was with James, so Mother finally got me on my cell phone."

"I see." He tipped his head toward the nurses' station. "I asked when we came in. They said they don't have any news yet."

"That's what they told us," James informed him. "Darius is in surgery now."

"They took him before we got here," Lily supplied.

Simon exhaled a long breath. "Prognosis?"

"Nobody's saying anything," Lily said. "I know Lavonia must be terrified. I feel so bad for her." She glanced at her across the room. "I wish there was something we could do besides just sit here. This has got to be the worst night of her life."

Simon had to agree. The one time he'd had to take James to the emergency room after James had gotten hit in the eye with a baseball, Simon had suffered all the anxieties of hell in the hour-long wait for a prognosis on the extent of James's injuries. He couldn't even imagine what was going through Lavonia's mind as her only child struggled for life. "We'll wait and see," he told them. "In the meantime, we'll do what we can to make this easier."

That seemed to please Lily. "What are you thinking?"

"Jorie's going to need a change of clothes," he told her. He studied Lavonia's bloodstained shirt. "So does Lavonia. I think they wear the same size."

"Close enough," Lily told him. "I have a key to Jorie's apartment. James and I can go get her clothes. I'll pick up something for Lavonia while we're there."

James nodded. "We'll get some food and stuff, too. It's going to be a long day."

"All right." Simon wiped a hand over his face. "Get back when you can. After that, we'll just have to wait and see."

* * *

An hour later, Jorie accepted a Styrofoam cup of coffee from him with a weary look. "Thanks."

"Drink it," Simon urged. "It tastes like hell, but you need it."

She took a tentative sip, grimaced, then cradled the cup in both hands. He took the seat beside her and stretched his long legs out in front of him. She'd never been as thankful in her life to have another person's supporting presence in an hour of crisis. Simon had taken over the situation in the hospital waiting room like a field marshal. After sending James and Lily to fetch clean clothes for her and Lavonia, he'd managed the steady stream of Lavonia's friends from church, assigning various tasks as needed. Thanks to Simon, Lavonia's bloody clothes had been sent home for washing, she'd been fed, comforted, and generally cared for during the small hours of the morning. He'd already placed a call to the night manager at her job and explained why she wouldn't be in the next day. He'd pressured the nurses for information, had kept Lavonia as isolated as possible from the relentless questions, helped her issue her statement to the police, and most comforting of all, he'd simply sat, holding Jorie's hand, and waited. "Thank you for staying here," she told him. "I think it means as much to Lavonia as it does to me."

"I like Darius," he told her. "And I like his mother. I'm glad I was here to help."

Jorie looked across the room where Lily and James were pillowed against each other, asleep in two of the waiting room chairs. They'd shown remarkable maturity tonight. Neither had been obligated to come to the hospital, certainly neither had been obligated to stay, but they'd risen to the occasion. Lily had seemed eager to provide whatever comfort she could, and James, too, had shown a depth of compassion Jorie found moving. She was sure the young couple could have thought of a dozen ways to spend this time that didn't involve the sterile, harsh environs of the hospital waiting room, yet except for the errands they'd run at Simon's request, neither had made a move to leave despite the realization that Darius's surgery would take hours. Though Jorie had encouraged them to go home and get some rest, James had insisted that they weren't leaving until they had news.

"They look exhausted," Jorie told Simon.

"I'm sure they are."

"They've really been wonderful."

"Yes."

She tucked a strand of hair behind her ear. "James is so good to her."

"She's good *for* him," Simon added. "I'm seeing things a new way." He folded her hand in his. "You do that to me."

"You don't sound like you like it too much."

"The jury's still out on that. I think I liked the old, cynical me better." He shot her a slight grin. "He was more predictable."

Her smile dazzled him. "You're a fraud, you know," she said.

"You think?"

"Sure. All this time you wanted everyone to believe that you were worried Lily was after James's money."

"I was."

"Maybe," she concurred. "You may have fooled them, but you didn't fool me. It's his heart you were really worried about."

Simon didn't respond to that. He looked at Lily and James again. "I think they'll make it," he admitted.

"I'm sure they'll be glad to hear that." Jorie leaned back in her chair and winced as her muscles protested the long hours in the uncomfortable seats. "I'm worried about Lavonia," she told him.

"She seems like she's holding up all right."

"That's why I'm worried." She turned to study her friend. She sat with her head tipped back against the wall, eyes closed. She wasn't sleeping, Jorie knew. The compression of her lips and the worry lines around her eyes gave her away. Though still and reposed, she was on full alert as every nerve and cell in her body screamed in protest at what was happening to her child.

She looked so utterly alone and desolate that Jorie's heart twisted. Though Andrew Tipton and several church members had come to sit with her and pray with her, and Simon had done his best to see that her needs were being met, she had withdrawn progressively as the time wore on.

As dawn came, the hospital waiting room had begun to fill with new patients and their families. Lavonia had remained in her chair, stoically silent and detached.

When Simon had gone to fetch the coffee, Jorie had attempted to draw Lavonia out of her self-imposed shell, but had gotten nowhere. Lavonia had answered her questions in flat, toneless monosyllables, while shadows of fear and anxiety crowded her dark brown eyes.

When she looked at Simon again, he was watching her closely. "You don't look so good, either," he told her. "Your eyes are bloodshot, and your face is too pale."

"Thanks," she muttered. "You're no prize yourself." His day-old whiskers had begun to look scruffy. He'd raked his hand through his hair so many times that it lay in tangled disarray.

"Are you holding up all right?" he probed.

She shrugged. "I don't know." She glanced at Lavonia. "I've been so busy worrying about Lavonia, I haven't really thought about it much."

"She's handling this better than I would," Simon said.

"Lavonia is one of the strongest people I know. Even if Darius—even if things aren't all right, she'll find a way to survive." She leaned forward and braced her elbows on her knees with a soft sigh. "God. I can't believe this."

The cry was as much a complaint as a conversation with the Deity. Jorie added this to her growing list of questions she planned to ask when she finally stood face to face with her Creator. Things like this weren't supposed to happen in a world that a God of justice and mercy claimed to rule. Yet in her experience, they happened more often to people like Lavonia than to people who seemed more deserving of God's wrath.

Simon rubbed his hand up and down her spine. "I asked at the nurses' station when I went to get the coffee," he said. "They still don't know anything."

Jorie shook her head. "Do you know I had arranged an audition for Darius a couple of weeks from now? Did I tell you?"

"No."

She'd searched for months to find a competent piano teacher who would agree to take him on scholarship from Art-Is-In. Finally one of her former classmates from Berklee had referred her to a former concert pianist who lived near Avon Hill. Jorie had spoken with the man several times on the phone, presenting her case for Darius's music education. She'd scheduled the audition for the week after the fund-raiser. "I found someone," she told Simon, "who'll take him on scholarship if he—" She couldn't finish the statement. Tears welled in her eyes and she struggled to contain the painful knot in her throat.

"He still might make it," Simon assured her. "Don't go there before you have to."

"Even if he survives this," she shot back, "he won't make the audition."

Simon shrugged. "So he'll audition later."

She gave him a bitter look. In her experience, people who lived in Simon's world where money and power opened doors and bought opportunities had no idea how the Lavonia Jacksons of the world had to live. They didn't understand that the people who most needed a break rarely if ever got it, and that life tended to deal its most wretched hands to the people who were already down on their luck. She was angry, she knew, not at Simon, but at the terrible circumstances that had put Darius in this place. And though Simon merely presented a convenient target, she couldn't keep the hard note out of her voice. "Don't you get it?" she charged. "This is going to cost Lavonia a fortune. The hospital bills alone are going to be bad enough. But by the time you factor in his recovery time, whatever physical therapy he might need, doctor costs and ambulance bills, she couldn't pay this with what she makes in a year. Then you have to consider what it's going to do to Darius's morale and Lavonia's. She'll have to take off work while he's recovering. She'll probably lose her job because of it. Retailers don't tend to extend family leave to employees who are easily replaced."

She took a deep breath and continued, "Families like theirs don't recover from a setback like this. They're small and they're already struggling, and something like this can wipe them out. I see it all the time."

"I wasn't trying to be cavalier," he said.

"I know you weren't. You were trying to put things in perspective. But the perspective on this right now just plain sucks. Darius will be lucky if he lives. All he was doing was getting the paper off his front porch. Any kid should be able to pick up the paper off his front porch without thinking his life is in danger. But now here he is just trying to stay alive."

Jorie wiped angrily at the tears that had begun to stream down her cheeks. "And what's worse is that it's going to be that way for most of his life. He might as well give up the piano now, because when you weigh it against the price of supporting himself and his mother"—she choked on a sob— "what does it matter? What does any of it matter?"

"Don't do this to yourself," he told her. "You don't know what's going to happen."

She mopped her eyes with the back of her hand. "You can't possibly understand what this is going to do to them," she charged.

She saw a subtle change in his expression. Something registered deep in his gaze that she'd seen the night he'd stood in his living room and told her about his mother's painting. "Yes," he said quietly, "I can."

Jorie sucked in a sharp breath as she realized the complete injustice of her comment. Simon had lived in the unstable environment that was the best his mother could provide until they'd moved to the Wells estate. She was certain he had memories of sparse meals and cold nights, of leaking roofs and faulty plumbing. There would have been the anxiety of the creditor notices that had piled up in the mail, of hiding from the sheriff's office when they'd come to serve papers, or from apartment superintendents to avoid eviction.

She knew from the children she worked with that the constant fight for survival didn't lend itself to dreams of the future. Most of Simon's dreams had probably been expended on finding the next meal or a place to stay where the roof didn't leak and the heat worked at least most of the year—or on using his last dollar to buy nylons to go with a stolen dress from a funeral parlor so his mother could get a job.

Feeling suddenly overwhelmed and inexpressibly sad, Jorie wrapped her arms around his waist. "Oh Simon, I'm sorry." She hugged him. "I'm so sorry. I shouldn't have said that."

"It's all right," he assured her.

"No, it isn't." She rubbed her face against his chest. "I didn't mean that. I'm just—"

"Hurting," he supplied. "I know." He cupped the back of her head in his large hand.

Jorie took a moment to absorb the comforting heat of his fingers. Finally she lifted her face. "Please forgive me."

"It's forgotten," he assured her as he pointed to Lily and James. Lily had awakened and was shaking James's arm. "Our friends have returned," he told her gently.

Lily and James had a brief conversation before they crossed the room to join them. Lily took the seat next to Jorie and wrapped her arm around her shoulders. "I'm sorry I fell asleep."

Jorie shook her head. "Don't be. I know you're exhausted. I didn't have a chance to thank you earlier for the change of clothes."

"No problem. It was Simon's idea." Lily looked at Simon. "No news yet?"

"Not yet," Jorie said. She gave James a slight smile. "You two really should go home and get some rest. We can call you when we have news."

"We're staying," Lily said firmly. "James was going to go find us something to eat. Do you need anything?"

"No. We're—" Jorie stopped abruptly when she saw a surgeon walking toward them. "Lavonia?"

Lavonia sat up in her chair, looked momentarily at Jorie, then stood to meet the surgeon. The doctor entered the waiting area, pulling his scrub hat from his head. "Mrs. Jackson?" he asked Lavonia.

Jorie moved quickly across the open space to take Lavonia's hand. "How is Darius?" Lavonia asked the doctor.

"I'm Dr. Hudland. I was the head surgeon on your son's case."

"How is he?" Lavonia asked again.

"We got the bullets out," he announced. Jorie felt her heart begin to beat again as she drew a thankful breath. The surgeon continued, "The wound in his arm isn't serious. The other." He shook his head. "It entered your son's abdomen from a side angle, which is probably what saved his life." He indicated the angle of the bullet on his scrubs. "It skidded across the top of his pelvic bone and lodged between the lumbar and sacroiliac portion of his spine."

Lavonia drew a steadying breath. "Is he going to be all right?"

"To be honest, we don't know yet. He lost a lot of blood, and he's still in very critical condition. There is considerable internal damage and bleeding from the wound. A lot can go wrong."

Simon wrapped his arm around Lavonia's shoulders. "What can we do?" he asked the doctor.

"The next forty-eight hours are crucial." The surgeon glanced at Jorie, then looked at Lavonia again. "Do you have any family here, Mrs. Jackson?"

"No," Lavonia told him. "Darius is all I have."

The desolation of that comment wasn't lost on Jorie. She squeezed her friend's hand and hurried to assure the doctor. "We're her family," she insisted. "Lavonia has a lot of local support. Between her church and her friends, we'll make sure she has whatever she needs."

The surgeon nodded. "Someone should stay with Darius, preferably around the clock. I don't always recommend that, but with a child, I think it helps for him to have familiar voices around him."

Lavonia shuddered slightly. "May I see him?"

"He's in recovery. As soon as they get him moved to a room, you can go in."

"Thank you."

Jorie wrapped her arm around Lavonia's waist. "Is there anything else we need to know?" she asked the surgeon.

"He's a tough little boy. I think he's going to make it." He patted Lavonia on the shoulder. "Just have a little faith, Mrs. Jackson. Your son came through surgery all right and that's the hardest part."

"Thank you."

"Talk to him as much as you can. If there are things he's familiar with, clothes, certain toys, anything, that'll help, too. His brain is alert even if his body isn't."

Lavonia nodded. "I understand."

"And if there's anything you need—" Dr. Hudland said.

"We need to know where we can get a piano," Simon said.

Simon checked his watch as he entered the hospital later that morning. He'd taken an exhausted Jorie home to her apartment where he'd insisted she get some rest. A quick stop at Art-Is-In had yielded the result he wanted. Jorie's boss had readily agreed that since Jorie had already laid most of the groundwork for the upcoming fund-raiser, they could try to get through the resulting media blitz without her. Simon had promised the help of Wells Enterprises' public relations department, and Jorie's boss had seemed relieved.

Simon made the call and put his best people on it. Two more calls had yielded a promise to cover Darius's hospital bills and recovery costs. The Wells Foundation had recently donated a wing to the hospital's critical care department, so Darius's medical bills were easily dispatched. Joe, who had taken the news about Darius harder than Simon had suspected, had been eager to help. Simon had sent James and Lily with him to arrange for purchase and delivery of a piano to Lavonia's apartment and a portable keyboard to Darius's hospital room. He had three more items on his agenda today. First, he had something to discuss with Lavonia. He'd stopped by the hospital knowing he could catch her there before Jorie came to relieve her after noon.

Second, he had a meeting scheduled with Mark

Baine that afternoon. Simon was going to demand some answers, fast, on just what kind of game the investigator was playing.

And third, he had decided during the still hours of the morning, as he'd watched Jorie agonize with Lavonia, her fear and anxiety almost as intense as her friend's for the life of the child she loved, that he had definitely gotten in over his head with her. This was a relationship he couldn't control. Jorie threw herself into the deep water of people's lives. His entire life, he'd wondered what it meant to love and be loved with that kind of reckless abandon. That's why she was scaring the hell out of him. He had a grim suspicion that she'd been trying to teach him a lesson last night when she'd made love to him on the carpet of his living room. She'd wanted him to realize that he couldn't always be in control with her. She wanted him to trust her enough to let a piece of himself go. Too soon, she'd realize that he probably couldn't give her what she wanted, that he wasn't even sure he had all his pieces anymore. He'd stored them away for so long, he was fairly certain that some had disintegrated. And if he didn't move immediately to bind Jorie to him as quickly and as completely as possible, he'd eventually lose her.

And in Simon's well-ordered world, that was simply unacceptable.

Chapter Fifteen

🎵

❬ WHEN JORIE ENTERED DARIUS'S HOSPITAL ROOM a little after noon, she gave Simon a surprised glance. He and Lavonia were deep in conversation. Lavonia still looked anxious, she noted, as she held Darius's hand tightly against the white sheets. He was hooked up to a myriad of monitors and tubes, with a mask over his face pumping oxygen into his little body. His stillness seemed odd to her. She associated him with limitless energy and perpetual motion.

Simon's head was bent close to Lavonia as the two discussed something of obvious import. Jorie noted the portable digital keyboard on a stand in the corner of the room. Top of the line, she observed. Simon had taste. "Am I interrupting?" she asked quietly, giving Simon a curious look.

His eyes were steady and determined when he met her gaze. "Not at all," he said. "I was just keeping Lavonia company until you got here." He stood and came toward her, bending to give her a light kiss. "Did you get some rest?"

"Yes." She looked from Simon to Lavonia and back again. "I guess you didn't," she said to no one in particular.

Simon shrugged. "I'm fine."

Lavonia turned to Darius and squeezed his hand. "Jorie's here," she told him. "You'd better perk up soon, boy, or she's not going to know who you are. Nobody recognizes you when you aren't shooting your mouth off a mile a minute."

Jorie smiled slightly. She leaned closer to Simon. "Didn't the doctor say one visitor at a time?"

"I got an exception." He didn't elaborate.

"And a keyboard," she pointed out.

"I thought you might want to play for him. He'll find it familiar."

"I'm sure he will." She wished she could decipher the enigmatic look in his eyes. "Did you and Lavonia have a nice talk?"

"Very," he assured her. He glanced at Lavonia. "I've got to get going," he told Jorie. "How long do you plan to stay here?"

"However long I can get Lavonia to take a break and get some rest. I doubt she'll agree to be gone long."

"I doubt it, too. I wouldn't if I were her."

"Me either," Jorie agreed.

Simon nodded and dropped another quick kiss on her forehead. "All right, then. I've got some things to take care of today. Why don't you call me when you're done? I'll come get you."

"I can take the T—"

"Jorie," he said patiently, "I will come get you." He cupped her face in his hand. "Promise you'll call me."

"I promise."

"Okay. Do you need anything?"

"No."

With a nod, he turned to go. "I'll see you tonight."

Jorie caught his arm. "Simon—"

He looked at her. "Yes?"

With a muffled cry, she flung herself against his chest and kissed him thoroughly. "Thank you. Thank you so much."

Simon kissed her back before gently setting her away from him. "You're welcome," he said, his expression inscrutable. "Call me when you're ready." And he left.

Lavonia was still talking to Darius, so Jorie approached the bed. "Any change at all?" she asked Lavonia.

Lavonia shook her head. When she met Jorie's gaze, her eyes seemed more hopeful than Jorie had seen them in hours. "Not yet." She squeezed her son's hand. "He's going to be okay, though. Everything's going to be okay, Jorie."

Jorie nodded. "I know." She laid her hand on top of Lavonia's where her fingers were laced with Darius's. "I know you don't want to leave—"

"I can't—"

"You have got to get some rest. You're not going to be any good to him if you collapse."

"What if he needs me?"

"I'm going to stay with him."

"I'm not leaving him."

"Then at least let the nurses tell you where you can stretch out for a little while. There may be an extra bed around somewhere—or at least a lounging chair."

She hesitated, but finally released Darius's hand. "You'll call me—"

"In a second," Jorie assured her. "If he bats an eyelid. I swear."

Lavonia stood and hugged Jorie fiercely. "I don't know what I'd do without you," she said.

"Or me you." Jorie held her friend close for long seconds. "So go get some rest. For me and for Darius."

Lavonia wiped at her tears as she turned to kiss her son's cheek. "Mama's right down the hall, baby. All you gotta do is ask."

Jorie waited for Lavonia to make her way out of the room before she sat in the chair by Darius's bed. Lavonia's parting comment haunted her slightly as she remembered the pained look in Simon's eyes when she'd accused him of not understanding what their family had to go through. There wasn't a lot of security in Darius's life, it was true. Bills piled up. Unexpected financial emergencies created unusual stress for a woman in Lavonia's position. But in one way, Darius's lot in life was far superior to what Simon's had ever been: Darius had the absolute and incontrovertible assurance of his mother's unconditional love. For all his accumulated wealth and success, that was a treasure Simon had never known.

The thought made Jorie inexpressibly sad. She took Darius's hand in hers and gently stroked the back of his fingers. "Here's the thing, D," she told him. "He doesn't have the best style in the world, and he can be really annoying at times, but I went and fell in love with him." She managed a slight smile. "Stupid, I know. You'd tell me I was acting just like a girl."

She squeezed his hand. "So you've got to get better so you can give me some of your sage advice. Simon tells me you're quite the man of the world these days. I can't believe you had a woman and didn't tell me about her. I thought we shared everything, D."

She waited, half expecting him to open his eyes and give her his usual impish look and a mouth full of stuff. The only sound in the dim room was the beeping of the monitors and the steady drone of the oxygen machine. Jorie struggled with a bout of tears. "Come on, D," she urged. "You're a fighter, and you know it. You can lick this. You've got to lick this."

When he still didn't respond, she moved to the top-of-the-line synthesizer sitting in the corner. "Okay," she told him, "but I'm going to break this thing in since you won't. And I am *not* playing that chopsticks duet by myself."

Simon dropped Nora Benton's picture on the small coffee shop table late that afternoon where Mark Baine was waiting for him. "Hard-looking woman," he commented. "Don't you think?"

Mark glanced at the picture, then at Simon. "I can explain."

"You'd better hope so." He sat down in the chair across from Mark and folded his arms across his chest. "You've got five minutes."

Mark held up his hands. "She came to me before you did. One of my clients referred her. She wanted me to look into her husband's dealings with Delitron and VanMetre. When you first talked to me about James, I didn't immediately make the connection between Benton Electronics and James's fiancée."

"And when you did?"

"I saw no reason why I couldn't give you and Nora what you both wanted."

"Didn't that strike you as a slight conflict of interest, Mark? Damn it, I trusted you."

"Take it easy, Simon. Had it come to that, you know I would have leveled with you. Hell, the Benton woman's a client. You're my friend."

Simon pushed the picture toward him. "So while you were looking into Benton's financial woes for his wife, you decided you'd tack your fee onto my bill."

Mark winced. "It wasn't like that. Honest to God, I didn't think the two things were even related until this week. You wanted me to see if Benton had some kind of deal with Howard to marry off his daughter and merge with Wells Enterprises. Nora Benton wanted me to check out her husband's Delitron connections. I never expected the two things to cross paths."

"But they did."

"They did." Mark reached for his briefcase and pulled out a folder. "And how."

Simon frowned. "You found something?"

"Yeah. Not what you were hoping for, I think." He pushed the folder toward Simon. "I brought it to you first. I haven't discussed it with Nora Benton."

Simon held the other man's gaze for long seconds, then accepted the folder. He flipped it open and studied the detailed accounting sheet and corporate memos it contained. He felt rage begin to eat away at the fragile rein he already had on his temper. "Where did you get these?" he asked Mark.

"Believe it or not, from Nora Benton."

"Where did she get them?"

"Swiped off her husband's fax machine. She has no idea what they mean."

Simon turned a page and read on. His teeth were pressed so tightly together his jaw was starting to ache. "The bastard," he muttered.

Mark nodded. "Exactly. And I'm beginning to suspect that's just the beginning." He extracted another file from the briefcase, checked it, and passed it to Simon. "That source I told you I had?"

"Yes?" Simon accepted the folder.

"Panned out. Take a look at that."

Simon opened the folder with resolute determination. What he found in the indexed reports confirmed his worst suspicions. He could feel the pulse throbbing in his temple. "Has anyone else seen this information?" Simon prodded.

"Just my investigator, me, and you," Mark assured him. "I swear, Simon. Since I was supposed to meet with you tomorrow, I was going to tell you about the Benton connection then. Had it not been for Delitron and VanMetre's indictment, I never would have put the two things together."

"Until you found Howard was the link," Simon stated flatly. "Do me one favor, Mark."

"Sure."

Simon scooped up the two folders and rose to

go. "Give me twenty-four hours before you talk to Nora Benton about this."

Mark's eyebrows rose. "Simon—"

He held up a hand. "If your information is correct, one more day isn't going to hurt."

Mark thought that over. "All right. Twenty-four hours, but then I have to tell her."

"I understand." Satisfied, Simon tucked the folders under his arm and headed for the door. That should give him all the time he needed.

Jorie stirred slightly when a wide band of artificial light from the corridor fell across her chair by Darius's bed. She glanced up to see Simon entering the room. "Hi," she said, rubbing her eyes. "What time is it?"

"After eleven."

"Where's Lavonia?"

"I sent her to get some coffee. She's going to stay through the night."

Jorie nodded and stretched her arms above her head. "I made her get some rest this afternoon. She came back around five, so we've been in here off and on." She glanced at the chair. "I must have dozed off."

"Any change?" Simon asked, glancing at Darius.

"Not yet. He's still critical, but he hasn't taken a turn for the worse. The nurses say that's a good thing."

Simon reached for her hand. "I'm taking you home."

"Someone should—"

"James and Lily are here," he informed her. "They're going to stay until two. Then Andrew Tipton's got another shift coming in for the early morning."

Jorie swayed slightly, exhaustion getting the better of her. "You're really amazing, did you know that?"

Simon smoothed her hair off her face. "I've been managing people's lives for a long time. I've got practice."

She tipped her head against his shoulder. "Can't you just accept that you're a nice person?"

He stroked her back. "I'm glad you think so."

"Simon, you bought him a piano."

"The doctor said he should have familiar things. I thought if you played for him, it would help."

With a slight laugh, she shook her head. "I'm not up to arguing with you."

"Good," he said, looping his arm around her shoulders and leading her toward the door. "Then I'm taking you home."

With a weary sigh, Jorie leaned on Simon's shoulder as they trudged up the stairs toward her apartment. Even though Simon had insisted she rest awhile that morning, she had not slept well.

She was bone-tired from the anxiety and emotional stress of the day. As bad as she felt for leaving Lavonia, she knew that Simon had done all he could to ensure that her friend was well cared for. She never had been able to get Lavonia to tell her what his visit that morning had been about, but she'd sensed a new determination in Lavonia for the better part of the day.

As for Darius, the prognosis was neither discouraging nor encouraging. Though he was still unconscious, his vital signs had stabilized during the day. Jorie had played for him for over an hour, but the lights and buzzers on the monitors had remained stubbornly unchanged.

In the intervals when Lavonia sat with him, Jorie had tried a range of conversations with the Almighty. When angry accusations had failed to work, she'd resorted to begging. Begging had seemed the best strategy as the afternoon wore on with no sign of change. Her heart ached as much as her body, and the sheer grief of the situation had taken its toll. If she hadn't had Simon to lean on, she probably would have collapsed on the stairs.

She'd had to struggle not to fall asleep on the ride home from the hospital. She'd even been too exhausted to protest when Simon parked in front of a fire hydrant outside her apartment building.

Simon shifted her weight slightly as they trudged up the stairs. "You're falling over exhausted," he told her. "Are you sure you're all right?"

She managed a slight nod. "You have to be more tired than I am." She suspected he had not slept at all that day.

"Don't worry about me. I'm fine."

When they reached the landing, Simon took her keys and unlocked her apartment door. He pushed it open and guided Jorie inside. She noted blankly that the pile of mail that should have accumulated that afternoon was missing, and that the lights in her living room were on. Confused, she glanced toward the kitchen.

Fatigue, she decided, was making her hallucinate. Her mother, clad in a traditional Dai homespun tunic, was walking toward her with a cup of tea and a worried look. "Good heavens, Jordan," she said. "You look awful."

Jorie stared at her for several seconds. "Mother?"

"We just arrived. Your father's gone out to find a newspaper." Amelia Morrison glanced at Simon. "We got the key from Lily."

Jorie swayed a little. "She didn't tell me. I saw her this afternoon and she didn't tell me."

"Hmm." Her mother pursed her lips. "I suppose she wanted to surprise you."

Jorie yawned. "I suppose." Simon's arm tightened around her waist.

Amelia set her tea down on the small end table

and crossed the room to her. She pulled Jorie into her arms. "It's nice to see you, dear."

Jorie patted her shoulder blades. "It's nice to see you, too."

"You're exhausted."

"Um hmm." Practically dead on her feet now, even the surprise of finding her mother in her apartment failed to stir her energy. Even her speech sounded slurred. She yawned again. "I'm glad you got in okay," she said. "I'm going to bed now. We'll talk later."

"Jordan—"

"I've been up most of last night, Mom. It's been a very long couple of days and I'm beat." Her eyes had begun to burn. "It's a long story." She waved a hand in Simon's direction. "If he's not too tired, Simon can explain it."

"Are you all right?" her mother insisted.

"Sure. Fine." Jorie tipped her head against Simon's shoulder. "Simon's probably even more tired than I am," she went on, "so you might want to cut him a break."

"I'm fine," Simon assured her.

"In that case, Simon, this is my mother. And I'm going to bed now."

Twenty minutes later, while Jorie slept soundly in the other room, Simon found himself seated across from her parents in what felt like a strange parody of a Victorian courtship ritual. Her father, owlish and scholarly-looking, had returned with the newspaper minutes after Jorie had stumbled to her bedroom to fall across the sheets. Simon had waited in the living room while her mother pulled Jorie's shoes off and helped her into bed. He'd tried not to feel jealous.

Jeremiah Morrison had come up the stairs bearing newspapers and doughnuts to find Simon pacing the living room. If Jorie's father was surprised at his presence, he showed no sign. He introduced himself, set the newspapers down, and offered Simon a doughnut. The two of them sat awkwardly eating the doughnuts in silence until Jorie's mother joined them.

She looked a lot like Lily, Simon noted. Her pale hair was pulled away from her face revealing features that, though sun worn and aging, were still classic. Once she'd been beautiful. He never would have guessed she was Nora's sister. A sudden insight told him that Nora, though attractive in her own way, had always felt inferior to her sister's physical beauty. He began to understand Nora's resentment of Amelia's marriage. Amelia had chosen Jeremiah because he was the love of her life. According to Jorie, her mother had joined him as his partner in the mission field for an uncertain and unstable future. Nora, on the other hand, had taken a conventional path with William Benton. From a good family, William had the ability to provide well for her. Nora had thought financial security would be enough to make her happy.

But she'd watched Amelia's marriage to Jeremiah from afar and found herself wanting more. No wonder, Simon thought, that Jorie was an emotional risk taker. She'd learned it from her parents. She'd seen them give themselves away countless times to the people they worked with and to each other, and they seemed utterly content. Nora, on the other hand, had kept every card to herself and was clearly miserable with her choices.

Simon's resolve from earlier that day strengthened: whatever it took, he couldn't lose Jorie.

"So," Jeremiah said, "You're a friend of Jorie's?"

"Yes."

Jeremiah nodded, thoughtful. "A good friend?"

"Yes," Simon said again.

"How good of a friend?" Jorie's father pressed.

"Jerry," his wife chastised as she entered the room. "Leave the poor man alone." She looked at Simon. "Jorie's dead to the world."

"I'm sure she is," Simon said. "She's exhausted." Briefly, he brought them up to speed on Darius's situation. "We've been at the hospital most of the night."

Amelia's face was a mask of concern while Jeremiah offered up a quick, heartfelt prayer for Darius's well-being. Jeremiah, Simon noted, talked freely and often with the Almighty. Lily had told once that Jorie was the same way. He'd never met religious people like these. He'd found that on many people, religion was an unflattering mantle of severity and criticism. In Jorie's family, they wore it like a comfortable old coat.

"Well, if you've been at the hospital with her all night," Jeremiah finally mused, "then you must be a close friend."

"Jerry, stop."

"I'm curious," Jeremiah insisted. "I think this is where I'm supposed to ask him about his intentions toward our daughter."

Amelia laughed. "Jerry, for heaven's sake. Jorie is thirty-two years old. You don't have to treat the man like her first date."

"It's the first one of her dates I've met," Jeremiah insisted.

That made Simon frown. Before this was over, he vowed, he'd have an explanation from the couple about how they'd managed to abandon their daughter without apparent guilt. Jorie had been more open with him on the ride to Rockport than at any other time, and he still felt a nagging suspicion that she'd internalized far more hurt than she admitted.

Amelia pursed her lips. Her eyes twinkled just like Jorie's. "You may have a point there," she told her husband, "but Jorie would kill you for that question." She looked at Simon. "How did you meet my daughter?"

All this scene needed, Simon mused, was a bright light and one-way glass. Jeremiah and Amelia had already mastered good cop/bad cop interrogation techniques. "James Wells is my responsibility."

Jeremiah raised his eyebrows. "Lily's fiancé?"

Simon nodded. "Yes."

"Your responsibility?" Amelia asked.

Simon nodded again. "Yes."

"I suppose there's a story in that somewhere." Jeremiah leaned back on the sofa and pulled one knee between his linked hands. "But I'm also guessing you aren't going to tell it to us."

Simon liked him. A quiet, intelligent man, he had his daughter's personality. "Not today." He leaned forward and braced his hands on his thighs. "Today the only concern I've got is helping Jorie and Lavonia do what they need to for Darius."

"Poor thing," Amelia mused. "And the doctors still haven't indicated how he's doing?"

"He's stable," Simon said, "but critical. The next twenty-four hours will tell."

"Jorie must be beside herself," Jeremiah concluded. "She gets so involved in the lives of people she helps."

"Yes," Simon agreed. "And she was closer to this one than most."

Amelia shook her head. "I'm glad we got here today. I don't like to think of her going through this alone. I'm sure she wasn't expecting us this soon, but we decided to take a longer furlough."

As she had so many other things, Simon mused. Jeremiah must have noted the doubt in his expression. He gave Simon a shrewd look. "You look grim, son," he said.

"Do I?"

Jeremiah nodded. "If you're as close to my daughter as I think you are, then I suspect you're thinking it's about time we gave her some attention."

"Maybe," Simon concurred.

"I can see it in your eyes."

"It's none of my business."

"I don't know about that," the older man stated. "From the way you look when you talk about my daughter, I think maybe it is your business."

Simon wasn't sure he wanted to have this conversation. He was tired, and his nerves felt raw from the long night. Fresh in his mind was the slightly hurt look he'd seen in her eyes when she'd told him her parents were coming for Lily's wedding. *Why hadn't they been there for her?* that look had asked. It had twisted Simon's guts. He knew the sting of disappointment too well, and instinct urged him to demand answers. He carefully considered his next words. "If anyone deserves an explanation, it's Jorie."

Jeremiah's expression turned pained. "Melly and I haven't been able to give Jorie as much of ourselves as other parents do. That's true enough. I've always worried that she might resent that."

Not enough to avoid it, Simon mused. "She's been hurt," he admitted, "but I don't think she resents it."

Amelia laced her fingers through her husband's. "Jorie is a remarkable person. We tried very hard to help her understand."

"It's been difficult," Jeremiah added. "Balancing the demands of our work with the demands of family is tough. I know a lot of people say that, but when your work involves feeding thousands of starving children a day, or trying to rebuild a village after an earthquake that wipes out half the population, it takes on a new dimension." He scrubbed a hand over his face. "As much as possible, we tried to involve Jorie in our ministry. As a child, she lived with us. Her mother homeschooled her, and she was a part of our life in China."

"It became too dangerous," Amelia added. "The political situation—"

"I couldn't keep her with us in good conscience," Jeremiah said. "It was the hardest decision of our lives, but we felt that sending Jorie to Boston was the best thing for her. I think generally she agrees."

"She does," Simon assured him.

Jeremiah nodded briefly. "I know there were times that Jorie felt we'd abandoned her. We considered moving back here, but the need always seemed so pressing where we were."

"Nora didn't make it any easier on her, I know," Amelia added. "My sister has never been nurturing, but Jerry has no close family, and as large as mine is, most of my relatives aren't really suited to raising a child."

Simon had to agree there. He thought of the eclectic mix of Jorie's extended family he'd met at James and Lily's engagement party with a slight smile. "I've met some of them."

"Then you know," Jeremiah said, "what we faced when we made the decision to send Jorie to the States." He sighed. "I'm not going to claim that I've always made the right choices. I don't think any father can claim that. But I loved my daughter. I wanted what was best for her. If I'd had my way, I would have kept her with us."

"Oh yes." Amelia patted her husband's knee. "We wanted her there, but there were so many other considerations."

Simon thought that over. "Couldn't one of you have returned with her?"

"It was never our intention to be separated for so long. We had no idea the political situation would remain so bad."

"We missed her so much," Jeremiah continued. "The work—" He shrugged. "I suppose that sounds like a poor reason to you, but I think Jorie understands. I pray that she does."

"More or less," Simon said. "She's missed having you involved in her life." He gave them a shrewd look. "You made it for Lily's wedding, but you missed your own daughter's high school graduation."

Jeremiah's expression saddened. "The political situation—that was right before Tiananmen Square."

"You can't imagine what it was like," Amelia added. "We were told we probably wouldn't be able to get back into the country if we left to return to the States."

"It stayed that way for a long time." Jeremiah rubbed his forehead as he relived the memories. "For years, everything was so precarious."

"We have always regretted that we missed that time in our daughter's life," Amelia said. "We never heard her recitals, and we were forced to miss her college graduation. I'll always regret that."

"She knows that," Simon assured him. "But it hurts."

"She told you that?" Amelia asked.

"I figured it out," he said.

Jeremiah nodded solemnly. "Simon, we've never pretended to be the best parents in the world—"

"You managed to give plenty of yourself to the children in your ministry."

Amelia linked her hands together in her lap

and gave Simon a stricken look. "I know it looks—"

"It looks like you cared more about your work than your child," he stated bluntly.

"That's a strong accusation." Jeremiah leaned forward and braced his hands on his knees.

Simon studied the man for long seconds. "I'm sorry," he finally said. "It's been a long day. I didn't mean to sound like I was accusing you."

"We understand." Amelia covered her husband's hand with her own. "You're obviously close to Jorie. I can see why you'd be concerned."

Jeremiah nodded. "I know." He looked at his wife. "Like every parent in the world, I know there have been times when I've failed my child. I wish that wasn't the case, but it is. The best I can do is apologize, ask God and Jorie to forgive me, and try to get it right the next time."

Amelia smiled at him. She leaned forward and lightly kissed his cheek. Simon watched the couple with a slight pang as he realized that the passion that had inspired Amelia Morrison to leave her comfortable world and follow this man halfway around the globe still burned brightly between them. It had deepened into an abiding love that both sustained and nurtured them. He'd lived most of his life afraid that no one would ever love him with that measure of devotion.

Jeremiah looked at Simon. "And as Jorie's father," he said, "I don't care whether my wife thinks it's my business or not, I want to know what your intentions are toward my daughter."

Amelia laughed. "Oh Jerry, stop."

Simon's expression remained utterly serious. "I'm going to marry her," he told them.

Amelia took a sharp breath. "Oh." She frowned. "Jorie never mentioned that she was— we didn't know."

A slight smile played at the corner of Simon's mouth. "That's because I haven't told her yet."

Chapter Sixteen

♪

"S IMON ?" J ORIE PRODDED HIS SHOULDER. S HE'D walked into Darius's hospital room late the next morning to find Simon asleep in the chair, his head on the side of the bed. "Simon, wake up."

He stirred, glanced at her, and waited a moment or two for his eyes to focus. With a soft smile, Jorie adjusted the glasses that sat crookedly on his nose. "How long have you been here?"

"Since four this morning."

Something melted in her heart. "Oh Simon. You told me you had people coming to stay with Lavonia this morning."

"I did," he assured her. "I told Lavonia I'd take the early morning shift so she could get some rest."

"Have you slept at all since yesterday?"

He glanced at the indentation his head had left on the bed. "Sure," he said, his gaze amused. "Like a log."

Jorie smoothed his hair back from his forehead. He was such a fine man. She'd been more accurate than she'd known when she'd first described his features as noble. "You're amazing."

"Nice of you to notice," he said.

"My parents inform me that the three of you had a nice talk while I was sleeping."

"We did."

"Anything I need to know?"

"No," he said gently. "Just things I needed to know." He took her hand and tugged her onto his lap. "There's something I've been wanting to ask you," he said.

She wrapped her arms around his neck. "Yes?"

"The night before last. At my apartment—"

Jorie shot a quick glance at Darius. "Simon—"

"Just tell me what you were trying to communicate when you ripped my clothes off."

She squirmed, slightly uncomfortable. She should have counted on his astute nature to know there had been more to her aggression that night than a severe case of physical desire. *Take the plunge,* she told herself now, *or you'll never know what the water feels like.* She drew a calming breath. "I needed to know," she said gently, stroking the side of his face with her fingertips, "that you trusted me enough to let something go with me."

Simon's expression turned thoughtful. "I wasn't in control."

She nodded. "You don't like that."

A slight smile played at the corner of his mouth. "I didn't have much of a problem with it, if I remember."

She laughed. "You fought me. You didn't want to surrender."

"You held on," he countered. "You made me do it."

"I had to."

He squeezed her gently. "Tell me why, Jorie."

She toyed with the earpieces of his glasses. When he stared at her with that intent look in his green eyes, she couldn't resist him. "I'm in love with you, Simon. It's probably foolish. I probably shouldn't have fallen for you. I know you never made me any promises. But I couldn't help it. I fell hard and fast the night I sat at Lily's engagement party with you and you told me about your life."

"Right then?"

She smiled gently. "I didn't know it for a while," she said. "I fought it hard enough."

"I think I should feel insulted."

She kissed his forehead. "Don't. I just figured you were the biggest risk of my life. You just had that look. I've never been able to resist that look."

He raised an eyebrow. "What look?"

"It's a vulnerable, wounded kind of thing."

"Jorie," he said patiently, "I have it on excellent authority that I can be a mean SOB."

She shook her head. "It's a façade."

"Speaks every woman who ever loved an unsuitable man."

"You're not unsuitable, Simon." She draped her arms over his shoulders. "Unattainable, maybe. Unconquerable, almost definitely. Unbelievable, unmitigating, unmanageable."

"Do I have anything to recommend me?"

She kissed him lightly. "Incomparable, indescribable, and incredible."

"I'm glad to hear that."

"I was feeling a little over my head, and I needed to know you could trust me at least enough to give me that little piece of yourself."

"I understand."

"Do you?" She framed his face in her hands. "You haven't had a lot of people to trust in your life, Simon. You've always had to take care of everything and everyone. It started with your mother, and it's spilled into every other relationship you have." When he didn't respond, she pressed a kiss to his forehead. "My parents made their share of mistakes—"

"Your father asked me last night what my intentions were."

She laughed. "They've been out of the country so long they don't know it's not 1965 anymore." Jorie brushed that adorable wave of hair off his forehead again. "But even though they disappointed me at times, and even though I struggled so much when they sent me to live in the States, they taught me how to live with abundance and passion."

"I saw that in you the day I met you," he confessed. "Do you know it's most obvious when you play the piano?"

He would probably never cease to amaze her. "Really?"

"Um. It's the way you play." He wagged his eyebrows. "It kind of turns me on."

A smile tugged at the corner of her mouth. "I had no idea."

"Don't use that against me, will you?"

"Don't count on it." She ran a fingertip along the edge of his collar. "But I have to confess something to you, too." Jorie carefully considered her next words. "Before I met you, I'd begun to feel like I was losing a part of myself. It had been too long since I'd taken an emotional risk. Without meaning to, I'd started falling into the same trap as my Aunt Nora. I had insulated myself from anything that could hurt me. You"—she drew a shaky breath—"you came in like a hurricane and threatened to knock me off a cliff. I started to feel like a part of me would die if I didn't take the leap."

Simon frowned. "Jorie—"

"I know that probably sounds crazy. I just needed to know that that part of me was still alive.

I've always defined myself with it." She touched his face gently. "I love you, Simon. I will probably always love you. And no matter what happens, I'll always remember that you're the man who gave me my passion back."

His eyes had taken on a gleam she'd never seen before. He cupped the back of her head in his large hand and pressed his lips to hers for a long, searing kiss that made her toes quiver. Tracing the contour of her lips with his tongue, he shifted her in the chair so she lay pressed to his chest. He kissed her leisurely, thoroughly, completely until she felt breathless and dazed. When he finally raised his head, her pulse was hammering. A slight smile softened the hard angles of his face. "Marry me, Jordan," he whispered.

Stunned, she looked at him for long moments, searching his eyes for any hint of what he was feeling. He had not said he loved her. He hadn't even promised he could love her. "Simon—"

He shook his head slightly. "No arguments. No discussion. Just marry me." He stared at her for long seconds. "Please."

She never, Jorie reminded herself, had been able to resist that look. With a muffled cry she pressed herself to him and kissed him again. The only noise in the room was the muffled beeping of the medical monitors.

Until a hoarse voice from the bed said, "Vanilla. I knew it."

* * *

Lily's face lit with unabashed joy. With a squeal of delight, she hurled herself into Jorie's arms. "Oh my God. I knew it. I just knew it."

Simon and Jorie had chosen to deliver the news of their engagement personally to James and Lily. Once Darius had awakened at the hospital, the resulting flurry of activity had momentarily overshadowed everything else. Darius had been the one to tell his mother. With tears in her eyes, Lavonia had given Jorie a fierce hug. "He's a good man," she told Jorie. "A little broken, I think, but then most men are."

Jorie had laughed. "You have a point there."

Simon had suggested that she go with him to James's apartment, where he and Lily had gone to crash after their stint at the hospital. Not only would it give them some desperately needed time away from the activity surrounding Darius, but they could deliver the news to the young couple personally. He had a feeling that Jorie would want to tell Lily first—even before her parents.

Though James had looked a little wary when he let Simon into the apartment, he and Lily both seemed genuinely pleased with the news. James extended his hand to Simon. "Congratulations," he told him.

Simon shook his hand and indicated the sofa with a nod of his head. "There are some things we all need to talk about." He held out a hand to Jorie, who joined him on the love seat. Simon waited until James and Lily sat across from them.

He looked at Lily first. "Lily, I want you to know that no matter what this may sound like when I tell you, I never had any personal reason to oppose your marriage to James."

James frowned. "Look, Simon—"

Simon held up a hand. "You'll understand in a minute, James." He looked at Lily again. "When you and James returned from Paris and announced your engagement, I was concerned."

She nodded. "You and I discussed it that day at your office. I told you I'd sign a prenup."

"I don't want you to," James said stubbornly.

Lily ignored him. "But you're still worried."

Simon shook his head. "Not anymore. And never about you." He took a deep breath.

Jorie tightened her grip on his hand. He'd already revealed the details of this to her in the ride on the way to James's apartment. She had told him then that James and Lily wouldn't want to hear the truth from anyone but him. He acknowledged her encouragement with a slight squeeze. "A month ago, I hired an investigator to look into some things for me."

James' expression turned fierce. Lily shot him a quick glance, then looked at Simon again. "What kind of things?"

"Financial things," James supplied. "Simon knows this guy who investigates businesses and businessmen to see who is stealing money from whom."

Lily's eyebrows knit together in confusion. "What's that got to do with James and me?"

"I wanted to know," Simon continued, "if your father had any reason to have orchestrated your meeting with James."

"Daddy? Why would he?"

Jorie leaned forward and touched Lily's knee. "Benton Electronics has been struggling for a while. Your father's doing everything he can to stay on top of it, but he could have benefited significantly from a merger with Wells Enterprises."

James turned to Lily. "I didn't know anything about any of this, honey. I swear."

Simon nodded. "That's true. I didn't tell James until Tuesday that I'd been investigating your father."

Lily's eyes remained closely on Simon. "And?" she asked quietly.

"And," he answered, "nothing. As far as anyone can tell, the only thing your father has done wrong is show bad taste in golfing buddies."

"It's Uncle Howard," James said. "Isn't it?"

Briefly, Simon explained Howard's connection to Bronson VanMetre and the Delitron scandal. "He was shuffling Wells Enterprises funds through several different accounts to disguise how much of the stock he was purchasing before the sell-off. VanMetre was the point man. He knew that the report on Delitron's failed micro battery experiment was going to be released, and he deliberately manipulated the stock to an artificial high in the weeks prior."

"Uncle Bill," Jorie explained, "plays golf with Howard Wells."

"And Uncle Howard," James guessed, "told Bill to buy Delitron stock."

"Exactly." Simon rubbed a hand over his face in frustration. "At the time, Howard didn't trust Bill enough to let him know about VanMetre's connection. I frankly think," he told Lily, "that Howard was trying to impress your father with his investment strategy. But when it became obvious that the bottom was about to drop out of Delitron's stock, he was trapped. Howard had to sell or lose his shirt, and since he'd given your father the tip, if he didn't tell him to sell, your father would have gotten suspicious."

"So Daddy sold his stock and sent me to Paris," Lily mused.

"He wanted you out of the country in case the initial investigation news about VanMetre implicated him," Simon told her. "I don't think he dreamed VanMetre would be indicted."

James put his arm around Lily's shoulders. "It's going to be okay, honey."

"So is Daddy going to be indicted, too?" Lily asked Simon.

"No," he assured her. "There's no evidence at

all to suggest that your father has done anything wrong." He glanced at James. "But Howard probably will."

Lily sucked in a sharp breath. "Oh James."

Jorie watched James's serious face as he considered what Simon had told him. "What about the company?" James asked.

"You're protected. I saw to it."

James's smile was simultaneously sad and self-effacing. "I should have known."

"But there's going to be a lot of publicity, isn't there?" Lily rubbed her hand on James's knee. "Right around the wedding."

Simon sighed and leaned back on the sofa. "Unfortunately, probably yes. I had hoped to spare you from that."

"Lily," Jorie said, "I know you planned on a big wedding—"

"But you think we'll be overwhelmed with media attention." Lily nodded. "It's possible."

"It's likely," Simon countered.

Lily drummed her fingers on James's leg. "I'm going to have to think about it."

"If you want a big wedding, then I want you to have one," James said. "We can control the media."

"James," Simon quipped, "nobody can control the media."

"You know what I mean. Hell, I'll hire every security guard in Boston if I have to."

Lily laughed. "I'll have better security protection than a Kennedy wedding."

"Right now," Simon told them, "you can afford to wait and see, but the story is going to break tomorrow or the next day. I wanted to warn you first."

James muttered a frustrated curse and rubbed his face with his hands. "Have you told Howard yet that you know?"

"Tonight," Simon said. "Mark Baine is going with me. We plan to confront him with the evidence."

"I think I should be there—"

Lily looked at him in alarm. "James."

"It's okay, honey. He's my uncle. He's trying to destroy my business and my life. I have a right to tell him what I think."

Jorie glanced at Simon. He was watching James with a strange expression on his face that Jorie recognized. She'd seen the same look mirrored in her own eyes when Lily had passed certain milestones: her first bike, her first date, her engagement. When Simon wasn't watching, James had made the transition to manhood. He appeared to have made it with grace and honor, and Simon, as he should be, was duly impressed.

"I think," Simon said quietly, "that's an excellent idea."

* * *

Lily handed Jorie a bowl of popcorn later that night and dropped onto the sofa in her living room. "Doesn't this make you nervous at all?"

Jorie nodded. "Of course it makes me nervous." She looked at her father. "Dad, can you turn that up a little?"

Her parents were watching a documentary on the breeding habits of the giant sloth. Jorie had noted over the years that her parents had an inordinate interest in the animal kingdom's breeding habits, but had never had the nerve to ask why. She remembered walking into the room once and hearing the calm, methodical voice of the television commentator announce, "The colossal bull has a penis to match." Her parents had been watching the program on elephants with their usual avid interest. She'd decided then and there that she never really wanted to know just what her parents found so intriguing.

Her father complied with her request by punching the button on the remote. Amelia was curled up beside him on Jorie's overstuffed love seat.

Jorie grabbed a handful of popcorn. "I have no idea how Howard is going to react," she told Lily.

Her father turned his attention momentarily from a particularly graphic image on the screen. "That's certainly true. Depending on how much James's uncle has at stake, he could do anything."

Lily frowned. "Do you think so?"

"Dad," Jorie warned, "you're not helping."

"I'm just so worried," Lily said, her face a mask of concern. She'd decided to wait out the evening with Jorie and her parents. James and Simon were supposed to join them there once they'd finished their meeting with Howard. During the afternoon James and Simon had discussed their potential responses to Howard's duplicity. The two had agreed that if Howard would turn over whatever evidence he had to the SEC, Wells Enterprises would not press charges of its own for embezzlement. Howard's stock would be seized and redistributed evenly among the stockholders, and his assets would be liquidated to cover the funds he'd stolen from the firm. If he refused, however, they had federal agents standing by to execute an arrest.

"I don't think it'll turn violent," Jorie assured Lily. "Howard's unscrupulous, he's not a mobster."

She shuddered. "I never liked that man. James didn't, either."

"It's hard to believe he's his father's brother. From what Simon says about Peter—"

"He's Peter's half brother," Lily clarified. "That's why James's grandfather left the bulk of the business to Peter. He never approved of his son's second marriage."

"Hmm." Jorie munched on her popcorn. "I'm sure everything will be all right. Simon knows what he's doing."

Lily hesitated, then nodded. "James does, too. It's just—oh, let's talk about something else."

"Good plan."

"Like your wedding," Lily said, prodding Jorie with her toe. "Have you thought about it?"

"Ezekiel's wheels, Lily, he just asked me today."

Jorie's father looked at her, his eyes twinkling. "Good thing, too, since he asked me last night. I didn't want to have to keep that a secret from you."

"Stop teasing her, Jerry," Amelia said. "He didn't ask you and you know it. Simon's not the asking type. He just sort of gives orders and expects them to be obeyed."

"Come to think of it," Jorie mused, "he did, more or less, order me to marry him."

Lily giggled. "No kidding. That's some story you're going to have to tell your grandkids." Her eyes turned slightly dreamy. "He must have fallen in love with you the night of the engagement party," she said. "I knew it the first time I saw the two of you together."

Jorie didn't comment. She wasn't prepared to admit that Simon had made no mention of love in his proposal, or since. He was marrying her for many reasons, but love wasn't one of them. "Well, I hate to disappoint you all, but I think we're going to have an extremely simple wedding with about ten people present. Family and friends only."

Lily gasped. "Oh, Jorie, you can't. Don't you remember when we used to talk about weddings?"

"I was nineteen, Lily. And you were seven. I don't think that counts."

"Every woman in the world dreams about her wedding," Lily insisted.

"I did," Amelia confirmed. She looked meltingly at Jeremiah. "Of course, I never dreamed it would be on top of a mountain in China."

Jeremiah wrapped his arm around his wife's shoulders. "Strange, maybe, but memorable." With a nod, he looked at Jorie. "You do what you want, dear, and don't let anyone tell you differently."

"I just think you'll regret it," Lily said.

Amelia glanced at Jorie, her eyes questioning. "I don't know," she said. "Jorie has never liked crowds."

"Got a point there," Jeremiah said. "Not since festival day in Tai-ling."

Jorie shuddered. "Getting separated from your parents in a parade crowd will do that to you. I was only six."

"And the Chinese found you fascinating," her mother said. "That hair."

Lily laughed. "I can imagine. From the pictures I've seen it was even redder—"

"And curlier—" Jorie added.

"When you were younger."

"It was. I can remember being in that crowd and having people tug at my hair."

"But this is your *wedding*," Lily insisted. "There has to be something you want. Even if it's just the dress."

"I don't know," Jorie demurred. "I'll think about it. And I'll talk it over with Lavonia. She's way better at this than I am."

"Speaking of Lavonia," Jeremiah cut in smoothly, earning a grateful look from his daughter for his change of topic. "Is there any more news about her son?"

"He's been improving steadily all afternoon," Jorie said. "I called her before we left James's apartment to come here. She was just getting ready to take a break. He's getting stronger, and they even expect him to take clear fluids on his own tomorrow."

"Amazing."

"It was very scary," Lily said. "It's hard for me to imagine that this could happen to someone I know."

"You were a big help to me," Jorie assured her. "And to Lavonia."

"Not as big a help as Simon. He's pretty amazing."

Jorie had to agree with that assessment. She was only now learning of all the things Simon had arranged during the crisis of the last few days. He'd sent James and Lily to make arrangements for Darius's piano to be delivered to his home by the weekend. He'd consulted with a physical therapist who'd confirmed that Darius would regain full use of his arm more quickly if he underwent physical therapy, and that the piano would be an excellent tool for keeping it limber. And, of course, he'd also been responsible for the digital keyboard in Darius's hospital room.

In addition to the help he'd organized for Lavonia while she was at the hospital, he'd contacted her employer, her friends, and Reverend Tipton to take care of the details for when Darius was able to return home. And, most significant to Jorie, he'd offered Lavonia a job as his personal assistant. He'd promised to help her get her GED and pay for her college education if she'd come work for him as soon as Darius was well enough.

When Jorie had questioned him on the unexpectedly generous offer, he'd passed it off as a simple matter of expedience. He'd pointed out to her the trouble he'd had procuring decent office staff.

She'd given him a knowing look that had finally yielded a confession. When he'd been Darius's age, he'd prayed fervently that God would give his family some kind of break. If his mother could get a decent job, if she could keep that job, if she had the opportunity to make some changes, things would be better. Finally, God had answered those prayers—and He'd done it through the Wells family. Simon had sworn to himself that somewhere down the road in life, he'd pay back the favor. Lavonia was an intelligent, capable woman who'd been dealt a difficult hand and had made the best of it.

Giving her a job and an opportunity had not really seemed like such a big sacrifice to him.

Jorie had fallen a little deeper in love with him in that moment, and though a warning continued to sound in her mind that he'd never promised to love her in return, she'd pushed it aside. Simon needed to be taught how to love, she had reminded herself. Everything was going to be all right.

Now she smiled at Lily. "Yes. He is pretty amazing," she agreed.

Chapter Seventeen

{ JAMES FROWNED AT HIS UNCLE. "UNCLE Howard, how could you do this?"

Howard Wells gave Simon a bitter look. "It's his fault."

"Interesting theory," Simon drawled.

"It is your fault, you bastard. After Peter died, you did everything you could to keep me from my rightful place in this business."

"Which," Simon said, indicating the papers on Howard's desk, "was obviously a very wise idea on my part."

Howard's face turned redder. "It was never my father's intention for Peter to shut me out of the business."

"It was never his intention," James charged, "for you to put the business in jeopardy by engaging in insider trading, either. My grandfather is rolling in his grave."

Howard glared at him. "Shut up, James. You don't know what the hell you're talking about. You're too young—"

"I'm old enough to know that if it hadn't been for Simon, you'd be taking Wells Enterprises down with you."

Howard's laugh was harsh. "What a loss that would be."

James shook his head. "I trusted you," he said. "You were all the family I had left, and I trusted you."

Simon put one hand on James's shoulder. They were seated in Howard's office at Wells Enterprises. The Boston skyline loomed in the background, providing the only other illumination for the room besides the lamp on Howard's desk. In the shadowy darkness, Howard's face looked flushed and threatening. Simon leveled him with a harsh look. "No matter what you intended, Howard, here's the way it's going to be." He glanced at Mark. "Mark's got all the evidence he needs to ensure that you're indicted and convicted on the Delitron matter."

Howard swore darkly, glowering at Simon. "You would, too, you son of a bitch."

"If I had to," Simon assured him. "But James and I have agreed that if you will go to the SEC voluntarily and cut a deal with them on the Van-

Metre issue, we won't press charges for what you've done to the firm."

Howard leaped to his feet. "It was my money, damn you. It should have always been my money."

"That's the whole problem, Howard," Simon said. "You wanted somebody to give it to you. You couldn't bring yourself to earn it like everyone else."

Howard looked at James, his eyes glittering with rage. "Like him, you mean? What did he do to earn it?"

James took a sharp breath. "My father—"

"Was an idiot," Howard snarled. "This business could have been twice the size it is now if your father had provided the right kind of leadership."

Mark Baine shot Simon a dry look. "Like illegal stock trading?" he quipped.

Howard's gaze swung wildly to Mark. Simon didn't like the look in his eyes. "Stay out of this," Howard demanded. "Haven't you done enough?"

Mark shrugged. Howard looked at James again. "And before you get self-righteous about any of this, just know that I can take down your precious fiancée's father. All I have to do is say the word. Is that what you want?"

"The only mistake Bill Benton made," Simon said quietly, "was taking investment advice from you. The evidence is clear. He had no contact with

VanMetre until after he'd sold his Delitron stock. You were the one who passed him the tip. He can't be faulted for selling stock that someone said might plummet."

"But the media won't see it that way," Howard insisted, "and neither will the SEC."

James leaped to his feet. "Damn it, Howard, for once in your sorry life can't you just take this like a man and admit that you screwed up. You screwed up. You got caught. Now pay for it and shut up."

Howard's face darkened even more. He turned on James, his eyes narrow and slightly wild. "You punk. How dare you? Do you have any idea what it was like around here for me when you were fourteen years old and everyone ridiculed me because you were my boss?"

James didn't reply. Howard laughed harshly. "When Peter got ill, I kept this company on its feet. I kept it moving forward."

Simon ground his teeth but let the lie pass. The board of directors had called him several times as Peter lay dying to advise him of Howard's attempts to seize control of the company. Only with careful negotiations and alliance building had Simon managed to protect James's interests until Peter's will went into effect.

"It was me," Howard was saying. "If it hadn't been for me, the only thing you would have inherited would have been a pile of rubble. Then you might actually have had to work for a living." He looked at Simon. "Or maybe you could get your whore of a mother to sleep with some guy who was willing to pay your way."

Simon's jaw clenched so tight his head started to throb. Beside him, James muttered an outraged curse. "That's enough," he told his uncle. "I've heard all of this I'm going to listen to. This is your last chance, Howard. Either you give me your word right now that you'll take what you have to the SEC, or I'm making the call and having you arrested. Tonight. You won't even leave this office."

Howard was breathing heavily. He mumbled something beneath his breath and reached for his briefcase. "Fine," he said, plunking it on the desk. He snapped it open and began tossing files inside. "If that's the way it's going to be. But don't think I'll go down quietly. I'm going to make sure you pay hell for this."

Mark Baine shook his head. "No, James is right. You can't touch him. Simon has him so well insulated that there's not a shred of evidence to suggest he had anything to do with this."

"No matter what you try to do, Howard," Simon said, "I'm going to be one step ahead of you."

Howard met Simon's gaze. He'd thrown more files into the briefcase, and his expression had taken on a menacing look. "Always have to have the last word, don't you?"

Simon didn't respond. Howard smiled a small,

malicious smile that made him look ugly and slightly crazed. "Well, this time, I know something you don't," he said.

"I doubt that," Simon countered. "You're not smart enough."

Howard's laugh sent a chill down his spine. "You don't think so?" he asked. He placed another file in the briefcase before he dug into the top flap. He removed a .45 caliber magnum from the case. "This time," he said quietly, "you're not going to win."

He pointed the pistol at James. Simon's entire body went on instant alert. He gripped the sides of the chair and gauged the distance between himself and Howard. He shot Mark a quick glance and realized Mark was thinking the same thing. Howard was shaking so much that the gun was wobbling in his hands. Simon made a slight move with his head. Mark nodded.

Howard laughed and waved the gun. "This time," he said to Simon, "I'm going to come out on top. You can't protect your precious James from everything, you know."

"Put the gun down, Howard," Simon said softly, his voice laced with steel.

Howard shook his head. "It's too late. If I'm going to go down for this, then he should pay, too."

"You don't want to do this," Mark argued. "You're going to make things worse than they already are."

"They can't get any worse," Howard screamed. "Don't you goddamned get it? They can't get any worse."

James held up a hand. "Uncle Howard—"

"Just shut up," Howard ordered. "Will you just shut the hell up? For years I've had to listen to stories about your father's wonder boy. Everyone was so glad that James would be at the helm of the company. Everyone was so relieved that Peter's legacy was in good hands. James is smart. James is talented. James will provide excellent leadership. Meanwhile, I was shuffled off to some meaningless vice presidency where I moved papers and drew a paycheck. It started with your grandfather. He didn't give me what I was owed. Then your father robbed me, too. And now you. You think you're going to take away what little I have left?" Howard glared at him. "Well, you're not. This time, you don't win." He raised the gun.

Simon edged to the front of his chair.

"This time," Howard said, "I win."

Simon launched himself out of his chair and made a flying leap for James. From the corner of his eye, he saw Mark lunge toward Howard. He heard the gun go off as he shoved James to the floor. After a moment of stunned silence, he reared up on his elbows and looked anxiously at James. "Are you all right? The shot—"

"I'm fine," James told him. "He missed."

"I don't think so," Mark said, rising to his feet

and dusting his hands off. He pointed to Howard, who lay on the floor with a pool of blood oozing from the gunshot wound to his chest. "I think he hit exactly what he aimed at."

"James! Oh my God, James." Lily hurled herself into James's arms when he and Simon entered Jorie's apartment late that night.

Jorie hurried across the room and wrapped her arms around Simon's waist. "Are you all right?" she asked.

He hugged her close. "We're fine. We just finished with the police."

Lily was weeping softly. "James, God, I was so worried. I'm so sorry. Honey, I'm so sorry."

Jorie's parents joined them from the kitchen. "You two are a sight for sore eyes," Jeremiah said. "We've been very concerned."

"We were, too," James said. He cradled Lily's face, wiping her tears with his thumbs. "Baby, I'm fine. I swear."

"I'll make some tea," Amelia offered.

Jorie smiled slightly. Her mother was of the opinion that tea fixed anything that needed fixing. Guiding Simon farther into her apartment, she pushed the door shut with her foot. "Both of you sit down. I know you're exhausted."

James pulled Lily onto his lap. She buried her face in his shoulder. He looked worn and pale,

Jorie noted. "I have to admit, once the adrenaline wore off, I felt like I was going to collapse." He rolled his shoulders and looked at Simon. "I think you knocked my back out when you tackled me."

"I was trying to keep you alive," he said. They'd called to report to Jorie and Lily why they'd be later than expected returning home. He'd given Jorie most of the details of the story and allowed her to convey them.

Lily looked up and rubbed her hand on James's cheek. "Do you really think he meant to kill himself?" she asked. "Jorie said you thought it might have been an accident."

"We did at first," Simon admitted. "It was possible that he was going to shoot James, but when Mark knocked him to the floor, he could have shot himself by accident."

"You don't think so now?" Jorie asked.

Simon shook his head. "We found a suicide note in his briefcase."

"But those threats he made to you," Lily insisted. "What did he mean by that?"

"Howard knew," James said soberly, "what was going to happen when he shot himself. He had planned to do it at the office tonight so the staff would find his body in the morning. He had gotten word today that the SEC was going to subpoena his records. He confessed his participation in the Delitron stock scandal in his note. He knew that the media would swarm all over Wells Enterprises and that the publicity would damage me." He looked at Lily. "And you."

She sighed and pressed herself close to him. "What about now?"

"We can control it a little better," Simon said. "The story will still break in the morning, but it's not going to take us off guard. James has everything he needs to issue a statement about Howard's involvement with Delitron and his confession. Most of the flak will get deflected to VanMetre."

"Daddy?" Lily asked.

"Not even mentioned in the note. There's no reason why his name should come up other than the fact that he's your father."

With a slight sob, she buried her face against James's neck. "I'm so glad this is over."

"Me too, baby," he told her. "Me too."

Three months later, Jorie accepted a bouquet from Lavonia at the back entrance of Andrew Tipton's church and waited patiently while the bridal march began. So far, there had been no sign of Simon, Lily, or James. The large crowd was beginning to get nervous, she noted. She seemed to be the only person in the room without a care.

On the bride's side of the aisle, her parents sat quietly, enjoying the ambiance and the moment.

They'd been traveling, visiting old friends for the past several weeks and returned for the wedding. At Lily's request, Jorie had worn the same gold dress she'd worn to the engagement party. Lavonia had helped her dress, commenting on how the gold color made Jorie's skin glow and her eyes brighten. The dress was Simon's favorite as well.

Darius, who sat perched on a pile of hymnals playing a somewhat revved-up version of the wedding march, shot her a sly look. His grin warmed her heart. He was recovering well, and everyone was thoroughly relieved he was going to be able to play for the wedding. He'd made his comeback the night of the Art-Is-In fund-raiser when he and Jorie had brought the house down with her chopsticks arrangement.

Now he was in his element in his royal blue tuxedo, tearing up the piano and grinning at Jorie as if he'd never suffered the agonies of the past few weeks.

Lavonia leaned forward and whispered to Jorie. "What is taking so long? Why aren't they here?"

Jorie gave her a slight smile. Lavonia, she knew, would forgive her later for the deception. The large crowd had gathered expecting Lily and James to get married today. Only Jorie knew that plans had changed. "Don't worry," she told her friend. "Everything's under control."

* * *

Across town at Logan Airport, James pulled Lily into his arms and gave her a close look. "Are you sure about this, babe?"

She smiled her dazzling smile at him, the one that never failed to melt his heart, and nodded happily. "Absolutely sure. Aren't you?"

James didn't hesitate. "Completely. I just don't want you to feel cheated later. I know we agreed that if we did this, we'd miss the publicity, but if you want to go to that church and have the wedding you planned—"

Her laugh delighted him as she covered his lips with her fingers. "Are you kidding? All I ever wanted was to be married to you, James. I don't need all the rest."

With a grin, he pulled the airplane tickets from the back pocket of his jeans. "Then here they are."

Lily took the tickets and pressed them close to her chest. "I've always wanted to see Las Vegas," she assured him.

"We're only staying there tonight. I booked us a suite at the Ritz in Paris."

She kissed him again. "Oh James, I do love you."

"I love you, too, baby. More than you'll ever know."

He looped an arm around her shoulders and guided her toward the terminal.

* * *

Simon flung open the side door of Andrew Tipton's church. Jorie stood at the back of the aisle, a small bouquet in her hands, and gave him an amused look. God knew, he thought, she should be outraged. He was late. He looked abominable. And she'd agreed to marry him simply because he'd told her she should.

He was a first-class fool, he told himself for the hundredth time that day. He had the love of the most amazing woman on earth, and so far he'd failed to tell her just what she meant to him. On his way from dropping James and Lily at the airport, he'd carefully rehearsed the speech he was going to make.

"Here, son," Clarence Hodges said, thrusting a white rose at him. Clarence wore a lime green suit. "At least put that in your pocket."

Clad in jeans and a denim shirt, Simon dropped the rose in his breast pocket and strode across the front of the church toward the pulpit. Damned traffic hadn't given him time to change. Jorie's eyes twinkled as she walked steadily down the aisle toward him. She looked breathtaking, he thought. As beautiful and radiant on the outside as she was on the inside. Darius picked up the speed of the wedding march.

When she reached him, she shook her head slightly. "I suppose you have a reasonable explanation for why you're late," she said.

Lavonia had followed Jorie down the aisle. She glanced disapprovingly at Simon's clothes as she took her place next to Jorie. "And why you're dressed like that. Where are Lily and James?"

Simon took the bouquet from Jorie and handed it to Lavonia. "They're not coming," he told her.

Lavonia's mouth dropped open.

"Not coming?"

"They're on their way to Las Vegas."

At his announcement, the large congregation erupted into a bevy of murmurs. "Don't worry," Simon told them, "There's still going to be a wedding here. Just bear with me a second."

He grabbed both of Jorie's hands and pulled her close. "Honey, listen to me. I took James and Lily to the airport like we planned."

She nodded. "I'm glad. I didn't want them to leave on their own. Was Nora upset?"

He laughed. "You don't know the half of it. I'll tell you about the argument later. The important thing is, Lily and James are happy."

"Good. They deserve to be."

"On the way back here, I got caught in traffic in the Callahan. So while they were trying to get the tunnel open, and I was sweating bullets knowing I was going to get here late, I had some time to think."

He kissed her lightly. "I was scared to death you were going to give up on me and leave."

"I'm never giving up, Simon," she assured him. "That's what love is. It never gives up."

"I know that," he said. "That's what I realized while I was sitting there. That I know you love me enough not to quit on me. Then I realized that if you had a brain in your head, you'd slug me for the way I've treated you."

"What are you talking about?"

"You were willing to love me, to risk everything to be with me, and I never even gave you a reason. Not one good reason."

"Simon," she said, her eyes slightly teary. "You gave me the only reason I need. You're you. And I love *you*. Not who you are, or what you are, or what you can do. Just you. Plain and simple."

Dear Lord, he thought, if he ever lost her, he'd die. "I don't know why," he said hoarsely. "And I know I don't deserve it, but my God, Jordan, I'm madly in love with you."

She smiled the most radiant smile he'd ever seen. "Oh Simon."

He squeezed her hands. "Tell me you'll marry me."

Darius jumped up from the piano bench. "You're supposed to ask, dimwit," he called to Simon.

The congregation, who had been watching the drama with rapt attention, laughed. Simon shook his head. He felt better than he could ever remember, almost light-headed with the sheer relief of knowing he was about to make this exquisite woman his own. On impulse, he dropped to one knee in front of her. "Out of the mouths of babes," he muttered. He gazed up at her with all the love in the world in his eyes. "Jordan," he said softly, "will you do me the very great honor of being my wife?"

A tear trickled down her face. "I'd love to, Simon," she told him. "More than anything in the world."

The congregation applauded. Clarence Hodges clapped Simon on the back so hard, he nearly lost his breath. Jorie leaned down and pulled Simon to his feet. She smoothed the wrinkles from his denim shirt with a deft swipe of her hands. "You're a mess," she told him.

"I'll change if you want. Whatever you want," he said quietly.

She framed his face in her gloved hands. "I only want you."

He nodded and covered her hands with his own. "I'm sorry it took me so long to realize it." He glanced at her dress. "I should have recognized the signs the night of Lily and James's engagement party."

"Signs?"

"Um hmm. The way you looked in this dress. You took my breath away." He gently stroked her fingers. "You always do. You always will."

"I'm too short to be glamorous," she reminded him.

"If you didn't have at least one flaw, you'd drive me crazy."

"I love you, Simon."

"I love you," he said solemnly. "I'm probably not very good at it—"

"I'll teach you," she promised.

"I'll look forward to it."

She smiled at him. "Then let's get married," she said gently. "I'm kind of looking forward to it myself."

"You gonna go back out so I can play the processional again?" Darius asked.

Simon stood, laughing. He reached for Jorie's bouquet. "No way," he told Darius. "I barely made it down the aisle the first time." He handed the flowers to Jorie. "I'm not risking it again." He looked at Darius. "Hit it, kid. I've got a woman to satisfy."

Darius grinned at him over the top of the piano. "Vanilla," he chided. "I knew it."